Rat

A Cop's Secret Weapon

Edmond Gagnon
Author of "A Casual Traveler"

ISBN 978-1-62646-441-4

Published by BookLocker.com, Inc., Bradenton, Florida.

Printed in the United States of America on acid-free paper.

Booklocker.com, Inc.
2013

First Edition

Dedication

This book is dedicated to:

Jesse William Trudell
1983 – 2006

Jesse passed well before his time
and could not follow in his father's footsteps,
fulfilling his dream
of becoming a police officer.

Acknowledgements

I'd like to acknowledge front-line police officers everywhere. Their unselfishness and dedication to duty played a major role in my inspiration for this book. I was proud to be among their ranks.

I'd also like to acknowledge the invaluable input that informants give the police. They are a *secret weapon* in the fight against crime. Their contribution is rarely known or publicized. Many serious criminal investigations would not have been brought to a successful conclusion without their input.

Finally, I'd like to acknowledge those people who have become "my fans" and have encouraged me to continue with my writing.

A special thanks to my creative team:

Cover photo – Angelica Lachance
Primary editor – Cathryn Gagnon
Technical Assistants – Larry & Kristina Greco
Final Editing – Angelica Lachance

Test Readers: Doug Herrmann
Jerry Arneaud
Glady Brindley
Kay Tall
Marcia Howe

Table of Contents

1
Crazy Jerry

"All that is necessary for the triumph of evil is for good men to do nothing"

- Edmund Kist

On June 1st, 1979, Norm Strom was promoted to the rank of Constable on the city police force. That title meant he'd be wearing a police uniform that included hand cuffs, a night stick, and a gun! He had been a police cadet for the two years prior, handing out parking tickets and serving summonses and subpoenas. The promotion meant he'd be a real cop, assigned to walking the beat downtown. Back then, the downtown core was divided into four walking beats with one man on foot in each area. The city is at the southern end of Canada; some folks like to call it the asshole of Canada because of its location.

Norm was actually born in a small town, just outside the city he grew up in. He worked from the age of twelve doing a couple different paper routes and cleaning up at construction sites. In his later teens, he put up aluminum siding until he landed a full time warehouse job. Norm was left to be the man of the house when he was eleven, after his parents divorced, leaving his mother with six children. Norm was the eldest and had the responsibility of looking after his siblings, while his mother tried to hold down three different jobs. It was his upbringing that gave Norm his fortitude and leadership abilities.

Norm was an all star jock in high school, but he found he would have to work for a living to get what he wanted from life. His mother had no time to be a soccer mom driving her kids all over the city. Norm learned to be independent and self sufficient. He was a big guy, but easy going and an attractive candidate for the police force. Long hair was in style back then, so Norm had to get the standard cop hair cut. It highlighted his baby face, making Norm look like he was twelve years old again! He was hired by the city police force a month before his nineteenth birthday.

The city was considered blue collar and a lunch bucket town. The automotive industry basically supported the city and employed most of Norm's buddies. Granted, the city changed dramatically over the last thirty-something years. It lays directly across the border from a gritty metropolis in the United States. The border city is a gateway to Canada, where tens of thousands of vehicles per day enter; most pass through, but many stay and play.

The makeup of the downtown area was much different in the days Norm walked the beat; there were dozens of shops and boutiques with a few large stores like Kresge and Woolworth. The sidewalks were bustling with people during the day, but deserted at night. There were no all night coffee shops, only one small diner that stayed open until 3:00am. After that, there were really only the cops on the beat, and criminals on the street. Police portable radios were something new at the time. There were no pagers, cell phones, or other mobile devices! It was a cold and lonely job at 4:00am in the dead of winter.

Walking a beat was pretty mundane and uneventful, but you got plenty of exercise being on your feet for eight hours. This was what Norm's training officer Andy Green told him on his first day as he tried to keep up to Andy's much longer stride. The training period lasted a whole two days! Andy was tall, dark, and handsome. He could have been a poster boy for police recruiting. He even had a perfect cop moustache! Andy taught Norm how to stroll, and look for anything that was out of the ordinary. There was no way Norm could learn to consume the amount of coffee that Andy did in one day, especially since Norm hated the stuff, go figure....a cop who didn't like coffee! Donuts were acceptable.

Welcome to the Real World

Norm's second day on the beat started the same as the first, but then it happened. The dispatcher called for every available unit to attend the east side of the city, where two small airplanes had collided in mid-air. Norm could feel his heart start to race as one of the patrol cars pulled up to the curb and the driver told him and Andy to jump in. It was Norm's first lights and siren experience. The police force had just gotten new patrol cars with fancy roof lights and sirens. The old cars had the single cherry on top and a wind-up siren. The ride to the crash scene was a blur! The driver never stopped for any reds lights. The siren was ear piercing. Norm hung on to the seat in front of him and the arm rest. He looked over at Andy to see how he should be acting. Andy just smiled.

The scene of the crash was complete chaos. More speeding police cars arrived after Norm's. People were crying, screaming, and running all over the place. A neighbor approached Norm carrying a piece of one of the airplanes that had fallen into his yard. Norm didn't have a clue as to what he was supposed to do, so he just shadowed Andy. Luckily, the bulk of the wreckage from the two planes landed in an empty field. The crash site was smack dab in the middle of a residential neighborhood.

Norm noticed that there was still some smoke coming from the fuselage of one plane. It didn't resemble an airplane in any way. The wings and tail were missing; the metal shell was torn, mangled, and charred from fire. Norm could smell burnt fuel and something else unfamiliar to him when he got closer to the wreck. It was burnt human flesh. He could see the charred remains of the passengers in the plane; there were no survivors. Norm watched in amazement as some grizzly bear of a man tore through the metal with his bare hands to get at the bodies. He was Ted Masterson, the one man body removal service. It was a horrific scene, Norm's welcome to the ugly side of police work.

Police work consisted of time at the scene, and time doing the paperwork. In many cases, street cops like Norm never saw the conclusion of a particular case. Follow-up and arrests were made by detectives, and cases could take several months to go to court. As in the case of the plane crash, Norm read the explanation of the event in the local newspaper the next day. He found that he was part of a team, and that everyone on the team had a specific job to do.

A Little Help from a Friend

As Normie new guy, you were expected to put your time in walking the beat. As you gained seniority and new rookies were hired on, you moved up the chain and eventually into patrol cars. Like the other rookies before him, Norm put in his time. He learned the basics of policing and who the bad guys on his beat were. Norm tried to get to know some of the local business owners. He proudly patrolled their neighborhood on foot. Norm would always smile and wave. Back then, people actually smiled and waved back to you. There was one day in particular where everyone was smiling at Norm, even before he made eye contact with them. Norm found out why later. He removed his hat at lunch and saw that a pigeon had shit all over it!

Norm got a call from his friend Jerry one day; he said he had some information for Norm. Norm had known Jerry for a few years before becoming a cop. He was a good guy, but not quite your model citizen. Gerald was his proper name, but he was known as Crazy Jerry on the street. He had some minor brushes with the law, but he was never arrested or charged with anything criminal. He was the guy to go to if you needed anything. Jerry knew people, who knew people, who could get you drugs, car and motorcycle parts, or even decoy ducks. Once, Jerry went to *borrow* some decoys from somebody's basement storage area, and he found three pounds of pot instead! Jerry, Norm, and all their buddies were high for days! Norm's came to realize his circle of friends had to change when he became a cop. He had to quit smoking up with the boys and stop hanging out with Jerry.

Anyway, Jerry said he had some information that would earn Norm some Brownie points at work. He made it quite clear that he wasn't a rat and that he just wanted to help Norm with his career. Norm already knew what a rat was someone who supplied information to the police. What he didn't know was how they would influence his police career. Jerry said he had been in a bar, and he overheard some guys talking about a heist they had pulled. The guys were talking about a tool and die shop they had broken into. They did the B & E, stole the company truck, and then filled it with stolen tools. Jerry gave Norm a pretty vague description of the guys, but he was sharp enough to copy the license plate number of their vehicle.

Norm wasn't quite sure what to do with Jerry's information, so he asked a senior guy for advice on how to write up the report. Norm was taught how to keep Jerry's name out of the report, referring to him only as a confidential source. Jerry had just become Norm's first informant. He submitted his report to the detectives and they issued a bulletin with the details that Norm had supplied them. The bulletin included the business that had in fact, been broken into. Norm blushed a bit when his Sergeant read out the bulletin, but he also felt a sense of pride. During roll call, patrol officers receive several bulletins prior to the start of their daily shift.

Norm went about his business that day, walking his beat as usual, when he spotted a truck bearing the same license plates as the one he had reported! What were the chances of that? He should have bought a lottery ticket that same day. Norm called the detectives and they told him to keep an eye on the truck until they got there. The detectives arrested the Duchene brothers when they returned to their truck. Some of the stolen tools were found in the truck, so the detectives got a search warrant for the Duchene house. They arrested a third dirt bag there. Norm and the detectives recovered over $10,000 in stolen tools from the house. All three men were charged with the B & E and possession of stolen property.

Norm cherished the fact that the detectives included him in the search of the house and the arrest, giving him credit for the bust. Norm was the rookie though and had to do the dirty work, like crawling into a dark and filthy crawl space. The veteran detectives were like Gods to a rookie like Norm, who was at the bottom of the totem pole. The detectives submitted a report to Norm's commander, and he received a divisional commendation for his devotion and dedication to duty. Norm scored some Brownie points thanks to Jerry!

Libation and Celebration

The least Norm could do to thank Jerry was to buy him a few drinks. The outing started in the city on Jerry's turf, but Norm thought he'd give his old buddy a glimpse of his new world and his new buddies in blue. There was a particular bar in the U.S. that cops from both sides of the border hung out at; it's a cop thing. When they let their hair down, they want to be among their own and someone they trust. If you've ever noticed an off duty cop in a public place, he will usually have his back to the wall with his eyes continuously scanning the room. They are trained to be aware of their surroundings at all times and to be prepared for any situation that might present itself.

On that particular night, Jerry was in for a treat. He got a few stares from some of the boys, but Norm gave them the nod to acknowledge Jerry was with him. Close friends were accepted as well as groupies and girlfriends. Wives were *not* allowed. There were only a handful of women on the job back then, so the room was full of cock and balls. You could pretty well smell the testosterone in the air. There were more guys than usual in the bar; apparently one of them was having a makeshift bachelor party. Jerry and Norm were working on their first beer when someone at the bar pointed up to the man of the hour. It was the future groom, Manny in all his glory. He was standing on the bar with his pants down around his ankles. Egged on by his buddies, Manny attempted to belly dance while someone tried to stuff a pickled egg into his navel.

Norm didn't know Manny that well. He was known as Mad Manny. The word was that the name came from his high school football days. He definitely had the build of a football player, and was louder than any sports announcer! The guys said he ran like a deer and was a good cop. Whether it was a police uniform, or an expensive suit, Mad Manny always looked like he had just slept in it. His true claim to fame was that he could stuff a whole Big Mac into his mouth without chewing it. Apparently, he once attempted a Whopper, but it started to come out his nose and he almost choked to death. Jerry nudged Norm with his elbow as Mad Manny posed on the corner of the bar. He was looking up at the ceiling and before anyone could catch on to what was about to happen, Mad Manny leaped up and grabbed the chandelier. He crashed down on top of the pool table to the cheers and laughter of the crowd. Without missing a beat, one of the guys playing pool tried to bank the cue ball off Mad Manny's ass.

The bar owner, who was usually pretty tolerant of his drunken cop patrons, was not impressed. He suggested it was time to take Mad Manny home. Norm told Jerry to drink up while he went to find their ride home. They had caught a lift with Franky on the way there. Norm had last seen Franky at the pinball machine where a groupie chick was working the game's flippers, and Franky was behind her working her titties. Norm couldn't find Franky anywhere in the bar…someone said to try Lola's place out back.

Lola was a big black hooker who serviced some of the guys when they needed to relieve a little stress. She lived directly behind the bar. Norm made his way through the poker game in the back room on the way to Lola's place. One of the guys had just thrown his pay check into the pot! Norm found Franky at Lola's, but he was preoccupied. His pants were down around his ankles and he was banging Lola from behind. Lola, in turn, was blowing one of the other guys. It was a tag team event! The threesome looked like an Oreo cookie in reverse. Norm's naivety was fading fast, with his new discoveries on and off the job.

Dogs and Guns

Jerry and Norm caught a ride with some other guys to grab a Coney dog on the way home. The Coney Island at 3:30 in the morning was always entertaining. Mad Manny was already there, wearing one of the waiter's aprons and taking orders.

The place was packed with drunks and very loud. Then Mad Manny said the word Nigger purposely loud enough for everyone, including the only black guy in the place, to hear it. The pure silence that followed made the room stand still. The black guy stood up and pulled out a huge silver gun and pointed it directly at Mad Manny. Only the black guy and Mad Manny remained standing, everyone else hit the floor except for Marty James. He casually positioned himself between the two men and then softly explained to the black guy with the big silver gun what Mad Manny had actually said was Pigger, ...which just happened to be the nick name of one of the other guys. It had to be the only acceptable explanation that the guy wanted to hear, since he didn't pull the trigger. The poor bastard probably realized he'd never make it out of there alive if he had shot Mad Manny.

Marty James should have been a hostage negotiator, but he was too much of a rebel. He could have been a company man, but his attitude changed years earlier after he shot a guy who charged at him wielding a hammer. It was one of those split decisions that didn't play out well in the media, and Marty was made out to be the bad guy. It's always easier to judge when you're not the one being attacked.

The police brass never did anything to back up Marty's decision. It was like they thought he should have taken a whack on the head before he shot the guy. Marty was left with a bad taste in his mouth; he lost his motivation and respect for the rules of the job. He grew his hair and moustache beyond regulation, and he only worked to rule. He would answer his calls for service, but never go out of his way to write any tickets. Rebels always were often looked up to within the ranks; it must have something to do with that bad boy image.

To add to his God-like status, Marty managed one more feat the night of Mad Manny's party. Norm went to take a piss before heading home and bumped into two other cops peaking through a hole in the men's bathroom door. They told Norm that Marty had announced a fugly contest earlier in the evening. That's where you pick the ugliest women in the place and try to have sex with her. Apparently Marty claimed his prize, and he was banging her on the sink in the men's room!

Sadly, Marty James died a few years later; his heavy drinking caught up to him one night when a hydro pole jumped out in front of him on his way home. Even in death, Marty was chastised by the media. Norm will never forget listening to the two veteran cops who got the accident call, telling the story. They didn't recognize the dead man until they rolled him over; his badge fell out of his pocket and on to the road. It was Marty James.

Gerry and Norm had their fill of beer and Coney dogs and decided it was time to head home. Somehow, there were now more passengers than there were cars; someone had obviously taken off, leaving the others behind. Seven guys packed into a compact car. There were three in the front, and four in the back. There were still two guys who refused to be left behind, and they climbed into the trunk. Apparently the second guy couldn't wedge himself into the trunk, so he decided to ride on the roof! Norm, the new guy, was told do drive the stick shift that he was not familiar with.

"No problem," Jerry said.

"You work the pedals, and I'll do the shifting!"

Sure, it all seemed like fun and games until the car pulled up to the Customs booth on the Canadian side of the border. The guy on the roof was wailing, pretending he was a police siren. The poor border guard just pretended he didn't see anything and waved the car through.

Norm was somewhat amazed that Jerry hadn't said much all night, although he seemed to be thoroughly enjoying himself. It wasn't until Norm dropped him off that

Jerry said, "Your cop buddies are fucking crazy, worse than my biker buddies!"

In all honesty, Norm had begun to wonder himself, exactly what he had gotten himself into.

It wasn't just a job…it was a fucking adventure!

2
The Rookie

"Courage, above all things, is the first quality of a warrior"
- Karl Von Clausewitz

What exactly is a *cop*? And where does the word come from?

Norm asked himself and others this question. Answers and definitions varied; nobody seemed to be really sure as to where the word came from. Some said it was short for *copper*, derived from the old copper buttons police wore on their uniforms, and some said police originally wore copper badges. Other definitions were: *constable on patrol* or *citizen on patrol*. It seemed everyone had their own definition.

Research the word on the Internet and "Snopes" refers to two different sources: "Chambers Dictionary of Etymology" and "Encyclopedia of Word and Phrase Origins."

According to these sources, the word *cop* evolved from 1844 to 1859 when cop meant to take or seize. Thus *coppers* were those who would *take into police custody*. The word cops has stuck with police ever since. A century later more colorful names like *fuzz* and *pig* were added to the list.

Normie New Guy

Even though Norm was promoted to constable, he was still considered a rookie by all who were senior to him. This not only meant he'd be doing the lowest job on the totem pole, but that he'd also be doing just about anything else that was asked of him by his seniors. This meant coffee runs for the boss and shuffling police cars around in the parking lot for the guys who actually got to drive them. Norm learned other jobs like relieving the station men or cell man when they went for lunch. This was a great learning experience at times but Norm felt like a yo-yo being called in and out of the station from his walking beat.

One of the jobs Norm hated the most was traffic direction. When a particular intersection would get backed up or there was a car accident, Norm would be sent to clear up the mess. This is when Norm learned how stupid some drivers really are; he had to have eyes in the back of his head so not to get run over. Norm found it especially fun having to direct traffic in the pouring rain without any rain gear. It was the job, and you had to stay put until the sergeant said you could leave. There were times where they would completely forget about poor Norm, and he'd have to call on the radio to be relieved. Standing in a freezing rain when your bladder was about to explode was not fun! Then every once in a while, someone senior would feel the need to break the rookie in and have Norm do something stupid, like attending all the offices in the building, asking for a left handed stapler!

Being a rookie full of piss and vinegar, Norm chomped at the bit hoping to get into some real action. Occasionally a patrol car on the way to a fight would come screeching up to the curb telling Norm to get in. He'd get all worked up racing to the call, only to find the fight was over by the time they got there. Norm was to discover that was a cop's real job....cleaning up the mess, sorting it all out, writing down all the pertinent information, and looking after the victims. Norm also learned that cops could become victims too.

While walking the beat one evening, Norm heard a dispatch over the radio that puts a knot in every cop's stomach.

"Officer needs assistance!"

The call was from an off-duty cop who was working a huge bash at the university. The city allowed the police to work off-duty at bars which, in effect, reduced calls for service to those particular establishments. The cops working off-duty get paid for the job by the owner of the business. Norm worked some of these jobs; it was a great way to make some extra cash and meet chicks!

Norm felt helpless as patrol cars replied to the dispatcher that they were responding to the call. Just as Norm was feeling completely useless, a patrol car came around the corner and picked him up. An officer needs assistance call means everyone drops whatever they are doing and goes balls to the wall in an attempt to get there and help. You never know when it might be you that needs help.

The driver of the patrol car said, "Hang on junior!"

The two veteran cops in the front seat had obviously done this before. The driver kept the gas pedal to the floor and the passenger called out *clear* at the intersections where there were traffic lights. Partners rely on each other like that; the driver relied on his partner to check the intersections, while he kept his focus up the road. It was the first time Norm had ever driven on city streets blowing red lights at 80 miles an hour!

The car Norm was in came screeching and sliding to a halt behind several other cop cars that had previously arrived on the scene. The two cops in the front seat bailed out and started to run, but the passenger had to come back and let out Norm who was locked in the back seat. The back doors of cop cars can only be opened from the outside…it keeps the bad guys in. Norm followed the senior guys into the crowd of hundreds. Some of the crowd started to disperse as the police presence grew. The focus was to get to the cop who needed help, so they had to just push and shove their way through the crowd. Finally, Norm saw a group of cops in the middle of the melee hovering around a cop on the ground. Norm was distracted by the shoves and shouts of the mob, but he noticed that the cop lying on the ground had his face and shirt covered in blood.

The group of cops in the middle of the mob formed a tight circle around their fallen comrade. Then they slowly expanded it, pushing the mob back and telling them to disperse at the same time. The mob was hostile and didn't budge; they yelled and shook their fists. Some of the cops picked up their injured brother, and then carried him up and over their heads to get him out of the mob. A few of the animals in the mob reached up and grabbed at the injured cop, trying to pull him down. The biggest cop led the way using his riot stick to push through the mob. Norm thought it was like following a snow plow! The injured cop's face and head were so swollen and bloodied; Norm couldn't even tell who he was.

Paramedics were waiting near the cruisers and they took the injured cop to the hospital. Norm and the others returned to the mob telling them to disperse and go home. Some men in the mob grabbed the loud mouthed antagonists and pulled them away. They knew they'd get their heads busted or asses arrested if they didn't. Norm had noticed the whole crowd was of a Middle Eastern descent. Apparently the off-duty cop was trying to break up a fight amongst them and they thought he was picking on the minorities. Others joined in the fight, and it escalated from there. It is a chain reaction where the mob mentality takes over. Norm found out later the injured cop was a fellow rookie who had been hired on after him. He actually flat lined on the table at the hospital; the severe swelling to his head and brain caused his heart to stop. A jump start from the doctor brought him back to life!

On the way back to the station in the patrol car, one of the veteran cops up front turned to Norm and said, "Did you learn anything junior?"

"You never let them get you down…they'll put the boots to you!"

Norm felt a little light headed and saw his hands were shaking a bit. He didn't know it at the time, but it was the after-effects of the adrenaline that had been pumping through his veins. When it subsides, you can be left with wobbly knees. "Wow," Norm thought to himself, "I'm sure glad that wasn't me!"

Saturday Night's Alright for Fighting

Most normal people run from a fight, but the police have a responsibility to break it up. Every police officer is taught defensive tactics in their initial training at the police college. Norm's instructor was a Kung Fu guy who taught the recruits a whole bunch of fancy moves to take down bad guys and how to protect themselves. A lot of the techniques seemed pretty cool, but Norm had to wonder how effective they would be on the street. The problem is the same with any sport; if you don't practice and use it, you lose it. Norm tried to practice on his younger siblings at home, but they went crying to mom. He tried using some of the handcuffing techniques while making arrests, but he found they were useless unless the bad guy cooperated. There were a few young women Norm met that wanted to be handcuffed, for other reasons.

You may wonder why it sometimes takes four or more cops to successfully take down and hog tie a suspect. It means he is not cooperating or submitting to the cops, allowing them to put the cuffs on. Superior manpower helps to ensure the suspect isn't hurt because that is not acceptable in this day and age, no matter what heinous a crime they might have committed.

Norm had been involved in a couple fistfights as a teenager, the kind where the guy pinned on the ground would say uncle. He had to stick up for his younger brother in a few neighborhood battles. Norm was a big kid; his size helped him get the police job. In reality, Norm learned to fight as a cop on the street and while working in the bars. Even though Norm was a big guy, there was always some other guy who thought he'd take the challenge and go for the title. Alcohol or liquid courage usually had something to do with it.

The first time Norm had to hold his own in a fight was after receiving a call for a large party at a housing project. Norm was working by himself and took the call while the afternoon and midnight shifts were changing over. This meant Norm was the only cop in service on the whole east side of the city! Norm responded to the call and saw about 50 to 60 teenagers drinking on the street. The party had spilled out from one of the townhouses on to the front lawn and the street. A couple of the neighbors approached Norm on his arrival and complained of the loud music, drinking, and public urination. Norm advised the dispatcher of the situation and asked for back-up while the neighbors continued nattering in his ear. Two guys started to fight on the front lawn in front of the townhouses.

One of the neighbors asked Norm, "Aren't you going to do something about that?"

Norm relayed the new information to the dispatcher, knowing full well the nearest help would be at least 10 to 15 minutes away. A few more kids got into the fight and the neighbors demanded Norm do something about it before someone got hurt. Norm got out and went to the trunk of the car. He pulled out a three foot hickory riot stick and swung it up in front of him, taking a defensive stance…that shut the neighbors up! Norm told the dispatcher he was going in and to keep the back up coming.

Norm waded into the crowd that had gathered around the five or six guys he could see fighting. He yelled for them to disperse immediately, but his demands were completely ignored. It was a sweltering summer night, and there was a light drizzling rain at the time. The rain didn't deter the crowd; they were drinking and yelling over the music at the combatants in the fight. Norm approached two guys swinging wildly at each other. They were all wet, covered in mud, and one of them had no shirt on. Norm got in between the two young men and pushed them apart. One of them disappeared into the crowd, but the guy with no shirt took a swing at Norm.

Norm avoided the punch and used the kid's extended arm to spin him around and put him in a head lock. Another kid charged at Norm and slammed into him and the kid knocking Norm off balance and causing him to lose his grip on his prisoner. Trying to hang on to the kid was like wresting a greased pig! His bare skin was wet and slimy from the rain and mud. The kid reached back in an attempt to pry himself loose, and he knocked Norm's eyeglasses from his face. Norm was in the middle of the front lawn and he tried to walk the kid back to the cruiser parked at the curb. He managed to get one handcuff on the kid when he was kicked on one leg by another kid. Norm reached for his radio microphone but someone knocked it from his hand; it dangled from his belt as he inched his way back to his cop car.

The same kid that kicked Norm came back at him with his fists raised. Norm held his prisoner with his left arm, and he swung the riot stick with his right. The blow struck the kid across is raised forearms. He still charged at Norm. He used his prisoner as a shield and whacked the kid with his riot stick again. The blow hit hard and the stick broke in half! Another kid hit Norm from behind knocking him to his knees; he managed to hang on to the one handcuffed arm of his prisoner. The kids kept coming, and Norm kept swinging the broken riot stick to keep them back. He heard police sirens coming from a distance…it was a welcome sound!

It seemed like Norm's car was parked a mile away…it was in sight, but it wasn't getting any closer! Norm swung the riot stick and broke it again on the same kid! He was relentless and wouldn't back off. The sirens got closer, but the hostile mob was oblivious. Two veteran cops were the first backup to arrive, they grabbed hold of two of the kids who were kicking and punching Norm. They used their prisoners as shields too. The three cops kept their backs to each other while fighting off the rest of the mob. More cops came and one of them chased the kid who was attacking Norm into one of the houses. The crowd started to thin as the thin blue line got thicker. Norm finished handcuffing his prisoner and put him in the cruiser. Four more kids were arrested by other cops. Norm retrieved his mangled glasses from the muddy front lawn and headed for the cop shop.

Norm had no memory of the ride back to the station. When he got there, one of the other cops laughed out loud when he walked into the report writing room.

"Here comes Buford Pusser!"

"You looked like 'Walking Tall' swinging that big stick!"

Another cop added, "Yeah, all we saw when we pulled up was a blue shirt in the middle of the mob swinging a broken stick!"

Norm laughed and sighed in relief at the same time.

Norm's boss asked, "Hey Norm how's your back?"

Norm was puzzled and said, "Fine, why?"

His boss said, "Go look in the mirror!"

Norm went into the locker room and looked at himself in the mirror. He had two big muddy running shoe prints on the back of his shirt! The shirt was also torn in the front, and there was mud, and someone else's blood spattered on it. His knees and his elbows were covered in mud but his only injury was a scrape on his left elbow. Norm smiled at himself in the mirror and took solace in the fact he made it out alive.

The case went to court several months later. Norm was questioned on the witness stand by the lawyer of the one kid who Norm whacked with his stick.

The lawyer asked Norm," Officer, is it true you hit my client with a large wooden baton?"

"Yes sir, a wooden riot stick"

The lawyer stepped closer to the witness stand and raised his voice a bit.

"And how many times did you hit my client with your riot stick officer?"

"At least three times sir…every time he charged at me!"

The lawyer stepped up right in front of Norm on the witness stand and raised his voice again for effect.

"And how hard did you hit my client with your riot stick?"

Norm leaned forward in the witness stand, looked over at the judge and said, "As hard as I could sir!"

The other cops and some of the audience in the courtroom broke out in laughter. The judge looked directly back at Norm from his lofty perch and just nodded his head.

The kid was found guilty of causing a disturbance by fighting and resisting arrest. The verdict was the same for the other stupid kids.

They fought the law, but the law won!

Bar Brawls

Norm worked *off-duty* on some weekends in one of the biggest bars in the city. On any given Friday or Saturday night, there would be seven to eight hundred rock n' rollers packed into the place. Even though it was a two-cop job, they were still vastly outnumbered. When cops were first introduced in the bar, Norm had to earn some respect and let the regulars know there was a new sheriff in town. After sizing Norm up, one of regulars, a local biker, thought *he* would decide when it was closing time. There was always one loud mouth in the crowd; the rest of the table waited to see how Norm handled their self-designated leader. Norm called a waitress over to the table and started taking their unfinished drinks away and putting them on her tray. The loudmouthed biker got up and retrieved his drink from the tray, but Norm beat him to his chair and pulled it away from the table as he went to sit down. The biker crashed down on the floor, and the whole room went silent.

Norm knew better than to let the biker make the first move, so he grabbed him before he could scramble to his feet and put him in a head lock from behind. Norm kept the biker off balance by dragging him backwards to the side exit, then he pushed him face first through the fire exit door. Immediately outside the door was a small porch with a railing. The biker's momentum took him straight into the railing, and then over it, head first. He landed upside down in the parking lot. Thinking the problem was solved, Norm was astounded when he got back to the table and saw the biker charging in through the front doors! All it took was a nasty Clint Eastwood glare from Norm and the rest of the biker's friends grabbed him and dragged him out of the bar. They got the message and the new sheriff earned some respect.

After closing, one of the owners said to Norm, “I’m glad you’re on my side; I wouldn’t want those big arms on me!”

Norm was working at the megabar one night when his partner showed up late and half in the bag. Poncho was not one of Norm’s regular partners at the bar, but he was filling in for another guy. He was actually a veteran of the fabled big brawl at another city bar where bodies got tossed through windows out on to the street. Norm considered sending Poncho home but cut him some slack and told him to grab a coffee. The bar was packed as usual. The owners would see how many people they could get into the place in the hopes they’d sell more booze. Dealing with the boozing mob was left up to a few bouncers and the two cops. Norm spent most of the night perched near the front door, coincidentally right beside the door to the women’s restroom. When Norm wasn’t watching the hottie parade, he was keeping an eye on Poncho and the alcohol absorbing crowd.

Even in a jam-packed bar with blaring rock n’ roll music; Norm got to know the sound of a fight: it was usually preceded by the sound of breaking glass. That meant a table had been knocked over and someone was about to duke it out. Scanning the room Norm saw the tell-tale crowd gathering around the combatants, not to far from him in the main ballroom. Norm pushed his way through the crowd and grabbed one of the combatants in his signature head lock. As Norm tried to back the guy out of the crowd, another guy came crashing into them, knocking Norm and the guy to the floor under some toppled tables. Remembering those words of wisdom he once heard, Norm thought to himself, “I can’t let them get to me while I’m down.” Norm hung on to his combatant, using the tables as a shield to fend off the kicks from those who were trying to free their buddy and take cheap shots at Norm while he was down.

Poncho had heard the commotion and came to Norm's aid throwing people out of the way. He grabbed hold of the guy that was after Norm. Norm will never forget what he saw when he got to his feet; he and Poncho were surrounded by at least 50 to 60 people who were all fighting…some were trying to help the cops, and others were fighting them. The crowd looked like a churning dark sea, with fists and elbows as the white caps. Norm and Poncho dragged their prisoners up front to the coat room using it as a temporary holding cell. Norm told the kids who worked in there to keep an eye on the prisoners until they got things under control. Norm could hear sirens in the background and knew that help was on the way. As the number of blue shirts multiplied, the crowd got the message that the fun was over. The band never even stopped playing the whole time; it was just another Saturday night fight at the rock n' roll bar!

Norm and his best friend Jesse James earned a good reputation at the bar. This became evident to Norm when he saw the regulars watching their backs when they tossed out troublemakers. The front lobby of the bar was laid out in such a way that it was perfect for bouncing idiots out the door. The walls were covered in thick stucco with sharp edges. It was great for getting someone's attention when they were shoved up against it. There were two steps going down to the front doors that helped the evictees gain momentum on the way to the doors. The doors opened out and that was a good thing. The fact they were glass was a bad thing. One night, Norm helped a drunken asshole out the doors, and the poor bastard actually smashed through one of the glass doors…oops! Miraculously he did not receive a single cut from the broken glass...until he decided to come back in the bar through the broken glass! It was a bloody mess!

The owner later said, "Oh my God Norm, what can we do so that won't happen again?"

"Plexiglas would work!"

During most nights at the bar, Norm and Jesse *almost* felt guilty collecting a pay cheque for hanging out, chatting about how to get out of police work, and admiring the scenery. Then there were those nights they had to wonder if it was worth the money. Like the night a group of five meatheads decided they owned the bar. They looked like the offensive line of a football team! Two of the five guys were larger than the table they were sitting at, the largest one being well over 300 pounds.

Jesse said to Norm, "I know which one you're getting!"

Three of the five were brothers; it was evident by their ugly similarities and girth. They argued with Norm and Jesse while being escorted to the front doors but eventually took great offence to being kicked out. The fight was on! Jesse started dancing with the medium sized triplet while the biggest one and another guy grabbed Norm. Jesse had a free hand so he swung his slapper and clipped the one guy in the forehead. Norm struggled with the big brother. He found it was impossible to use his famous headlock…his head was attached to his shoulders; the guy had no neck!

Jesse held his own with his brother, but Norm had a hell of a time…his punches just bounced off the guy like he wad wailing on a Popeye punching bag. The guy was built like a brick shithouse without a door! Norm was thankful the other guys stayed out of it, and he was encouraged by that joyful sound of police sirens in the distance. The big brother was so large the cops had to use two pair of handcuffs linked together to restrain him. The brothers got to spend the night in jail. It was closing time, so Norm had one of the waitresses patch up his bloody elbow. Then he and Jesse enjoyed a couple cold beers to celebrate another night of staying alive.

Shots Fired

Cops working the street never know what's waiting around the corner for them. Norm and his veteran partner were just loading up their cruiser in the parking lot at the start of a midnight shift when they heard, "pop, pop…pop." There was no mistaking that sound; it was gunfire. Norm told the dispatcher they were going to check the area for *shots fired.* The shots sounded close. Norm's partner went up the block, turned right, and slowed down in front of a neighborhood tavern.

Norm looked to his right, down a dark alley and said, "Down there."

His partner drove down the alley, the cruiser's headlights lit up two men fighting up against the building. One man had the other pinned up against the wall. He was punching and kicking him. As Norm's partner pulled closer to the curb, Norm saw something shiny tucked in the back of the one man's waistband.

"Gun!" Norm shouted.

The man's movements seemed in slow motion as he reached back for the gun. Norm was already out the passenger door, charging the two men. He grabbed the gun a split second before the guy could and flattened both men against the wall. Norm tucked the revolver in the back of his pants and cuffed the guy before he had a chance to turn around. Norm's partner had the other guy by that time and both men were arrested. Upon closer examination of the gun, Norm noted that it was a snub-nosed .38 caliber, 5 shot revolver. There was one empty chamber, and one bullet that had not been fired.

Interviews of witnesses and the two men laid out an unbelievable sequence of events. The two men started fighting inside the tavern, and then one of them went to his room upstairs and retrieved his gun. The fight continued outside where the guy with the gun fired two shots at the other, but he missed both times. Even more amazing was the fact that the other guy took the gun away from him and he fired back, also missing his target! Learning that neither of them could shoot to well, they got back to fist fighting. That's when the cops pulled up.

I See Dead People

Norm saw his share of blood and broken bones while growing up, most of it his own! He will always remember his dad bringing him next door to see what a dead man looked like. His elder neighbor had passed away with Norm's dad at his side. At the suggestion of his dad, Norm reached out and touched the man. He was intrigued by his cold skin and perfect stillness. Cops get to see more than their share of dead people, and Norm was no exception. In most cases, the police are called to investigate and to rule out foul play.

It didn't bother Norm, although it was difficult at times trying to pacify the deceased's loved ones who were complete strangers. Norm was also intrigued by the different circumstances in which some people died. He found people on the toilet, in the bathtub, and in one case…in bed with their spouse who had actually slept the whole night with her dead husband! He was an alcoholic, but she felt bad about calling him a drunken lazy bastard when he refused to get out of bed.

Everyone knows how smelly someone can be when they are alive and drop a rose. Anyone who has ever smelled a rotting corpse will never forget the distinctively pungent odor that is ten times worse! Norm's worst dead body was one found by the landlord of a high rise apartment building. The neighbors had complained of a foul smell, and he went in to investigate. At first glance, Norm thought the body was a 300 lb. black man, the skin was chocolate brown and there appeared to be male genitalia visible. It appeared that the man had died after getting out of the shower; his bath robe lay open and underneath him. Closer examination revealed the body was actually that of a female; her breasts were stretched beyond recognition and her inner female parts were hanging out. The real shocker to Norm was when the landlord said the body belonged to a white woman in her mid 40's!

Ted Masterson explained to Norm how a dead body decomposes: first it bloats, and then it bursts. He was kind enough to warn Norm of this before he attempted to move the body; he said it would undoubtedly burst. Norm was a little grossed out by the whole ordeal. It was more disgusting later when Norm ate lunch and could detect the odor that had permeated his clothes.

Ted Masterson was a piece of work. Norm recalled seeing the body removal guy in action for the first time when he clawed his way through the airplane wreckage at the crash site. It was the most gruesome job Norm could ever imagine, but this man was a seasoned professional. Norm still laughs out loud when recalling a war story he heard from one of the veterans. The police were called for an apparent suicide, and accordingly Ted was called for the body removal. One of the cops asked Ted to have a closer look at the victim; there appeared to be a piece of paper in the guy's mouth. Ted diligently opened the guy's mouth, and then he retrieved and unfolded a note. Ted read the note out loud.

The note said, "When you're dead, call Ted."

Night of the Living Dead

Seeing dead people really didn't bother Norm; maybe it was because they weren't bleeding all over him and screaming in agony. Seeing someone in that situation was different and a bit unnerving. One midnight shift, Norm and his partner were cruising through a residential neighborhood on a dimly lit street. It was a quiet and warm summer night, but then all of a sudden there was a naked woman standing in the middle of the road…like a deer caught in their headlights!

She was a beautiful blonde wearing what looked like a crimson scarf. A click of the high beams revealed that her throat was cut from ear to ear, and blood was gushing down the front of her bare breasts. It looked like a scene from a horror movie, but unfortunately it was real, and she needed help.

Without hesitation, Norm shifted into cop mode; medical help was summoned and an investigation was launched. At the hospital, Norm saw the curvaceous young woman unconscious and laying tits up on a gurney. The doctor said she had bled out and another minute or two unattended would have cost her life. He pointed out to Norm what he called a *hesitation mark* along side the cut on her neck. This was proof the victim inflicted the injury upon herself. According to the doctor, the amount of narcotics in her system kept her up instead of collapsing. As luck would have it, she ran into the cops.

Who said the cops are never around when you need them?

Twas the Night before Christmas

There was another night Norm will never forget; it was on a Christmas Eve. Cops are usually busy during the holidays when people are stressed and depressed. Norm received a domestic disturbance call that was elevated to a stabbing en route. It was a quaint little house in a quiet neighborhood. The house was moderately adorned with colored Christmas lights around the front porch. Norm and his partner were the second two cops to arrive, at the same time as the ambulance. The other cops were coming out the front door with a guy in handcuffs as Norm went in.

The ambulance attendants followed Norm in and immediately attended to a man clad only in sweatpants lying on the living room floor. The man had several puncture wounds to his abdomen, and he was covered in blood. Norm's attention turned to the distraught blonde woman who started to spew out an explanation for what had taken place. As she started to talk, Norm noticed her matted hair with streaks of blood in it. There were also spots of blood all over her pink house coat, and her hands were covered in the sticky substance that gave off a sulfuric smell. She explained to Norm how her boyfriend was helping her wrap the kids presents when her ex-boyfriend came crashing through the front door, drunk and looking for a fight.

The two men got into it…words turned into shoving…that turned into punches…then the ex-boyfriend pulled a knife and plunged it into her boyfriend's abdomen several times. As the woman described the fight, Norm's eyes drifted around the room…the Christmas tree had been knocked off its stand, and it was crushed up against the wall. Some of the presents were trampled, but even worse, they were all spattered with blood! Norm asked about the kids. The woman said they had been spared from seeing the fight; they were secure in another part of the house. She broke down and started crying. She said, "What am I going to tell the kids? Look at this place!"

One of the other cops, Richard Cranium, overheard the woman and said to his partner,

"We've got to do something about this."

It was well into the night, all the cops involved in the stabbing were busy doing the paperwork back at the station. Norm asked out loud, "Where the hell is the Dickhead?" *(Richard Cranium)*

Someone answered and said, "He's on a mission."

Norm assumed he was on a coffee run and thought nothing more of it until the end of the shift when the dickhead returned. He came into the report room with his arms full of toys he had scrounged from the local hospitals, and one store owner who he apparently dragged out of bed. Yes, the sarcastic bastard that the other cops loved to pick on actually went out and rounded up some new presents for the kids so they'd have something under their tree!

He looked at all the other cops in the room and said, "There's no way those kids are gonna miss out on their Christmas!"

3
Working the Street

"He Who Knows Others Is Wise. He Who Knows Himself Is Enlightened."

- Tao Te Ching

The best thing about being a rookie is that in time, you won't be one anymore! Somewhere along the line, rookie cops lose their virginity, and the experience they gain turns them into seasoned veterans. This was the case with Norm. From walking a beat, he moved into patrol cars as a relief man, filling in for the regular district guys on their days off. That meant Norm got to work with a different veteran almost every day. That could be good or bad depending on who he had to work with. Even with a few years under his belt, Norm was still the rookie in the patrol car. The veterans called the shots on everything, including who would drive and what was for lunch.

The midnight shift was the worst shift to get stuck with a bad partner. One old navy vet was a raging alcoholic who'd hide booze in the glove box or in his locker. Norm only had to work with him a couple times. He was almost killed by him early one morning, on the way into the station after the midnight shift. The drunken ex-sailor had been out all night and was driving into work pissed drunk. Norm was on the one way street leading to the station when a car came at him head on going the wrong way! Norm swerved to avoid a collision and saw that it was the drunken sailor behind the wheel of the other car. Norm felt obligated to do something, so he reported the matter to his sergeant. The sergeant sent the drunken sailor home.

There was another old war vet that Norm had to work with far too often. He always smelled of booze and smoked like a chimney, but nobody ever saw him drink on the job. Perhaps he just came to work that way. Smoking was quite acceptable at the time, so non-smokers like Norm got to inhale the crap for eight hours in the car. On one night in particular the guy threw Norm the keys saying, "You can drive junior."

Norm was excited since the vets usually chose to drive, leaving the rookies to write all the reports. There were no service calls waiting, so Norm headed out towards their district only to have the guy direct him to a dark parking lot. Norm couldn't believe it; he was ready to rock, but his partner just wanted to park and sleep all night! Norm only put up with that once; the next time, Norm waited for the guy to doze off, and then he drove around their district hitting every curb and pothole he could find. The guy was using his hat as a pillow, but one curb finally bounced his head off the window and woke him up! Norm tried not to smile; the old guy just scowled and went back to sleep.

There were those quiet nights, where the guys would get bored and play games to amuse themselves. On one such night, Norm's sergeant picked him up from his walking beat. They drove around for a while, and then the sergeant pulled up behind another patrol car, purposely rear-ending it.

He grabbed the microphone, and said over the radio, "You're it!"

The sergeant then turned the corner, and raced down an alley. It was called bumper tag…something you could do before they invented air bags. It was also fun "poofing" snow drifts on the side of the road, plowing through them with the car, and watching the fresh snow fly all over. One of the guys was doing it in a store parking lot one night; it was all fun and games, until he hit a shopping cart that was concealed in the snow. Door riding was the most fun, in fresh snow. It was something like bumper riding, when you were a kid. In this case the passenger would open the car door, and then hop out using the door for support. The leather soles on your police boots glided perfectly across the packed snow!

Rookies walking the beat were always fair game for the veteran car crews. They would pull up to curb and wave over the rookie. Just when the rookie bent over to talk to them, they would blast him with a giant syringe, fully loaded with water. They would also sneak up from behind, and toss firecrackers out the window. It passed the time. On the rare occasion, a car crew would take orders, then drive over the border and pick up a pile of Coney dogs.

Tommy Gunn

Norm got to work with other guys who liked to dig and look for shit to get into. That was just fine by him. Stopping suspicious people and cars would make the time pass by quicker. Midnight shifts were brutal when it was quiet. Norm got to work with Tommy Gunn quite a bit; he was a go getter but his nickname was for his big mouth and the fact he loved to bullshit. Tommy would tell a war story, and guys who were actually there would laugh because it was nowhere near the truth. Regardless, Tommy liked to work. Norm learned how to, and how not to, working with Tommy. Working as partners, Tommy and Norm received two separate commendations for their diligent police work during a break-in at a business and a robbery at a gas bar.

One night while Tommy and Norm were on routine patrol, the dispatcher sent them to assist the fire department at a house fire. Usually that meant the police were needed for crowd control or traffic direction. They were only a couple blocks from the call, Norm just about shit when they drove around the corner and he saw the house was on fire with no fire personnel on the scene! Norm saw thick grey smoke coming out of the upstairs windows and the open front door of the two story frame house. A woman stood on the front lawn waving frantically and screaming that her children were in the house. Tommy and Norm ran to the front door and then into the front hallway. The woman had told them her children were upstairs in the house.

A wall of thick black smoke knocked Tommy and Norm to the floor. They tried to crawl up the stairs in the hallway, but the smoke and heat from the fire drove them back outside. While Norm gasped for air, Tommy screamed on the radio for the dispatcher to send the fire department, police back-up, ambulances, the media, and the National Guard! Well, maybe he didn't ask for the army, but Tommy did get overly excited! As Tommy called for help, two young boys appeared in the upstairs window, up above the front porch and door. Tommy waved and yelled for the boys to jump out the window to him and Norm on the porch. Just then a long haired, skinny white guy pushed his way past Norm, running into the house. Norm pursued and tackled the guy in the hallway inside the house.

The guy resisted and yelled, "Let it burn, let it burn!"

As Norm dragged the guy out the door, one of the boys was climbing out the window. Norm tossed the guy over the porch railing like he was a sack of potatoes; he landed on the front lawn.

One of the young boys jumped from the window into Tommy and Norm's arms. They handed the boy to their mom, and Tommy yelled up to his brother to jump down. Norm saw an orange glow in the room behind the boy and thick black smoke billowing out the window over his head. The boy looked terrified, and he was crying; he disappeared from the window. The mother and Tommy both went berserk! The mother screamed for her son, Tommy screamed for an oxygen mask so he could go in the house. Norm looked into the hallway…it looked like the gates of Hell…nothing but fire and smoke…there was no way to get in the house without getting cooked alive! Just then a fire rescue truck pulled up. Tommy just about pulled a mask off one of the firefighters; he told them there was a child upstairs in the house.

Most people run out of a burning house. Norm gained a new respect for firefighters that day as two of them ran into the burning house. They disappeared through the gates of Hell.

The guy on the front lawn got back on his feet and charged back up the porch. Norm grabbed him again, then cuffed him and stuffed him into the cop car. More fire trucks and cops arrived; the boy upstairs was still not visible. Norm saw that flames had broken through the roof and were now coming out of the window above the porch. The heat was intense; Norm felt like his forehead was melting. The firefighters appeared to be running around aimlessly while they tried to establish water lines. Nobody reacted to the oxygen tank alarm going off inside the house. One of the firefighters inside the house was waving out a side window from upstairs; he was out of air! Two cops ran to a fire truck and grabbed a ladder; they helped firefighters prop it up to the upstairs window.

The firefighter in the window had the other little boy in his arms; he hung him out the window by one arm, he looked like a rag doll dangling there. The boy had only his pajama bottoms on; he was blackened with soot from the waist up. He was handed down the ladder to the other firefighters and cops below. The firefighter on the ladder then reached up to help his comrade out of the window. He had his mask off and his head out the window gasping for air; thick black smoke billowed out the window over his head. Orange flames chased him out the window and on to the ladder. Backing down the ladder, the firefighters slipped and came crashing down on top of the other guys below.

Norm could hear the aluminum siding on the house crackling from the intense heat. He heard the sound of glass breaking, and then someone shouted, "Look out!"

A giant black and orange fireball blew through the front picture window, over the porch and across the front lawn. The scene unfolded in slow motion as Norm watched the glass flying through the air, and everyone diving for cover. The fireball mushroomed out into the night air, barely over the heads of firefighters and police sprawled out on the front lawn. The roaring sound almost popped Norm's ears! It was ten times louder than that *whoomph* sound you hear after pouring gas onto a bonfire. Everyone had to back off because of the intensity of the heat. The house was lost; it went up like the cardboard schoolhouse fireworks you lit up as a kid. The house burned to the ground.

Both boys suffered from smoke inhalation, and a couple firefighters got banged up, but there were no serious injuries. As it turned out, the dirt bag Norm arrested was who actually set the fire! He was the downstairs tenant, whom the mother had left in charge of her two boys upstairs, while she went out. He intentionally set the fire and was subsequently charged with Arson. Months later in court, the prosecuting attorney pulled Tommy and Norm aside asking if they had been at the same fire. It seems Tommy got on a roll trying to impress the jury with his heroics, telling them how he dashed through the flames and saved the day. In reality, it was a scary experience for everyone involved, but it was a great combined effort by the police and firemen. For years, the two organizations had an ongoing rivalry, so it was great to see how well everyone worked together.

Tommy's naked curiosity caught up to him several years later when he got himself arrested for allegedly sexually assaulting female prostitutes. Norm had never thought much about Tommy's curiosity when he'd search dark city parks or the "passion pits" looking for couples getting it on in their cars. He would say they had to check for under age women or possible rape victims. Tommy would make them get out of their cars before they had a chance to put their clothes back on. Norm did think that part was a little strange, especially on one occasion with two gay guys.

Motor Town

Norm worked downtown and on the west side for his first seven years in uniform, then he was transferred to the east side station. The east side was mostly quieter, with the exception of the Ford road area in Motor Town. The area was actually a city itself prior to an annexation decades earlier. It was a gritty neighborhood surrounded by three automotive manufacturers and some of their parts suppliers. Ford road ran down the middle. At one time, it was lined with a dozen bars and bootleggers in less than a quarter mile! Some private citizens would have make shift bars in their homes where the factory workers could grab a couple beers on their lunch…day or night! Illegal booze flowed through the city since the days of Al Capone; he actually frequented the city back in the rum running days of prohibition.

Working out of a new station meant a new totem pole to climb. Being the junior man on the platoon also meant you were last to pick vacation time. Norm was actually told he could pick any weeks in November or February that he wanted; that was it. The bottom job on the night shifts was working in the office doing mostly secretarial work. The only time Norm would get out of the office was when someone called for the paddy wagon.

On one particular night Norm and the paddy wagon were called to a large house party that had gotten out of hand. All the east side patrol cars were on scene trying to coral hundreds of party goers who had spilled out on to the street. On arrival, Norm saw some of the neighbors sitting out front of their houses on lawn chairs watching the action. Several of the neighbors had complained of the loud music, noise, and fighting along with kids urinating and vomiting on their property. The first responding patrol car had asked the house owner to turn the music down and disperse some of his guests; the request was ignored.

The east side sergeant was also on the scene and he called for a team huddle. He told Norm to back the paddy wagon up to the front of the house.

He said to the guys, "Shut it down!"

Norm backed the wagon up as ordered and opened up the back doors for business. Some in the crowd saw that as a good time to leave the party, but a hard core group of assholes near the front porch started hurling beers and obscenities at the cops on the street. The boys in blue moved in and started to clean house. The boys in blue moved up to the porch and into the house, pushing and shoving stubborn partiers aside. Pushes and shoves escalated into punches and kicks. Norm began to receive his first paddy wagon guests as the party idiots and morons were arrested and handcuffed.

Norm heard a God awful commotion coming from inside the house; the fight was on between the blue and the bad!

One of the cops came out the front door and yelled, "Hey Norm, catch!"

Some poor bastard got tossed across the porch and over the first three steps without touching down. He bounced off the bottom step and landed in a crumpled heap at Norm's feet. Without hesitation, Norm snatched him up and tossed him head first into the paddy wagon. One by one, more bodies came flying out the door, air mailed to Norm. Norm thought all the action was pretty cool until the paddy wagon was full and the idiots inside started fighting with each other.

The downtown paddy wagon had to be called while Norm took the full load to the east side station. The brawl in the back of the paddy wagon got so bad they almost tipped the van over in one turn…two wheels came right off the ground! Norm freaked a bit but just laughed it off.

The officer in charge of the station greeted Norm in the garage, asking him how many prisoners he had. Norm admitted he really didn't know! Fifteen drunken, beat up, dirt bags were removed one by one from the wagon. The problem was there were only seven, single jail cells in the whole station. They had to be stacked two and three to a cell….while some of them were still fighting!

Once the whole gang was locked up, Norm had to register them all in the cellblock ledger. The first guy stepped up to the counter; he was bleeding from his nose and had a swollen lip and right eye.

The straight-laced officer in charge said, "What happened to you, young man?"

The guy replied, "I fell down the stairs."

The second guy stepped up with soiled and torn clothes, a big clump of hair missing, and a big scuff mark on his left cheek.

The boss asked again what happened, and the second guy said, "I fell down the stairs."

The third guy stepped to the counter; he looked like he had just been run over by a truck!

The boss asked him to sign some paperwork but the third guy said, "I can't, my fingers are broken!"

The boss asked, "I suppose you fell down the stairs too?"

The third guy answered, "Yeah, how do you know that?"

Norm just about pissed himself right there! The boss walked away shaking his head in disgust. Norm wasn't laughing too much the rest of the night as he processed the piles of paperwork. He had the arresting officers' parade through the cell block claiming who arrested who. There were a couple poor bastards left unclaimed. Norm just assigned them to someone.

Ford Road

Police work wasn't all about fighting. When Norm wasn't doing paperwork, he put in hours and hours on patrol. Sometimes he would drive for eight hours, not receiving a single call for service. Lunch hours were an hour long so Norm was able to work out in the gym at the station and keep himself buffed up. As the years passed, the city got busier and Norm was sent from call, to call, to call. Back when Norm was hired, there was no driver training, so cops learned how to drive on the job. Sure, anyone with a license can drive a car, but only race car drivers and veteran cops know how their cars really perform and how they can drive them aggressively at excessive speeds. Race car drivers are confined to a racetrack, but cops have to get places as quickly and safely as possible while dodging a myriad of obstacles and some other, very stupid drivers.

On one nice, sunny summer day, Norm was dispatched to a motor vehicle accident with injuries. That meant lights and sirens en route. Norm sped down a multi-lane road where everyone ahead of him was pulling over into the right lane….like you are supposed to do. Well, not everyone has common sense; one woman driver who was already in the right lane decided she'd pull out into the left lane….directly into Norm's path. There was a solid row of cars to the right and a huge cement pole on the left; Norm chose the path of least resistance and plowed into the rear end of the stunned woman's car. That was to be Norm's only motor vehicle accident in his entire career, and it wasn't his fault!

Norm liked the action that came with working the Motor Town district. It wasn't a steady assignment for Norm until Buck Flynn's partner booked off with a long term illness. Norm asked and Buck agreed to take him on as a temporary partner. Buck was a hard nosed cop from the old school. His Dirty Harry stare alone could frighten the bad guys, but he had a heart of gold when it came to helping others. Buck could be moody so Norm would get in his face and say, "So what's the bug up your ass today?"

It would be just the elbow to the ribs Buck needed to open up and get the problem off his chest. Buck liked sticking it to dirt bags and that was just fine by Norm. Their strategy was to try and make their lives as miserable as the victims of their crimes. Norm always hated being assigned to things like parking or radar enforcement…..he just wanted to lock up bad guys!

There was no shortage of prey for Buck and Norm around Ford road. It was like shooting fish in a barrel at times! There was even a biker clubhouse in the neighborhood to keep an eye on. The city had three biker gangs, one with a clubhouse on Ford road. Buck and Norm stopped one of the other gang's enforcers one day and welcomed him to the hood with a ticket for not wearing his seat belt. The biker was no stranger to getting hassled by the cops. Norm was puzzled when he handed him the ticket and the biker said,

"Why don't you just airmail me like everyone else does?"

Buck and Norm had a good chuckle. Some cops would write a dirt bag a ticket and then not turn it in. The ticket would then become an arrest warrant when it went unpaid, and the dirt bag would land in jail for a ticket he never got! The law worked in mysterious ways.

One hot and sticky summer night, Norm was called to the biker clubhouse for a murder. A couple of the neighborhood punks lured the club president out of the clubhouse and to a vacant lot where they beat his head in with baseball bats. It was a tough neighborhood where the kids weren't even afraid of the bikers! The two killers were arrested and sent to jail with life sentences. In Canada that means you can be out in seven years with good behavior. Thus was the case with Donny Gates, he was a convicted murderer, allowed back in the very neighborhood where he killed a man.

Donny had parole conditions, one being not to associate with any other know criminals! What a joke that was…all of Donny's friends were known criminals! Norm made it a point to keep on Donny's ass, and he arrested him for breaching the conditions of his parole on three separate occasions. Each and every time the courts put him back on the street; his lawyer said that Norm was picking on his client. A few years later, Donny Gates savagely beat his girlfriend to death during a drug induced rage. He went back to jail for his second murder. Society finally realized Donny was a bad man and he was designated as a dangerous offender. This meant he'd have to spend the rest of his life in jail…for real!

On the Light Side

Cops are only human. Seeing the things they do and dealing with people at their worst can take its toll on anyone!

Veteran street cops become seasoned, but also callous. When was the last time you called a cop when you were having a good day? They deal with all the world's ills and yet are expected to remain polite and courteous at all times. You always hear about someone who ran into a cop having a bad day. For all you know, his previous call could have been a sexually abused child. Cops have feelings too; they are only human!

Cops do have a sense of humor, and so did Norm. For that matter, Norm found it broke the tension in many situations, and it helped him deal with the worst in people he saw on a daily basis. Some people would appreciate Norm's sense of humor in the right situation; others just thought he was being sarcastic. Norm got to work with the king of jokers one Halloween. Cuckoo Connors brought in a Porky Pig mask to wear while out on patrol…yup, a uniformed cop, wearing a Pig mask! Norm had to play the straight guy, driving the cruiser, with Cuckoo as his pig-headed partner. The reactions from the public were off the charts! Norm would stop at a red light beside another car and the driver would casually glance over…nobody likes to eyeball the cops directly. Some people laughed so hard they forgot to move when the light changed.

While driving past other cars, some rubber-necked so hard they swerved into oncoming traffic. Cuckoo and Norm stopped at one of the bars and did a walk through…Norm keeping his dead serious cop look, and Cuckoo just being…Porky Pig!

Eyes popped out of heads, jaws dropped, and one guy spewed his drink all over his friends! Oddly enough, there were a few people who obviously had *no* sense of humor; they just stared in disbelief with a look of horror on their faces. Who said cops don't have a sense of humor?

Practical jokes were always a great way to pass the quiet time and to have some fun! Norm loved a good practical joke, especially if it was at someone else's expense! Lucky for Norm, Richard Cranium was on his shift one year. The Dickhead was everyone's favorite target! Norm and his partner Digger Daniels secretly played pranks on Dickhead's partner, and then on him. It was hilarious because one always expected it was the other that was doing the pranks. It started with packing the partner's car full of leafs, collected from bags placed at the side of the road. The cops in on the prank hid in the parking lot watching the poor bastard try to pull all the leaves out of his car so he could go home.

Naturally, a payback had to be planned, so Digger rigged the Dickhead's car with a special device. Again, the other cops hid in the parking lot while the Dickhead tried to start his car. A shrieking sound came from the engine, followed by a popping sound and a bunch of smoke. The Dickhead leaped from his car running in circles with his hands in the air. He gingerly approached the hood and then stopped to look back…he could hear the howling coming from the other parked cars. Simple and/or elaborate, the pranks carried on. Norm tried to rig the partner's locker with firecrackers but accidentally set his uniforms on fire. Retaliation was shoe polish rubbed around the inside brim of the Dickhead's hat. After he removed it, he had a lovely black ring around his forehead!

The Dickhead and his partner continually denied pulling pranks on each other and decided it was best to call a truce. Norm and his partner left the station early one day and went straight to the local variety store where the Dickhead stopped for a cigar every day. Digger convinced the store clerk to let him put a special load in the Dickhead's cigar, then place in back in the box. It was too bad only the Dickhead's partner got to see it. He went to the store as usual and purchased his special cigar. His partner had no problem keeping a straight face since he didn't know what was about to happen. The two cops started gabbing while on patrol and the Dickhead lit up his cigar. The dickhead was on his third big puff when *kaboom!!!* The cigar blew up in the Dickhead's face, and his partner lost control of the car when he burst into laughter. The peace talks were over!

Gut Instincts

Seasoned street cops develop a sixth sense when it comes to things like cruising in a patrol car and seeing someone run a stop sign four blocks up the road. Seasoned cops use their peripheral vision noticing things that anyone else would take for granted. It is the same with gut instinct. Norm was told when he started on the job that good common sense would carry him through his career. Good instincts made him a better cop. Anyone can have a gut instinct about certain things; the key is to learn to rely on those instincts since they are usually well-founded. Norm always remembered one of his old war vet sergeants who would pick him up on the walking beat. It would be the middle of winter and the sergeant would have all the windows down.

He'd say, "It's to hear the sound of breaking glass, my son."

This was the same man who would take Norm to a coffee shop, and he would suck back a piping hot coffee before Norm even got his coat off!

Buck and Norm were less than an hour into their afternoon shift, just cruising up Ford road into the bowels of Motor Town. Both cops' eyes locked on to a beater entering an alley from a hotel parking lot. Seasoned dirt bags frequently drive the back roads and alleys to avoid any attention from the police. Buck and Norm made a point of driving down those back roads and alleys. Norm drove parallel to the beater for the length of the block where it turned on a side street off Ford. There were two guys in the beater, and they didn't see the cops until they crossed Ford directly in front of them. Buck and Norm had already made their decision to pull the beater over so Norm switched on the roof lights.

The chase was on!

The driver accelerated and ran a stop sign on the first side street. The beater slid sideways making a right turn; the passenger lobbed full beers like hand grenades back at the cop car! Buck radioed in the chase while Norm focused on the beater and the road. The driver circled around the neighborhood trying to lose the cops; they were hot on his tail! Speeds got up to 60 miles per hour on the residential streets. The driver lost control at one point and drove over the front lawns of three houses. One horrified resident ran for cover. The spinning tires on the dirt and lawns caused such a dust cloud Norm could hardly see the fleeing car. At one point, an apple and banana from Norm's lunch bag rolled up from the back seat and got lodged under the gas pedal.

Buck just gave Norm his Dirty Harry scowl and said, "Don't lose this guy!"

The driver of the beater barely let up off the gas pedal as he blew through stop signs and slid sideways around corners. Norm was driving a shitty cruiser that stalled in one turn....he had to drive with two feet to keep it from stalling again. The adrenalin pumped through Norm's veins; he noticed he was barely sitting on the seat as he handled the steering wheel and pounded down the accelerator. Norm looked up ahead of the beater and saw another cruiser had blocked the road. The two cops were on either side of their cruiser with their guns aimed at the speeding car coming at them. The fleeing driver continued accelerating, and he aimed the beater at one of the cops. The cop dove behind his cruiser to avoid getting run down; the beater drove over the curb and sidewalk continuing down into a viaduct and intersecting road. He went north on Ford and then turned east on the River road. Rush hour traffic clogged the eastbound lane so the driver passed traffic in the oncoming lane forcing westbound vehicles off the road.

The beater then turned back south, Norm was gaining on him and he told Buck he'd try to take him out if he turned. Buck was busy hanging out the passenger window shooting at the beater as Norm sped up and tried to P.I.T. the car. Norm saw one of Buck's bullets hit the trunk dead center as the beater missed his right turn. The beater crashed through some construction barricades in the oncoming lane, and it sideswiped an eastbound car that was stopped at the traffic light. Pieces of broken barricade rained down on the cruiser. Norm slowed down thinking he couldn't make it between the cars and median.

Buck shouted, "Go, Go!"

Norm sideswiped the same cars and continued the pursuit.

The beater only went a few more blocks, and then wheeled it into a parking lot. Both the driver and passenger bailed out on foot and ran. Buck fired another shot through the passenger door, and the guy stopped dead in his tracks. Norm had to chase the driver on foot. The guy ran down an alley and then into some back yards. He hopped fences, going from yard to yard. Norm tried to keep up; he got yelled at by an old lady as he ran through her garden. In the next yard, the guy caught a Pit Bull's attention on his way over the fence. Norm couldn't stop; the dog nipped Norm's ass as he ambled over the fence.

The young dude was too quick for Norm, but he couldn't outrun the police radio. Jesse James and two other cops were waiting for the guy at the end of the block, and they put the grab on him. Norm was so jacked up on adrenaline he just about tore the back door off Jesse's cruiser after stuffing the guy in the back seat!

Jesse asked, "Are you okay Norm?"

Norm could only manage a grin and nod while trying to catch his breath. Jesse just shrugged and laughed out loud.

Buck and Norm sat down on a curb in the parking lot near the beater with the fresh bullet holes. They wound down, nodding at each other in satisfaction of a job well done.

Norm pointed at the bullet hole in the car's passenger door and said to Buck, "So that's how you got him to stop!"

Buck just smiled and gave out one last order.

He waved a neighborhood kid over and said, "Here kid, take two bucks and go buy us a couple Pepsi's."

During a search of the beater, the cops found more beer and a replica hand gun in the glove box. Why did they run and what were they up to? Those were the questions that had to be addressed when Buck and Norm reported to their boss. The only excuse the driver gave for running was that he didn't have a license or insurance. Their gut instincts led Buck and Norm to believe there was more to his story, but it remained a mystery. About an hour or so later, the cell man came into the report writing room with a big shit eating grin on his face. He said the driver had confessed to him. The driver was on the lam; he was an escaped convict from a prison in British Columbia!

The chase made the local newspaper; they quoted Buck saying, "The guy driving the car was as dangerous as a guy waving a machine gun."

That quote saved Buck and Norm from any criminal or police act charges for the shooting and property damage. High speed chases were being seriously scrutinized by politicians of the day; they were trying to outlaw them completely. Shortly after the chaos, new government legislation was passed prohibiting the police from shooting from their moving vehicles. Further guidelines were attached limiting the police as to who they could and could not pursue. It was one more advantage the system gave criminals over the police!

4
Squeaky Sally

After fifteen years in a police uniform Norm was transferred to the Drug Squad. Now he got to work in plain clothes and do investigative work! It took Norm a few years longer to get into the Drug Squad than the others who were junior to him and already in the unit. He was never an ass kisser and had apparently burned a few bridges along the way.

The man in charge of the whole Investigation Division, Ash Kist was one for sure. Norm got this first hand from a guy whose job in the Surveillance Unit was up for grabs. Norm went right to Kist's office, closed the door, and asked him what the problem was. Kist turned beat red and squirmed in his chair. He was adamant there were no ill feelings, but he was more interested in where Norm got the information from. Not an hour after Norm left his office, Norm's source called back asking what the hell he had said to Kist. He was now on a witch hunt to find the leak. Norm had repeatedly applied for other plain clothes jobs; thanks to a different boss, he eventually landed the job in the Drug Squad.

On his first day in the Drug Squad, Norm felt a bit lost, but he knew he would flourish there. The squad was filled with type A personalities. Norm had never really considered himself to be in that category, but he later learned that he was. Everyone had their own files and conducted their own investigations into suspected or known drug dealers and their associates. Norm got to know the specific bad guys in the areas he worked, but the new influx of drug information was overwhelming. The veterans in the office always seemed to be on the phone talking to someone named Buddy. Norm learned that this was the common nickname used for all informants, so that their true identities could be kept confidential. This had to be done to ensure the safety of the confidential informants, or C.I.'s.

Norm learned how not to act, or look like a cop, to be able to blend in while doing surveillance. He thought it was great to be able to go to work in jeans and a t-shirt! Norm also had to learn a whole new language: drug names, terms, slang, and the sub-cultures that went along with drugs like heroin, cocaine, and marihuana. Like so many other honest professionals, Norm had experimented with some drugs prior to becoming a cop. He was not naïve but admittedly amazed at the amount of drug trafficking in the city. The Drug Squad was the only place Norm ever worked where everyone scrambled to answer the phone. You never knew if that big tip was the next incoming call.

For the most part, the Drug Squad was a self-motivated unit. Officers received information on drug trafficking from various sources, and then they investigated. The main source of good information came from informants; they are the lifeblood of good drug investigators! As an investigator, you have to consider the informant's motivation, or reason for supplying the police with information. There is always a reason! Motivators can be money, revenge, elimination of the competition, dismissal of or leniency on existing criminal charges, or sometimes they are just do-gooders. It is important to know exactly why someone wanted to become a rat.

Piccadilly Circus

After about three months of learning the ropes, Norm got his call. It was from a woman who identified herself as Sally. Sally told Norm she was an opiate abuser who had turned to prostitution to supply her daily dilaudid habit. She was sick of the lifestyle and wanted to get into a methadone maintenance program. Norm met Sally, and she supplied him with 26 names of people who were involved in the dilaudid sub-culture, dealers and users. She explained to Norm how heroin was almost impossible to get in the city, so everyone turned to dilaudid. You could take the pills orally, but the method of choice was by injection.

One paragraph drug lesson: heroin, opium, morphine, dilaudid, oxycontin, and methadone are all opiates, meaning they are derived from opium poppy, or the seed resin of the poppy plant. Heroin and opium were actually prescribed for pain by physicians around and after the turn of the century, but they found the drugs could be addictive. Morphine was widely used during the Second World War for serious battlefield injuries; they found it was also addictive. Synthetic heroin or dilaudid is six to eight times more potent than morphine! It is prescribed to terminal cancer patients. Addicts discovered that dilaudid was easier to get than heroin and much safer to use. Oxycontin is the new dilaudid on the streets today. Methadone is a legally prescribed substitute drug used to wean addicts off the illegal drugs.

Norm was mesmerized as he listened to Sally ramble on for two hours. Her daily routine consisted of working the street, finding a John to have sex with, and then using the money to make a buy so she could get high. She would repeat this cycle throughout the day, every day! She was physically addicted to dilaudid; she would get sick if she didn't get her fix. Sally knew where, and from, whom to buy dilaudid on the street. Norm took all the information Sally gave him and created an intelligence file that he called, "Piccadilly Circus." It was a binder full of dilaudid dealers and users with their names, photos, and addresses. On one occasion, Norm and his file were called to court by the defense counsel in a murder trial. A dillyhead had murdered an old man for his money and pills. The arrogant lead detective *(Richard Cranium)* didn't have a grasp on how desperate a dilaudid addict could be. The defense lawyer was fishing to see if his client was in the Piccadilly Circus, file, but privacy issues prevented him from actually looking in the file. Norm found it was all quite interesting. The Dickhead wasn't amused!

A Bulge in his Pants

The day after meeting Sally, Norm put her to work. She went about her day hooking, and getting high, while gathering information as to who was holding dilaudid. Sally paged Norm around mid-day and said that Paula Watson was selling #4 dillies *(four milligram pills)* for $50 each. Information had to be recent and confirmed before a search warrant could be obtained to search someone's home. Norm got $50 in buy money from his boss and went out to meet Sally. Norm drove her to Paula's house and gave her the fifty bucks to make a buy. Within five minutes, Sally returned to the van with one #4 dilaudid pill. She said that Paula retrieved the pill from a bottle she was hiding in her bra.

Norm had been working the day shift which normally ended at 5:00pm and that was only fifteen minutes away. If Norm wanted to bust Paula, it meant obtaining a search warrant to search her residence. It was quitting time at any other normal job. In the drug cop world, you don't go home until the dealer is locked up and the paper work is done. It was time for Norm to write his first search warrant. Granted, warrants were much easier to obtain way back when, but this was B.C. *(before computers)* and Norm had to type everything in quadruplicate, using carbon paper, on a typewriter! Thank God he had taken one year of typing in high school. Norm was the only male in the class; it was now paying off!

The next obstacle to obtaining a warrant was getting it signed by a judge; they all went home at 4:00pm. That meant Norm would have to drive a half hour out of town to see the judge at their home. Norm waited while the judge read the warrant and decided whether or not it met the criteria for them to sign it. The warrant was granted, and at precisely 6:35pm Norm and the Drug Squad pushed their way through Paula's front door. Stealth is very important in entering someone's house if you want to grab them before they dump or destroy any of the drugs or other evidence. In this case, Paula's father-in-law Brownie answered the door for the female squad member, and they pushed their way in past him.

Searching someone's home for drugs is not fun by any means; just try to imagine someone hiding small pills about the size of kiddy aspirin somewhere in their house, and then you have to find it. It could take hours, and experienced drug dealers like Paula don't offer you any help whatsoever. Believe it or not, Norm actually found one dilaudid pill in the pants of a clown doll that was on a display stand in the bedroom. He later found some more hidden in the hem of her living room curtains! Now picture this: several months later during Paula's trial, Norm was on the witness stand testifying in court as to how and where he found the pills. There he was in the hushed courtroom, holding the clown in his hands, showing the courtroom how he had felt a lump in the clown's pants. Norm heard more than a few chuckles from the audience in the court room, but his colleague Bongo burst out in laughter. He had to leave the courtroom.

Anyway, Sally had now proven herself as a reliable source and valuable informant. Sally was probably cute in her younger days with blonde hair, blue eyes, and a few freckles. Hard living aged and ravaged her girlish appearance *(you would never imagine that men actually paid her for sex!),* but she had a big heart and was soft spoken with a squeaky voice.

When she called the office for Norm one time, one of the guys said, "Hey Norm, there's some squeaky chick on the phone for you."

Thus, she became "Squeaky Sally." Sally seemed quite simple to Norm. He later learned from her mother that Sally suffered from fetal alcohol syndrome, one of those lovely things you can pass on to your children when you abuse alcohol while you're pregnant. Sally managed to get by with government assistance in the form of a disability check.

Ma Barker

Norm's next target was a crotchety old woman people on the street referred to as Ma. Her last name really wasn't Barker, but it will be used here to protect the identity of the nasty old bitch. Ma was a grandmother and second generation welfare scammer who abused the system any which way she could. Out of the kindness of her heart, she would let street people shack up at her place. Of course, they were expected to chip in and help pay the bills by either selling drugs, stealing shit, or by prostituting themselves. Norm referred to her place as Ma's half-way whorehouse. Sally occasionally stayed at Ma's when she was down and out. Ma was also a supplier for Sally's addiction.

Sally supplied Norm with information on Ma Barker that led to her arrest on three separate occasions. Ma never got off the couch the whole time her home was being searched. On one occasion, it was because the dilaudid was hidden in the hollow leg of the coffee table directly in front of her. Ma called Norm everything but a white man that day!

Ma's drug charges piled high enough that she eventually had to appear in court to answer for her lawless ways. It was a sight to behold; Ma was decked out in her best Sunday church dress and carrying an oxygen tank. Norm suggested to her she might want to put out the cigarette she was smoking before she blew up the courthouse. The swift hammer of justice came down on Ma and she was sentenced to a lengthy term of double secret probation! Heaven forbid they would even consider locking up such a softhearted, poor grandmother on her deathbed!

Mack Attack

Sally continued to feed Norm intelligence information for the "Piccadilly Circus" file. She told him about a well-known, weasel of a dirt bag Norm had arrested back in his uniform days. Mack Crow was one of Sally's steady suppliers of dilaudid. She said he especially like dealing to the hookers so he could try and get his dick licked in the process of making a drug deal. Mack was a guy who probably always had to pay for sex; he was butt ugly! Really, his face looked like a can of smashed ass! He was short and skinny with lots of tattoos, and his long hair was greasy enough to be a fire hazard. He had a Pee Wee Herman voice and a downright bad attitude toward everyone and everything. Mack's record card consisted of pages of criminal convictions for stuff like theft, robbery, assault, and drug trafficking. Calling him a shit bag would be considered being polite. Oh yes, and one more thing....Mack just happened to be Ma Barker's son! It seemed Ma was too ill to carry on the family business so Mack took over.

Sally told Norm that Mack was running a shooting gallery *at* his house. Another pre-cursor to searching an unknown house is that you have to do some reconnaissance of the building and surrounding area. You can rely somewhat on a description of the building interior from the informant, but someone has to physically *recon* the area to find the best approach, and point of entry. Some of the many things that have to be considered are:

Where do you park the vehicles so your presence won't be compromised?

Where do you stage or get the team into formation prior to entry?

Which door will you use to get into the building?

Who is in the house?

Are there any children?

Are there dogs, firearms?

The list goes on. Then, no matter how perfect the plan is, you have to be prepared for something to go wrong. For drug cops, it seems something always goes wrong!

Sally supplied Norm with a rough layout of Mack's house. Norm drew it and the operational plan on an eraser board to brief the other officers. Mack was known to have or carry guns, so in this case, the S.W.A.T. team was called in to assist with the initial entry and clearing of the house for possible threats. It's nice to have the S.W.A.T. team if you think there is a weapon involved; if someone is going to take a bullet on the way in the door, it will be one of them! Some of those guys actually get off on that thought. Because of the weapon threat, the decision was made to use a stealth approach to the house and then a dynamic entry. The S.W.A.T. team loved dynamic entries because they got to don face masks and automatic weapons, then crash through the door scaring the shit out of everyone, and throwing them to the floor at gunpoint. It is a rush for adrenaline junkies!

The approach to the house had to be done very quietly as not to tip off the occupants and have any potential evidence destroyed. It was also a very busy neighborhood with lots of pedestrian traffic, some of which was going in and out of Mack's house. Norm's drug team followed the S.W.A.T. team from the dark alley at the rear of the house and into the back yard. Now this is where that bull in a china shop saying comes in. The S.W.A.T. guys get all geared up and geeked up in preparation for a raid. It's just like a football team getting pumped up before a game. They have about thirty pounds of special equipment on, and their adrenaline starts pumping through their veins as they anticipate the start of the game. Adrenaline is a wonderful drug, but rising levels in your bloodstream can actually cause tunnel vision, and in some cases partial hearing loss. This is the reason why many people who have been involved in a shooting say they never heard the gunshot.

So, what happens some times, and what happened on that night, was that one of the S.W.A.T. guys was so geeked up he didn't realize how noisy he was being when the teams lined up along the side of the house; he slammed up against the house instead of leaning against it. Norm had been listening to the action inside through an open window, but all went silent. In a dynamic entry, you have six to eight seconds to get in and get control before you lose the element of surprise.

Norm shouted, "Go, Go, Go!"

He waved the S.W.A.T. guys up to the front door. They crashed through the door and did their thing inside, clearing any potential threats. Norm and his guys then came in and found everyone spread eagle and face down on the living room and kitchen floors.

Bathing Beauty

One of the S.W.A.T. guys was standing in the bathroom doorway, and he motioned his head for Norm to come over. He was pointing his gun into the bath tub that was partially obscured by the shower curtain. Norm could see that someone was in the tub and he pulled back the curtain. There was Squeaky Sally, naked as the day she was born. She was on her knees with her cottage cheese ass sticking up in the air and her face down covered by her hands. Apparently, she was trying to be invisible…like when you were a kid. It was a sight; she had more stretch marks around her mid section than a thirty year old leather sofa! Norm tried not to smirk when he told her to get up and put her clothes on *(he remembered her saying she had to give up her child when she gave birth at sixteen).* Upon exiting the tub, Sally told Norm that Mack made her strip naked to check for wires or to see if she was bugged. It was his way of getting a cheap thrill.

Sally briefed Norm as to who was who in the house, and where she thought the dope was hidden. You would think with Sally's profession, she would be comfortable being naked in front of a man, but she was quite shy, and she tried to cover her important parts as she clumsily got dressed. Poor Sally, she was always the victim.

Ice Capades

To be a good drug cop, Norm had to learn how to play the game. The way the game worked was that when ever you busted someone with drugs, you made an attempt to roll them and turn them into your rat. This was easy bait to take for some if they didn't want to end up in jail. It was a *little* more difficult to obtain drugs in jail. Sally told Norm about a father and daughter duo she was buying dilaudid from. She said the father, Duke Delaney, was supplying his daughter Denise. She, in turn, would run the shooting gallery from her house. Another one of Norm's rats told him that Duke was one of the main dilaudid suppliers in the city. According to that source, Duke had befriended a cancer patient who was selling him his excess pills.

Norm put together enough information to obtain search warrants for both Duke and Denise's houses. They searched Denise's house first and seized fifty dilaudid pills, six vials of liquid dilaudid, and some weed, all worth about $4,000 on the street. With Denise and her boyfriend under lock and key, the squad went outside the city to search Duke's house.

It was a cold and shitty winter day with freezing rain. The Drug Squad pulled into Duke's driveway, and the entry team bailed out. Norm stayed dry in the van with his sergeant. The team ran from the gravel driveway onto the sidewalk and the Ice Capades began. The freezing rain had turned the sidewalk into an ice rink! Norm's buddy Jesse was first in line and carrying the battering ram; his feet went up over his head and the ram went flying through the air, nearly taking out Blackjack who was second in line. He ducked and was thrown off balance; Blackjack went down like a bag of wet cement. The third guy tried to stop and not run over the Jesse and Blackjack, it was just like watching a set of dominos fall. They all tried to get up, but they kept falling down, their feet were spinning on the ice like Fred Flintstone running in his car. Norm and his sergeant were still in the van laughing their asses off but had to get out so someone could get to the front door of the house.

The Ice Capades continued for what seemed like an eternity, until the front door opened and Duke Delaney said, "Can I help you guys?"

Everyone was out of breath and laughing so hard, Jesse could barely utter the words, "Yeah, you're under arrest!"

Another $13,000 in dilaudid and $4,000 in cash was seized from Duke's house. Thank God Duke didn't make the team search the whole house to find the pills. The house and garage were huge; he had the pills hidden in one of his sockets, in his tool box. The team might have searched for hours and never found his stash. People like Duke would sometimes cooperate like that, upon the threat of having their whole house trashed by the cops. A proper and complete search ended up looking like a bomb exploded in the house!

Norm managed to arrest Duke a couple more times before he finally saw the light and joined the team, becoming a rat himself. Norm now had a pack of rats that were all squealing on each other, and the dealers higher up the food chain. Even Sally's boyfriend joined the team; he wasn't a user, but he was trying to guide Sally down the right path. He figured if he ratted out Sally's sources, she'd have nowhere to buy her drugs. It got complicated and difficult at times when information flowed in from multiple sources. Norm had to learn how to sort and prioritize it all.

Dinner Time

Norm wasn't the only cop in the Drug Squad executing search warrants. He learned the ropes from the veterans in the unit; the pace was unforgiving. It wasn't a good job for family men; they tried, but many struggled with their marriages. The long hours and crazy shifts were not conducive to family life. Many days were so busy the cops in the unit didn't even have time to eat. Norm had to laugh at one veteran Banger, who for some reason always planned his raids around dinner time. Norm soon learned there was a method to his madness.

On one raid, the guy arrested left a half of a dozen, big and juicy cheeseburgers on the barbeque upon being arrested. Guess what the team had for dinner? Later, during the guy's interview Banger told the guy he let his dog outside and fed him the burgers.

The guy said, "Really, you guys are the greatest!"

Banger could make a meal out of just about anything! He would always volunteer to search the kitchen.

He hollered out at another raid, "Hey Norm, you want some soup?"

Hungry and curious Norm went to see Banger in the kitchen. There he was, eating cold mushroom soup out of the can!

Banger saw Norm' look and said, "What? It tastes just like pudding!"

Judging by the size of Norm, he didn't look like he missed too many meals. The crazy hours, junk food, and lack of work-outs added several pounds to Norm's once svelte shape. The late night parties had tamed down over the years, but there were still plenty of victory beers and pizzas after work. The Drug Squad worked very hard, but they played hard too.

The boys thought they'd give Norm a hint one day. He came into the office and found his desk rigged for special activity. They put a work-out bicycle in place of the chair and duct taped his phone to the handle bars. The emergency snack chocolate bars in his drawer were replaced with rice cakes!

Salvation

Sally helped to educate Norm in his new found dilaudid expertise. On one occasion while out on the road with Norm, she needed to *fix* and asked to be dropped off. Norm was curious and wanted to learn, he asked Sally if he could watch her fix. Sally told Norm to wheel through a coffee shop's drive-through where she asked for a cup of hot water…free to everyone including junkies! Norm parked the van and Sally asked for some paper money. She took the dilaudid pill and crushed it in the $10 bill, the raised ink edges helped break it down. Then she pulled her *kit* from her purse; it contained a syringe, spoon, rubber hose, and cigarette filter. Sally dissolved the pill in a spoon of warm water and placed the cigarette filter in it. Then she filled her syringe through the filter and tied off her arm. She stuck the needle into her vein and pulled back a bit of blood into the syringe *(this ensures no air)*. Sally then injected the dilaudid into her vein. The drug's effect took hold almost immediately, Sally began to mellow, and she spoke with a slight slur. She said it made her feel at peace.

Sally finally got into the methadone maintenance program, and her life slowly came together. The program was new to the city, and it was met with some resistance from certain citizen groups, especially the neighbors where the clinic was set up. Norm was offered a spot on a committee which comprised of the doctors and pharmacists who were prescribing, and dispensing the methadone. The committee was a conglomerate of other groups such as the AIDS committee, and the needle exchange program.

At first, Norm didn't believe in a program that freely gave addicts one narcotic to get them off another at the tax payers expense. But Norm learned that the program really did work. The addicts were not reliant on committing crimes to support their drug habits. The methadone kept addicts feeling good, but not actually high, and they didn't have the constant addiction cravings. Basically, it let them function normally in society, and it kept them off the street.

The committee was having problems convincing the rest of the community that the program worked, so Norm floated an idea at one of the meetings. Sally was interested in helping other people like herself; she volunteered to help Norm produce an informational and training video. She agreed to be on camera and interviewed. Sally openly talked about how she lost her baby, and eventually, her life to drugs. She explained how she had to sell herself to men to supply her daily drug habit. It was not a pretty story. Norm supplied copies of the video to the committee and police so it could be used for police training and public awareness.

Sally kept in touch with Norm on and off over the years. She would probably live on government assistance the rest of her natural life. The last Norm heard, Sally had moved into a better neighborhood, gained some healthy weight, and had taken on a part-time job. She considered tracking down her abandoned child, but she knew it was better off without her. She told Norm she would always consider him a friend. He tried to drop by her place a few years later, but she had moved away.

Sally openly admitted that if it wasn't for the methadone program, she would be dead! Methadone was her new lease on life.

5
Hanna and Helen

Everyone on the street has nicknames, making it difficult for the police to figure out who was who at times. The cops in the Drug Squad had nicknames too; they were called handles, used so true identities could be kept private, especially over the police radio. Norm Strom was "Stormin Norman" during his childhood; the name carried over to the police force, then Drug Squad shortened it to "Storm."

Actually, all Drug Squad talk over the radio was in code: street names, directions, vehicles, and license plates. S*ample radio transmission*: "The B52 and a mouse are six on the view in a blue skate; they're on the inside track with a half a buck in the till, I've got two for shade." Translated this would mean: "The black male and female are south on River road in a blue car, doing 50 km/h in the inside lane, I'm hiding two cars back." It was a whole new language that Norm had to learn after many years of using the standard police "Ten Code" system *(like 10-4).*

Many people listen to police scanners strictly for entertainment, but criminals use them to monitor the cops in the case they might be in the neighborhood and they had to shut down their operation. Some criminals seemed to be one step ahead of the drug cops; Norm had to juggle different means of communication to level the playing field. On one occasion, Norm coordinated a surveillance team over the Mountie radio while staying in contact with the city dispatcher over the city radio. Besides juggling the two radios, Norm kept in touch with his rat by cell phone. This was quite a feat when you consider the fact that Norm was also driving a car at the time!

The city Drug Squad was small, but it was able to share intelligence information and sometimes resources with other agencies such as the provincial police, the Mounties, and border services. Special projects or joint force operations would sometimes be put together to target high level drug dealers or organized crime groups. In the spirit of cooperation, some of these agencies would share personnel….i.e.: the city would trade people with the Mounties and the border folks. This cooperation led to better information sharing and better end results.

Having a good relationship with the border people meant their frontline officers could target or profile potential drug smugglers acting on information from police. One night Norm got a call from the border; they had three females in custody for being in possession of crack cocaine. The city was introduced to crack by American dealers from the metropolis directly across the border.

For those who don't know, crack is cocaine that has been purified and cooked into a solid rock form so that it can be smoked. The high is immediate and more intense; it is also highly addictive! A gram of powder cocaine would go for eighty to a hundred bucks on the street depending on quality and supply. For crack dealers, the amazing part of the conversion is that they could get five rocks of crack from that one gram of powder, and a .2 gram piece of crack went for fifty bucks! You do the math. It's a very profitable trade!

In this particular case, three young women from the city were returning from the U.S., and they were caught with the crack cocaine stuffed in their bras. Hanna, Helen, and Holly were all young girls who had no criminal records or prior contact with the police. Norm explained to the girls individually how the game was played; it was obvious they were being used as drug mules. What Norm really wanted was their supplier.

The Fila Boys

Two of the girls saw the light and decided to cooperate so that they might get on with their lives and not have a criminal record. Hanna and Helen told Norm similar stories of how they had met some young American black guys in the city one night at a dance club. This was not unusual; one of the downtown clubs catered to a totally black crowd. Hanna and Helen were lonely white girls who were a tad on the chunky side, apparently a good grab for the Americans Dwayne and Darnell. Anyway, the boys and girls all got to banging each other. Then the boys asked the girls to carry packages across the border. The boys said they were routinely searched at the border, and the girls were less likely to get checked. The boys were wrong!

Dwayne and Darnell came over to the city on a regular basis to see their women and to sell crack. Hanna and Helen were aware of this but turned a blind eye to it because they were infatuated with their American men. The boys came across the border with a couple of other homies. They were easy to spot because of their *Fila* sports attire; they wore hundreds of dollars worth of it, along with lots of gold bling. They became known as "The Fila Boys" to the Drug Squad. There were other guys that were part of the group, but Dwayne and Darnell were the common denominators.

The city Drug Squad had two separate teams working opposite shifts. Norm was told by the opposite team that they had run into the Fila Boys one night on the west side. They said the boys were trying to set up a place to deal. The Drug Squad searched them for crack but came up empty handed. The Fila Boys were then voluntarily deported that night, with a warning not to come back to Canada. The cops were given some attitude by one guy with a braided pony tail; his name was Tyrell. Tanker, one of the Drug Squad sergeants, told Tyrell if he ever saw him in the city again, he'd cut his balls off!

Good Girls

Even though Hanna and Helen were best of friends, they couldn't have been more different. With the exception of their attraction to the Fila boys and their personal physiques, they were two totally different chicks. Hanna was brought up in a loving, middle class family with strong moral values. Granted she was a big girl, but she was pretty, well-dressed, soft spoken, and intelligent. Helen on the other hand, was more the plain Jane who was brought up in a dysfunctional family and lived on government assistance. Where she lacked in intellect, she excelled in street smarts. Both girls had been ignored by local boys, so they savored the attention they got from the Fila boys. They really had no idea they were just being used for sex and as drug mules.

Hanna was very close to her mother, and they attended the cop shop together to speak with Norm about the mess Hanna was in. Mom told Norm she was not happy about the relationship Hanna had with Dwayne, but she wanted to be supportive of her daughter. Mom dropped a bomb on Norm telling him Hanna was pregnant with Dwayne's child. Being pregnant would make staying away from, and ratting on, Dwayne much more difficult, but Hanna wanted to do the right thing. She decided to stay on the team and help out in any way she could. Hanna telling Norm when Dwayne was on this side of the border helped. The Drug Squad needed to know where the Fila boys were to be able to conduct surveillance on them.

Dance Party

When investigating drug trafficking there are two types of information rats can give the cops: nice to know, and need to know. Hanna was great in giving Norm lots of nice to know information....like full names, descriptions, and even when the Fila Boys were coming to town. Helen on the other hand, was able to give Norm need to know information.....like where the boys were staying and if they were holding. She knew their street names, who exactly was in town, and usually where they'd set up shop. It was common practice for crack dealers to set up in a user's house; it put the dealers out of sight, behind closed doors. The host/user would get a commission in dope for supplying the place and other crack heads as customers. If the dealers couldn't find a private home to work from, they'd set up shop in a hotel room. In both cases, the cops needed search warrants to enter these places.

The girls both called Norm one day and said the boys were in town. Helen was able to elaborate saying Tyrell was with Dwayne and Darnell, and they were staying at a local hotel. Norm informed his boss who told him to come in early. It wasn't unusual for informants to call at any hour on any day, whether Norm was working or not. The boss mustered up enough guys from both teams to work the case. Norm started working on the paperwork required for a search warrant, and the rest of the team headed out to the hotel. Hotel management confirmed the Fila Boys were in a ground floor room, and they supplied the Drug Squad with a room directly across the hall. They set up surveillance on the parking lot entrance to the room, as well as the door inside the hotel. Hotel management was usually very cooperative with the police when they found out what sort of guests were staying with them.

The warrant process takes time, but time seemed to be in Norm's favor since all was reported quiet in the Fila Boys room. Helen called again, telling Norm that the boys were waiting on the delivery of their crack supply. Hurry up and wait. That was the name of the game in the drug business. Drug time meant never being on time. The cops had to sit and wait.....and wait! While poor Norm typed his fingers off in the office, the guys doing surveillance in the room napped and watched cartoons. They did have to take turns watching the Fila boys' room through the peep hole in the door. The poor bastards out in the car were jealous when they saw a pizza being delivered to the cops in the room. The guys in the cold van had to take turns pissing in a bottle, while the guys in the nice warm room enjoyed pizza and television!

Norm's buddy Jesse was one of the lucky ones in the room... and Jesse loved pizza! Norm once saw Jesse put away a whole large pizza by himself, with a cheeseburger to warm up. He was really hungry, and the pizza was taking too long. You never wanted to share a pizza with Jesse; he would use two slices to make a pizza sandwich, and he could inhale four slices to your one!

Norm's fingers were cramped and his stomach was growling, but he finished the search warrant and got it signed. He hadn't heard anything from the girls, so he joined the guys in the motel room. Jesse didn't even save Norm a single pizza crust! A short time later, the action picked up across the hall in the Fila boys' room. They had gotten their crack delivery and were open for business. Jesse gave Norm the key that the manager had supplied.

The cops out in the van were given the green light and the team stacked up in the hallway. Norm quietly opened the door with the key and the drug cops charged into the room. The Fila boys were caught by surprise! Jesse took Darnell out at chest height with a flying tackle; the two of them crashed into the T.V. Blackjack dove and belly flopped on to Dwayne who was lying on one of the beds. Bongo rammed Tyrell face first into a wall. Norm had to let the two cops from the parking lot in through the patio doors so they could join in the action. The room was in chaos…crack and money and bodies were flying all over the place! It looked like a shark feeding frenzy. The Fila boys had no time to escape or dump the evidence.

When the dust settled, the room was in shambles. The crack and money was scattered all over the floor, furniture was broken, and there was Fila blood dripping down one of the walls. Tyrell pulled a knife on Bongo who now had his snub nosed 38 revolver shoved so deep into Tyrell's mouth you could see the outline of the gun in his throat!

Bongo screamed at Tyrell, threatening to kill him.

Tanker rescued poor Tyrell but then asked, "Do you remember me?"

"I told you I'd cut your balls off if you ever came back here!"

He grabbed the knife and started to undo Tyrell's pants.

Tyrell screamed like a baby, "No, not my balls, please, please!"

Tanker then grabbed Tyrell's braided pony tail in one hand and sawed it off with the knife.

He tossed the pony tail to the evidence officer and said, "Here, exhibit this!"

Norm reached down and picked up a pair of broken sun glasses from the floor. One of the lenses was missing. Darnell was handcuffed, lying face down on one of the beds.

He looked up at Norm and said, "Those are mine."

Norm put the sunglasses on Darnell and told everyone, "Hey, look at how cool Darnell is!"

There was Darnell, looking through the broken sunglasses with a stunned look on his face. Everyone laughed out loud…even the other Fila boys!

Norm then said to Dwayne, "Look at you…who said you can't give a nigger a fat lip?"

The boys were a bit beaten and bruised, but everyone had a good laugh…until the hotel manager came in and saw the room. The poor woman looked horrified as she scanned the room from the doorway. Norm later asked Tyrell in the cell block if he regretted coming back to Canada.

Without hesitation Tyrell said, "What you guys did was nothing compared to what the cops on our side of the border would've done!"

"Shit!"

Dance Party II

The Fila boys whizzed through the revolving doors of the justice system and were back in action in no time. A few months later, the girls told Norm that Dwayne and Darnell were now working on their own. Tyrell never did come back to the city! The lure of the women and the easy money they made selling crack was just too hard to refuse. The girls had worked off their charges by that point. Hanna landed a good job but had the baby. She visited Norm again with her mother; they gave him a bottle of Crown Royal and thanked him for all his help. Hanna didn't have a criminal record to haunt her, but she still had to deal with her baby's criminal father.

Helen needed money, and she decided to stay on the team. Norm signed her up as a city police informant so she could receive cash for the information she provided. Her personal information was locked in a special vault controlled by the officer in charge of the Intelligence office. Only he had access to the identities of the individual police informants. The money informants received from the police was a joke, but it was money just the same. The police held auctions a few times a year to sell off unclaimed seized property. The proceeds would go into a special fund that informants would be paid from. After making a bust, Norm had to submit a written request to the officer in charge of the Investigation Division requesting payment to the informant. Norm then paid the informant, and they'd have to sign a receipt. They were allowed to sign a fictitious name, but it always had to be the same name.

Helen called Norm and told him that Dwayne and Darnell were selling crack from a guy named Rick's house. She even provided the address. It was only a few blocks from Norm's house…on the same street! You just never know what goes on behind the closed doors of your neighbor's house. Rick was an average, hard working family guy…but he had a crack addiction. He had no criminal record, but his addiction had taken him to the point where he was now letting criminals deal crack from his home. Norm tickled the typewriter keys once again and got a warrant to search Rick's house.

There are basically two different ways to raid a house: dynamic and stealth entries. The latter is obviously where the cops sneak up, trying not to be detected. When there is a locked door with the unknown waiting behind it, a dynamic entry is required. Locked doors are opened with the master key, a one man battering ram made of solid steel. The recon at Rick's showed there was a Pit Bull in the residence. A fire extinguisher usually worked quite well on vicious dogs.

The plan was put into play with Jesse being the ram man. The Drug Squad quietly surrounded the house and Jesse hit the front door with the ram. The wooden door had a glass window in it, and it shattered upon impact. The loud crash scared the dog so bad it puked right there by the door, then ran for cover.

On the way in Bongo shouted, "Hey, remember us?"

The cops charged into the living room and tackled the Fila boys. The boys didn't want to dance like the last time, so they surrendered and submitted. The boys also had to surrender their crack and cash, once again!

While searching the house, Rick's wife came home with a bucket of fried chicken…Norm's favorite meal! Everyone in the house was technically in possession of the crack, so they all were arrested. Guess what Norm had for dinner after everyone was hauled away? Rick broke down while being interviewed by Norm. He said his crack addiction had ruined his life. He was about to lose his house and job. He said he was relieved when the cops crashed his door since he had run out of money and he was about to let his wife have sex with one of the Fila boys when she returned home. It's a sad fact…a crack addict will do anything for that next high!

Helen got herself a new black stud, and she stayed in touch with Norm for a while. She helped Norm bust a few more of the Fila boys. They eventually got the message they weren't welcome north of the border. Helen got the odd part time job, but her life pretty well remained the same…it went nowhere. She was quite content with that, and the few bucks that she made from being one of Norm's rats. She eventually stopped calling; Norm never heard from her again. Norm always thought Helen was like the two huge turtles she kept in an aquarium in her living room. Like them, she lived her life from within the box. Life offered her a few treats for sustenance, but she was quite content in her environment with no desire to change things.

Norm ran into Hanna a few years later. She was doing well as a single mom, and she had a good job. She finally dumped her Fila boy and got on with her life. Unlike her friend Helen, Hanna was raised to expect more from life. She set her sights on a brighter future somewhere down the road and then she set out after it.

6
Cracker Jack & Ronny the Robber

Jack was a crack head. If you look up crack head in the dictionary, you'll see a good description of Jack. He was from a poor black family, second generation welfare folks who lived in the city's worst housing projects. The whole family was dysfunctional. Jack supported his drug habit by shoplifting and petty thefts. Jack would sometimes boost enough groceries to feed his whole family, but he traded the food for crack. Yes, some dealers take cash or trade! Jack even looked like a crack head…he was skinny with sunken eyes and the trademark rotting teeth. The hot smoke from the crack pipe had deteriorated his voice to the point where Norm could hardly understand him at times.

Cracker Jack was another rat, who called the Drug Squad one day, and Norm answered the phone. There was no mistaking the motivation behind his call; Jack wanted money so he could by crack! He rambled off some familiar names to Norm, most who were known crack dealers. Unlike the Mounties who gave their informants incentive money for information, the city drug cops needed product before payment. Giving a crack head money in advance of information was like throwing it out the window! Working with a crack head is something like training a dog…you give him a treat only after he does a trick. Crack addicts will lie, cheat, steal, or even suck cock for that next rock!

The problem with working with Jack was that he would only call when he had the itch to get high or he already was. Since getting high was his number one priority, Norm had to learn not to expect much reliability from Jack. His information was great, but once he got high, he would just disappear.

One of Jack's regular suppliers was Fat Fiona, well known to the Drug Squad. Fiona was very sly and usually one step ahead of the cops. Sure she'd been busted before, but she learned from it and knew how to play the game. She even pretended to supply the Drug Squad with information so they would leave her alone. She would rat out some of her competition or give nice to know information that never really amounted to much. Fiona was a single, black, welfare mom who graduated from the projects into a special city owned private home. To her credit, she never held or dealt drugs from her home. Unlike the majority of other welfare homes, her place was immaculate! Fiona used stash houses or had others hold the crack for her. She stayed mobile, making deliveries with her car. She'd put the rocks in the back of her mouth, or stuff a baggie up her twat. Crack is not water soluble, so her moist hiding places worked to her advantage. Only desperate crack heads would eagerly accept a rock that had just been inside one of Fat Fiona's dirty holes!

Jack gave Norm information on Fat Fiona a few times, but it never amounted to anything. It was like that with Jack, hit and miss. He tried to set up one of the Fila boys too, but that didn't work out either. Trying to catch crack dealers was tricky; the shit sold faster than cold beer at the ball game! The dealers would set up at someone's house with a pile of rocks and then the crack heads would flock there and smoke it all before the Drug Squad had time to react.

Roof Goofs

Surveillance was always a challenge for the Drug Squad. Officers would grow their hair or dress down so they didn't look like cops. Cars were another challenge. It didn't take long for the bad guys to catch on to the particular vehicles the Drug Squad used.

Sometimes when the Drug Squad drove through the hood, the locals would yell out, "Five-Oh" ...after recognizing the car.

Parking a shiny new car in the projects made the cops stand out like black jelly beans! On one occasion, Norm had been set up doing surveillance in the projects watching a crack dealer whose name had been provided by Jack. Norm and his partner Missy watched the house for over an hour, but there was no action. All of a sudden, Norm saw the target standing beside Missy's window.

She froze when he asked, "Are you cops?"

"What? Do we look like fucking cops?" Norm barked back.

"Well, we're really the compensation cops...we're watching those roof goofs over there working on that house; there's always one of them faking injuries!"

The target returned to his house. Norm discussed his options with his partner. She was sure they had been burned, but then Norm noticed the roofers were packing up and leaving. The word was out...the compensation cops were in the hood!

Roll another One

Cracker Jack finally came through; he delivered up a crack house in the downtown projects where he and his fellow crack heads had been smoking all night. The Drug Squad shut it down, arresting the female prostitute who lived there and the American crack dealer. Jack was completely fucked up that night. At one point, he looked like the silver ball in a pinball machine; he bounced from car to car in the parking lot trying to find Norm. His eyes looked like two glass implants, and he blurted out broken sentences at a hundred miles an hour. Having completed his mission, he got a cash advance from Norm and was off to the next crack house.

You could never have too many rats if you wanted to be an effective drug cop. This was the case with Norm; he was always on the look out for new sources. Cracker Jack dropped a dime on a crack dealer in the west side projects. Norm raided the house and arrested the owner with some dope.

Ronny the Robber was a rounder from way back who was selling crack and weed to supplement his government disability income. He was an old, hardcore criminal, doing robberies when Norm was still playing with G.I. Joe's. To Norm's surprise, Ronny rolled over and joined the team. He said he didn't want to be seen with cops in his hood, so he met Norm and Jesse at a local bar. He even bought Norm a beer!

Ronny the Robber looked more like your grandpa than a drug dealer. His hard lifestyle had taken its toll; he was sixty but looked seventy-five! Ronny knew everyone and he dropped Fat Fiona's name right off the bat. He said she was now a mid-level dealer who was selling to the little guys, like himself. Norm had only caught Ronny with a few rocks and a little weed, so he was surprised that Ronny wanted to work his patch. He was probably afraid of losing his monthly government check! He got to be like Jack, giving Norm lots of the nice to know, too late, kind of information.

Brotherly Love

Just when Norm thought he had seen it all, Cracker Jack called with a tip on another crack dealer...his own brother Jamal! Yup, for the price of a $50 rock, Jack gave Norm all the information needed to bust Jamal...in their mother's house! So much for brotherly love. They say there is honor among thieves, but there is definitely no honor among crack heads! Ronny never asked, nor ever found out, who ratted him out. He and Jack often gave Norm the similar information on the same dealers. It was all good.

Up Yours

Ronny the Robber was able to help Norm move up the ladder targeting some of the mid-level dealers. It was the specific mandate of the city Drug Squad to target street level drug dealers. Higher level dealers were targeted with special projects by joint force operations between the city and other police forces. With the help of the customs officers at the border, Norm was able to intercept one of Ronny's American dealers. Customs officers made the bust look like it was border related. It took the heat off anyone "like Ronny" who knew that the dealer was holding and coming across the border.

Customs did their due diligence and pulled the dealer over on Norm's information. They found nine rocks of crack in his pocket and some other indicia of drug trafficking, a pager and price list. Norm and Jesse got the call to retrieve the dealer from customs. Jesse made the formal arrest and searched the guy in the cell block at the cop shop. Having already found some crack on his person, and knowing there was more somewhere, Jesse conducted a strip search.

Norm was collecting the dealer's identification and property when he heard Jesse ask, "What's that?"

The guy was bent over already, Jesse asked, "What is that in your ass?"

The dealer remained silent. Jesse demanded, "Take that out of your ass, or I will!"

The guy then pulled a twisted paper lunch bag out of his ass and placed it on the counter. Jesse looked at Norm and said, "You're the exhibit officer…it's all yours!"

There were another forty-eight rocks of crack in the bag that had been concealed in his ass. Yes, it was a shitty job…but someone had to do it!

The Brady Boys

Being a hardcore west ender, Ronny the Robber knew all the other hardcore families in the hood. He gave Norm information on all three of the Brady boys: Greg, Peter, and Bobby. The Brady boys were part of a dysfunctional west end family. Nobody really knew what ever happened to their father, and their mother was as useless as teats on a bull! She was a welfare queen who kept a pig sty for a house. The kids virtually raised themselves in the tough neighborhood. Basically, they were fucked for life from the moment they were born. There was a girl too…Bobby's twin sister Betty, but she managed to stay off the cops' radar screen.

Norm decided to pick on Greg first, the eldest brother. Ronny said that Greg was the main weed dealer in the hood and that everyone went to him on welfare check day to buy their weed. Ronny pointed out Greg's house to Norm. Norm had a flashback to his uniform days when he responded to a fight call directly across the street from Greg's house. That house belonged to another crazy west end family. When Norm arrived on the scene there was a bright orange Firebird doing donuts on the front lawn of the house. That was a normal everyday occurrence in that neighborhood, but on that occasion, there was a guy wearing only cut off shorts hanging out the driver's window.

The car's engine was revving, the loud exhaust pipes were roaring, and the tires were kicking up grass and dirt all over the place. There was crowd on the porch yelling and screaming at each other and at the driver of the car. The guy hanging from the car window had the driver in a head lock. The driver had the steering wheel completely turned to the left so the car kept going in circles as he accelerated, going nowhere. Norm thought about selling tickets to the circus event! Then the guy hanging on flew off the car. It raced around the corner and into the high school parking lot. Another police cruiser headed the car off, and Norm boxed it in.

The driver was from a rival clan in the hood and he immediately engaged in a fist fight with the other two cops. One of them pulled out Excalibur and whacked the guy over the head with it until he stopped punching and kicking. Norm was in on the action at that point; his right hand got in the path of Excalibur while trying to cuff the guy. The blow almost broke two of Norm's fingers…he wondered how the guy's head must have felt. Everyone broke into laughter later at the cop shop, when the guy stepped up to the registration counter in the cell block. The guy was beaten and bloodied.

Norm noticed the guy's shirt and commented, "Hey, I like your shirt!"

The front of the t-shirt read, "Welcome to the city, home of police brutality!"

The guy smiled and said, "Thanks, I thought you guys would like it!"

Greg Brady

Ronny the Robber told Norm that Greg Brady always had weed to sell from his house, but check day was the best time to raid him; he could have up to a pound on hand. Greg had a lengthy criminal record as well as some biker connections. He was a feared man in the hood; nobody messed with him. Rumor had it that he kept a gun in the house. Greg looked and dressed like a dirty old biker; his hair was greasy and always tied back in a pony tail. He had two young children that lived with him. Norm had no idea what happened to their mother. Like all other dirt bags in the hood, Greg had a big bad ass dog. It was a German shepherd that ran free in the back yard, barking at anyone that came near the house.

Norm got a search warrant on Ronny's information and raided Greg's house promptly on check day. The Drug Squad found about a pound and a half of weed, mostly divided up into nickel bags, ready for sale. They also found some ammunition for a 12 gage shot gun but couldn't find the gun to go with it. After arresting Greg, Norm asked where his kids were. Greg said they were upstairs, but the cop who cleared the upstairs said he didn't see them. Norm went upstairs and looked in the bathroom. He noticed the shower curtain was drawn closed. Norm pulled back the curtain and saw Greg's kids hiding face down in the bath tub. Norm identified himself and asked the kids why they were hiding in the tub.

The older girl said, "Dad told us to hide here if we ever hear gun shots."

Apparently the kids thought the sound of the front door getting smashed in was the sound of gunfire.

That tactic saved the boy's life some years later when Greg Brady was shot dead in his own house during a drug deal gone bad. The shooters didn't think anyone else was in the house, but the boy was hiding in the tub like he had been instructed to do. Greg continued to deal drugs right up until the moment of his demise. Norm busted Greg two more times before he left for that drug infested, biker party place, in never-never land.

Peter Brady

Peter Brady was the middle boy and by far the craziest brother! He was probably crazier than he was dangerous. Either way, nobody messed with him either. He too had the biker look, with light brown frizzy hair that he usually tied back in a pony tail. He sported a Colonel Sanders type of beard, minus the moustache. Peter lived in jeans and a white t-shirt, and he always wore the trucker type wallet and chain rig. He lived alone. Ronny said Peter usually had drugs in the house too, but he sold on a smaller scale than Greg, who he probably bought them from.

Norm whipped up another search warrant on Ronny's information and raided Peter's house. As it turned out, Peter was growing his own weed. There were seedlings, marihuana plants, pots, and drying leaves all over the house. One of the drug cops called Norm into the den; it was kind of freaky. Peter had all kinds of newspaper clippings pinned up on the walls. The clippings were all about the mayor, police chief, and other political figures. Peter made a point of being a one man political activist…fighting for causes like…the legalization of marihuana. He proudly displayed his threatening letters to city officials in a scrap book! He also kept copies of his trespass notice…he was barred from go anywhere near any city hall!

Norm gave Peter the team speech and explained to him how he could help himself if he wanted to. Norm knew it was a waste of time, but he did it anyway and he gave Peter his business card as he left the house. About a month later, Norm got a call from a traffic cop who wanted to know why Norm's business card was displayed on the windshield of Peter's illegally parked car!

Bobby Brady

Bobby Brady looked like a sickly albino and runt of the litter. His skin was fair, and he was really skinny. Like his brothers, he favored the long-haired pony tail look and was known as a drug dealer. Bobby also lived alone. Once again, Norm applied for, and was granted, a search warrant acting on Ronny's information. Raiding Bobby's house was like going shopping at a drug store. Bobby had marihuana, hashish, magic mushrooms, acid, mescaline, opium, and an assortment of legal and illegal pills! He also had a collection of legal and illegal knives…pocket knives, switchblades, daggers, hunting knives, and even a machete! He could have easily opened a booth at a gun and knife show.

Norm didn't hear much about the Brady boys after Greg was murdered until after he retired. Norm read in the local newspaper that Bobby had just been sentenced to three years in jail for possessing another assortment of drugs and a sawed off shot gun. The family business was alive and well!

Austin Grey

Cracker Jack eventually faded away. Norm heard he may have gone back to school, who really knows? Ronny the Robber worked his patch and his charges disappeared. He called Norm from time to time while trying to keep his grandson on the straight and narrow…he too was of the silly belief he could keep him out of trouble by having his dealers arrested. Ronny had proven himself a reliable informant, so Norm had to give his information serious consideration. This was the case when Norm reached out to Ronny after being transferred to the B & E Squad. Norm was working a case where a fellow police officer's home was broken into. His gun and bullet proof vest were stolen.

Ronny said that he had heard that one of the neighborhood punks was showing off a gun he had stolen. The kid was also dealing weed, so Norm had enough grounds to obtain a search warrant. Since there was a gun involved, Norm called in the S.W.A.T. team to handle the entry. The townhouse was in the middle of the west end projects, and it would be tough to approach undetected. A plan was hatched where the drug guys would drive the S.W.A.T. guys, and then they could bail out of the vehicles on the roll. It looked just like the movies as the cop convoy came around the corner, then S.W.A.T. cops in combat fatigues bailed out and rushed the house.

By the time Norm got in the house, all the occupants were hog tied and face down on the basement floor. During a search of the house, the Drug Squad recovered the cop's gun, vest, and some ammunition. They also found a quarter pound of weed! Norm went over to chat with Austin Grey, the kid who had the gun. He was laying face down on the floor near the couch. When Norm rolled him over, a few of the cops started to laugh out loud…it seems that somehow during the take down Austin ended up face first on a huge, pink, rubber dildo! Austin was a tough kid who didn't seem to care about anything. His parents were great people; they always wondered where they went wrong. Austin's dad told Norm he had to take a pellet gun away from Austin; he was shooting anything that moved in the neighborhood. The kid was just plain bad news, Norm knew he'd run into Austin Grey again.

Solve no Crime before Overtime

The next time Ronny the Robber called Norm, he said he had been approached by some of his old buddies; they were looking to pull a robbery. The guys knew Ronny was a stand up guy with big balls, so they wanted him in on the score. Ronny stayed in the loop long enough to supply Norm with all the details, then he told his buddies he couldn't go through with it. The plan was to rob a local strip bar early in the morning before the owners made their bank deposit. They were going to use guns and jump the janitor when he arrived early in the morning. It had to be done on a weekend when the safe was full of cash.

Norm ran the information up the ladder to his boss, and then his boss' boss. The problem was that nobody in the B & E Squad was scheduled to work on the Saturday or Sunday night when the robbery was to take place. That meant a team of officers would have to be paid overtime to do an overnight stake-out. Cost usually overruled everything else, but the decision makers couldn't take the chance that someone might get hurt. It wasn't going to be just a property crime. Ronny said the heist was a go, so Norm and his fellow officers staked out the bar for two nights. Norm's boss was his old training officer, Andy Green. Andy enjoyed the chance to get out of the office and to make some overtime. Nothing ever happened, but all the cops involved got a little extra cash in their Christmas stockings that year!

Ronny called Norm back a couple days before New Years Eve. He knew all kinds of heavy hitters, and for some reason they still included him in their plans. Ronny told Norm a couple of his buddies were going to take down a biker out of town. He was sitting on two hundred pounds of weed. Apparently the club was going to leave just one guy to babysit the stash while the rest of the gang was out partying for New Years Eve. They knew the biker would be armed, but they were prepared and quite willing to take him out for the considerable amount of weed they'd get in return.

Andy Green rolled his eyes, but he smiled when Norm told him, "More holiday overtime boss!"

The rip off turned out to be out of Norm and the city's jurisdiction, so the information was passed on to the provincial police. They were anxious for more information, but Ronny's wife died and he didn't call back. Norm didn't hear from him until New Years day. He said the rip was postponed, but it was still being planned. The provincial police had lost interest since the information didn't pan out. Someone in the biker gang made a good New Years resolution by deciding to move the load of weed. Ronny's buddies missed their window of opportunity and that was that!

Ronny the Robber was legally a senior citizen and now a widower. He turned his attention to his crack head grandson, feeding Norm the odd tidbit of information in the hopes he could help keep the kid away from the wrong sort of people. Old age and grandchildren finally slowed Ronny down. Ronny had some great stories to pass on to his grandchildren. He lived a hard life, and life was hard on him. He will probably out live Norm!

Some informants come and go like a cold sore; you never know when one will show up. That was the case with Cracker Jack. It was not unusual; other guys in the Drug Squad had informants like him. The cops use their informants, and the informants use the cops…it is the circle of life in the drug world.

Cracker Jack bounced from one crack house to the next in search of his next high and the true meaning of life. Life itself eventually caught up to Cracker Jack and his American cousin on the other side of the border. The two men were unceremoniously gunned down in a dark alley by the police. It was a drug raid that went terribly wrong for Cracker Jack. A six line story on page five of the newspaper was his eulogy. It was no surprise to Norm; Cracker Jack lived hard…it was only fitting he died the same way. His brother Jamal carried on the family name; he beat a guy to death on the street. He went on to spend his life in jail, where he killed someone else. Jamal will reside there for the rest of his life.

7
Danny Dugan

During the fifteen years Norm spent in uniform, he locked up more than his fair share of bad guys. On one particular shift while working Motor Town, Norm was partnered with a rookie female. On the first cruise up Ford road, Norm spotted one guy who was wanted for outstanding arrest warrants. While affecting that arrest, Norm noticed another neighborhood dirt bag that was breaching his parole conditions. As the paddy wagon and Norm drove up the street with their prisoners, he spotted yet another wanted person to add to the load.

They hadn't even been on the road an hour yet and the rookie said, "Are you just about done?"

The one thing that frustrated Norm and all other cops was that no matter how fast you locked the bad guys up; the system would put them back on the street. It was not unusual to see a criminal with a three page record card; thirty percent of their charges were listed as either dismissed or withdrawn.

The Game

Working in the Drug Squad gave Norm a whole new perspective as to what kind of deals were made behind the scenes and how some charges *disappeared* from record cards. It was the game. A guy would get arrested for a criminal charge, and he would trade information on other criminals or criminal activity in consideration for leniency on his charges. If the police came up with something good enough, their charges could disappear. This was not always easy to pull off; the trade off had to be worthwhile and any deals had to be cleared through the prosecutor if the charges were already laid. Basically, it's just like you see on TV. If you help the cops before you're arraigned on your charges, you have a chance at walking out the door. That is how the game is played and many career criminals are quite aware of it.

One night, Norm got a call from Kirk Westwood, the Detective Sergeant. Westwood was known as the Dirty Harry of the city police force. When Westwood barked, even the brass jumped! He was a legend in his own time. Westwood was known for solving some big murder cases, and the way he took charge of an investigation.

If he got a call for a serious crime he'd stand up and shout across the office out loud, "Nobody's going home!"

Anyway, Westwood told Norm to grab a notebook and meet him upstairs in one of the interview rooms.

Norm met Westwood outside the interview room and got the scoop. He said the guy inside the room had been arrested for breaching his court imposed conditions. It was his third offence for the same thing, and he knew he'd be going to jail this time. Westwood told Norm that the guy was a long time informant of his and he knew how the game was played. The deal was that this guy gives Norm the name of ten separate drug dealers or guys who could be arrested for anything else; that was the trade for his freedom. Norm just about shit when Westwood opened the door and introduced him to Danny Dugan! Norm had arrested Danny on at least three prior occasions in Motor Town.

On one particularly hot and sticky summer night, Danny and his brother got into a shoot out in the alley behind their house that ran parallel to Ford road. By the time Norm arrived, Danny was sitting on his back porch drinking a cold beer, pretending that nothing had happened. It was like the Hatfield's and McCoy's with the Dugan's and another neighborhood family, the Molnars. The feud had been going on for years. Some said it was over one of Danny's brothers molesting a young Molnar girl.

This time Danny pulled out a shot gun, shot at, and chased one of the Molnar boys down the alley. Norm and the other cops searched for hours but couldn't find that shot gun anywhere in the dark alley. Danny just sat on his back deck grinning. Norm felt like he was playing that old childhood game of *hot and cold* with Danny. Every time Norm got near a certain garden shed, Danny would take notice then look away. Something was up with that shed. There was nothing inside but garden shit.

Norm's partner Digger said he was going to have another look. Norm thought it was time for a different perspective. He went over to Danny's and climbed up the stairs to chat with him on the back deck. From the deck, Norm shined his flashlight across the neighbor's yard over to the shed where he saw something shiny on the roof. A smile appeared on Norm's face. He hollered at Digger to check the shed roof. Digger climbed up the fence and reached up on to the shed's roof.

Digger hollered back, "Look what I found Norm!"

He was holding up a long barreled shot gun.

Norm looked at Danny and said, "Finish your beer Danny, you're going to jail!"

Danny had a long history with guns. When he was a young boy, he hid up in the attic after his drunken father chased him through the house, threatening another beating. As the story goes, Danny dropped his father with one shot right between the eyes, when he kicked in the attic door. The shooting was ruled self-defense.

The Trade

Danny just smiled as Norm sat down and placed his notebook on the table in between them. Danny's record card looked like the classified section of the city newspaper. He had been in and out of jail since he was a teenager. He was a tough guy who grew up in a tough neighborhood. The constant beatings from his father probably had something to do with it. He went to the school of hard knocks and was educated on the street. It all made sense then to Norm when he looked at the number of charges that were stricken from his record card.

Before Norm could get cordial Danny said, "Ok, let's get to it so I can get out of here."

"I need a phone to make some calls and see what's up."

Norm had a phone brought into the room, and Danny went to work. Norm had to use one hand to stop his jaw from dropping on to the table. Danny dialed up guys and asked who was holding or who had what. When someone questioned him, he simply said he was trying to set a deal up or he wanted to rip them off. He laughed and carried on with the guys on the other end of the phone while Norm played secretary scribbling names and details in his note book.

Within twenty minutes, Danny was able to supply Norm with nine separate names of guys who were either were wanted by the law, and/or were holding large amounts of cocaine or marihuana. Norm knew Danny wasn't bullshitting because the Drug Squad already had investigative files on half the names he supplied. Norm figured nine out of ten names was a pretty good trade, and the info sounded solid. He gave Westwood the green light to release him.

Danny had proven himself reliable to Westwood in the past so Norm got busy doing some follow-up investigation and search warrant preparation. It was a bittersweet relationship for

Norm since he'd spent over two years trying to cultivate an informant in Motor Town. Who knew that a man he had arrested before would already be on the team, just with a different coach?

As a result of Danny's information, Norm was able to execute three separate search warrants that led to arrests and large seizures of marihuana in each case. Another guy was arrested for outstanding warrants. Some of the other targets on the list were eventually busted. Danny was considered a hard core criminal on the street. He was associated to biker gangs. If anyone knew how Danny dealt away his charges, the police would have found him laying face down in a shallow grave somewhere. It was a deadly game he played, but he knew exactly how to play it! He never considered himself a rat, just someone working a patch and trying to keep himself out of jail.

Norm ran into Danny a couple more times over his career. Danny just smiled and nodded to Norm; his way of saying hey. He's still out there somewhere. With Kirk Westwood and Norm both retired, Danny will need a new coach.

8
Special Projects Part 1: Getting Wired

"A man must know his destiny. If he does not recognize it, then he is lost. By this I mean once, twice, or at the very most three times, fate will reach out and tap a man on the shoulder. If he has the imagination, he will turn around and fate will point out to him what fork in the road he should take. If he has the guts, he will take it."

-General George S. Patton Jr.

Norm loved a good challenge...both on and off the job. Normal sports like bowling, baseball, football, and water polo were challenging. Motorcycle riding, the demolition derby, sky diving, and bungee jumping were even better. Just becoming a cop was a challenge for Norm; he didn't know anyone on the job, and he really knew nothing about the job. After high school, Norm swore he'd never work in a factory. Policing looked much more interesting and challenging!

Admittedly, Norm floundered somewhat his first half dozen years on the job. He caught the seven year itch and almost quit the job while contemplating buying a fishing lodge up in northern Ontario. It wasn't until he got steady partners and worked a steady district that he found some purpose. It was his time to get serious about being a good cop. Those years in uniform gained him a reputation as a good street cop. He was praised by his colleagues and even the defense attorneys who represented the criminals he locked up. But after fifteen years of working the front line on the street, Norm grew weary and bored. There had to be more!

Only Dopes Sell Dope

After getting a taste of working in plain clothes, Norm spread his wings. He excelled in the Drug Squad and became an expert witness for marihuana, cocaine, and dilaudid trafficking cases. Being an expert meant you could give your opinion while testifying. Norm had to admit, it was kind of cool when a judge accepted his opinion over the lawyers. In some cases, if Norm couldn't dazzle the court with his brilliance, he could baffle them with his bullshit!

The city police didn't have any written policies or directives for its officers to do undercover buys at that time. Norm asked his sergeant if he could try to make a buy from a target in one of his files. The guy was reportedly selling crack from his house. All the guy had to do was say no to the stranger at his door, but greed is a wonderful thing. Norm did a simple door knock, dropped a name, and asked if he could buy some rock.

When the guy said he didn't sell that, Norm asked for some weed instead. Norm got invited into the house and had to wait in the living room with his wife while he made a phone call.

Norm tried not to freak-out when the woman said, "You look familiar!"

Then she added, "Do you go to the bar down the street?"

"I'm in the wet t-shirt contest there every weekend."

Norm was disgusted just by looking at the woman's big floppy titties through her sweat shirt, seeing those in the flesh would truly be repulsive!

The target said he had to go out for a minute, so the woman continued to babble on. She asked if he had heard about the big fight out front of their place where the cops had beat the shit out of one of their friends. Norm's partner Missy asked if she knew who the cops were! Norm saw the puzzled look on the woman's face and cut Missy off.

"Yeah those fuckin cops, they're all power trippers!"

The woman agreed and continued to babble on until the target returned and sold Norm a nickel bag of weed. Norm's co-workers later arrested the guy for trafficking and sat him in an interview room at the cop shop. When Norm walked in the guy put his head down and melted into his chair. He said he knew Norm was a cop, but he needed the money! It really didn't matter, he was going to jail and Norm had now made a drug buy.

Jesse James

Normally, undercover work was done by out of town cops. It only made sense for officer safety reasons. That was easier said than done for street level buys in the city so Jesse and Norm improvised; sometimes using their own vehicles to make buys. The Drug Squad cars were heat scores, well-known by too many criminals. The force was tight fisted with their cash so Jesse and Norm made their own flash roll of counterfeit cash. It was used when trying to make drug buys...sometimes the dealers wanted to see the cash first.

Even though Jesse and Norm were the best of friends, they had two completely different styles of policing. Jesse James was a cowboy, born a hundred years too late! He loved kicking in doors and pushing the envelope. There was no doubt Jesse could handle himself...Norm had seen proof of that way back in their old water polo days during a bench clearing brawl where Jesse took on three guys at one time...in the pool! Jesse wasn't impressed that Norm stayed on the sidelines with the women. Norm saw that Jesse was fine and holding his own.

Jesse had a heart of glass but an iron fist. There was one poor bastard who made the mistake of jumping Jesse from behind in an alley one night. Jesse reached back and pulled the guy over his shoulder. He instinctively punched him in the face three times and then handcuffed him. The kid later complained of police brutality. There was no brutality, but the kid's face looked like it was hit by a baseball bat! Norm was always glad that Jesse was his friend…and not his enemy; Jesse was one of the toughest bastards he knew.

Ignoring Norm's concern for his personal safety, Jesse set up a weed buy through a police agent from some unknown dealers. Jesse was using the flash roll to make the buy, and the team kept surveillance on him while he drove around the city trying to make the connection. The team lost sight of Jesse when he pulled in an alley to make the deal. Jesse tried to arrest the guy on his own during the money exchange when the guy caught on to the fake cash. The fight was on!

It was quite a scene when Norm pulled up. Jesse had the guy pinned to the ground with his knee on his back and a bowie knife to his throat. The agent was running around trying to collect all the fake money that was blowing all over in the alley and parking lot. Jesse and Norm were not afraid to break new ground in the pursuit of making drug busts. Besides, it was fun!

Eavesdropping

One day Norm's boss Teflon Tim asked him to join him in the wire tap room up in the intelligence office. The detectives from the B & E Squad were doing a wire tap on a group of guys responsible for a string of break-ins. The detective running the investigation asked Norm if he'd be interested in listening to the tapes and reading the transcripts to see if there was any drug talk going on. The civilian monitors transcribing the tapes didn't understand what they were listening to, and the B & E detectives didn't have the drug expertise to pick up on the coded drug talk. After one night of listening to the tapes, Norm was on his way to writing the first drug wire tap ever to be done by the city police. Normally the Mounties handled the drug wire taps from their office.

Norm wrote what is called a Part VI wire tap authorization allowing him to legally tap ten different telephone lines for a period of ninety days. This had to be approved by the brass, then read over, and signed by a judge. The judge was not impressed that one of the names listed in the authorization was a city cop. The B & E Squad had suspicions because of Matty Allen's connections to two of their targets. His voice was identified by an Intelligence investigator on some of the taped conversations. Norm found the wire tap was kind of cool; you got to listen to people's private conversations.

One target in particular *(Jimmy Smith)* was quite hilarious. He'd tell callers not to say anything over the phone because the cops were listening.

Smith would say, "Listen, you can hear the tape recorders."

Then he'd openly make a drug deal during the same call. A few calls later, Smith's wife got on the phone with her girlfriend and talked about some other guy she was banging! The drug investigation took on a life of its own. Norm had to try and identify all the incoming and outgoing calls. With a legal wire tap, the phone company was obliged to supply the owners of the land lines, but cell phones and pagers were becoming more widely used at the time. Instead of talking on the phone, perspective drug buyers would call dealers on their pager, leaving a code that would identify them and what they wanted. It was just one more way drug dealers stayed one step ahead of the cops.

Norm had a buddy at a local telecommunications company. He and Norm planned and implemented an idea that hadn't been done before. Legal authorization was not required to intercept pagers, so Norm's buddy cloned the pagers that were being serviced through his company. So in substance, Norm had six pagers the same as his targets' that would go off whenever calls came in. Between the tapped phones, and the pagers Norm was better equipped to track the movements of the drug dealers. So that his co-workers weren't disturbed by the beeping pagers, Norm switched them all to vibrate mode. It was hilarious one morning when Norm came into work and saw that the pagers had vibrated all over his desk and on to the floor during the night.

By using the intercepted calls as pieces of a puzzle, Norm was able to figure out that there was one main buyer who was making regular trips to Montreal and bringing large quantities of cocaine back home with him. It was great to acquire such information on paper, but live surveillance and some arrests would have to be made to prove Norm's theories. As with any organization, the bosses always want to see results; patience was not one of their virtues. Human tape monitors cost money, and Norm's big boss wasn't happy about the added cost of manpower.

Making Friends

The problem with Norm going out and making a bust simply on the wire tap information meant that the whole investigation could be compromised…and essentially, over. Norm identified a splinter group, operating separately from the main targets, and he was able to get a search warrant for Jake

Lamar's house. Jake and his wife Laura were arrested with cocaine and charged with possession for the purpose of trafficking. Jake was no stranger to the system, and he had four words for Norm:

"Lawyer" and "Go fuck yourself!"

Laura, on the other hand, cried like a baby. That is why it is important to interview people separately. Jake could be a hard ass, but he had no idea what his wife would say. She was embarrassed and worried about her family finding out…she worked at her family's restaurant, a successful business in the city. Laura helped connect the dots on Norm's flow chart of names and who was who from the wire tap information. Regardless of what her husband thought, Laura wanted on the team and to make her charges go away.

One late night at work, Norm cut through the gym on the way into the locker room. Matt Allen was working out. On the way to the toilet, Norm heard a pager vibrating on a bench in the aisle, he glanced down and took notice of the number displayed on the pager…it was a target number from the investigation. The pager belonged to Matty. Norm kept his boss, Teflon Tim in the loop, but Tim really didn't want to get involved. Norm was uncomfortable with the whole situation since Matty was of the same rank, there should have been a senior ranking officer involved in the investigation.

Good or Bad?

After only thirty days into the ninety day authorization, Norm returned from a weekend off to find the big boss had shut the wire tap down! The senior officer explained to Norm that is was his belief that the whole investigation was only about *steroids* and not cocaine or marihuana. He said he further believed that the connections to Matty Allen were only coincidental and that he might be using some mild steroids to enhance his workouts. Norm was pissed! His boss Teflon Tim just shrugged it off.

Norm went on a mission; he executed search warrants at the homes of two of the main targets of the investigation. At Jimmy Smith's house, cocaine, a loaded rifle, and a loaded hand gun were found. Smith's room mate was caught in the web and became another one of Norm's rats. At Craig Santos' house, two pounds of weed and a sawed off shot gun were seized. Smith was arrested later that night coming home with even more cocaine and a wad of cash on him. Norm made a special trip to the big boss' office in the morning and apologized for finding drugs and guns, but no steroids!

There was one nagging concern for Norm after the wire tap was shut down: what about Matty Allen? Norm might have had to work with this guy some day. Allen could have simply been high school friends with the guys. Then again, maybe there was more to it. Norm wanted to know if Allen was good, or bad.

One of the legal requirements of a Part VI authorization is that the people whose phones were tapped have to be personally notified of the interception. Allen was brought into the chief's office where he was notified of the wire tap. They asked him directly if he knew Jimmy Smith or Craig Santos. Allen admitted he knew Santos from high school, but not Smith. They asked if he was involved with or dealing drugs and he said no. That was it!

Norm was then called to the chief's office for a project debriefing. The chief told Norm that Matty Allen denied any wrong doing and he only knew Craig Santos from school. They hadn't asked him if he knew Smith by his previous surname of Jones. Norm knew that Smith had in fact installed an appliance at Matty's house. It was also Smith's phone that the cop was recorded on while he talked about *funny money*...some kind of code word.

A sergeant, who was responsible for getting the listings from all the phone numbers that came up on the wires, was found to be derelict in his duties and transferred out of the intelligence unit. There were too many coincidences that Norm could not explain, but the investigation was done as far as the powers to be were concerned! In his own mind, Norm would never be sure one way or the other, whether Matty Allen was good or bad. Everyone said he was a good cop on the street, and Norm could not dispute that fact.

Years later, Jesse James' twenty-one year old son died of cancer. It was the first time Norm saw Jesse cry; his glass heart was shattered. It was the day of the funeral and Jesse was a mess. Norm told Jesse to cowboy up and put his game face on. Norm had to put his money where his mouth was and address the congregation with a eulogy. The room was packed with all of Jesse's family...relatives, cops, and friends. Grief and silence hung heavy in the air, you could have heard a leaf fall from one of the trees outside. The silence was broken by Jesse's grandson who went running by the family seated in the front row...it was a welcome reprieve that earned a few chuckles.

At the luncheon, after the service someone approached Jesse and asked him where his brother was. He had chosen not to attend the funeral because *he* thought it would be too emotionally difficult. He and Jesse were like night and day. To answer the question, Jesse looked around the room and pointed to Norm.

"There's my brother right there."

After the luncheon, Norm brought the leftover food platters to the police station. He went in through the main lobby and saw something was amiss; some uniformed officers were openly crying and others were running around the main office. Norm put the food down on one of the tables in the report writing room.

He stopped in the staff sergeant's office doorway and asked, "What the hell is going on?"

The staff sergeant said, "Didn't you hear? Matty Allen's been shot!"

Norm thought his heart had absorbed enough sorrow for one day; he left the building in shock. Norm couldn't bring himself to tell Jesse, he would find out eventually on his own.

On the day that Jesse buried his son, Matty Allen was celebrating the birthday of his son. He was working, but he was on the way home for the birthday party. Matty stopped at a party store only a few blocks from his home. Upon exiting the store he saw two youths out on the sidewalk, near the road. Matty's cop instincts told him they were up to no good, so he approached them on foot. Matty was working in plain clothes. He asked the two youths for identification as he approached them; he pulled out his wallet badge to indentify himself. Instead of his identification, one of the youths pulled out a gun and he shot Matty point blank. Instinctively, Matty pulled out his gun to return fire, but something was terribly wrong; he was dying. Matty collapsed and died on a street corner, in his own neighborhood, with his gun and badge in hand. The two youths fled on foot.

Every cop that was working that day felt like they had a rusty steel spike driven through their hearts. They flooded the area and commenced a city-wide man-hunt. Citizens called in with sightings of the two suspects. The cops finally caught and arrested both suspects. The kid who shot Matty Allen was Austin Grey.

Even though Matty Allen was on the way home for his son's birthday, his cop instincts steered him to the place he would give up his life. He interrupted a drug deal; Austin Grey was selling crack, and carrying a gun for protection. Matty Allen made the ultimate sacrifice that day, in the line of duty. The city was outraged and still mourns to this day. Austin Grey never showed any sign of remorse; he will spend some time in jail, but will one day walk the street again as a free man. That is the Canadian justice system.

Was Matty Allen good or bad? The question really doesn't matter now. To his friends, family, co-workers, and the city, Matty Allen is a hero.

Driving School

Norm's wire tap investigation was done, but Jimmy Smith's coke dealing was not. Smith's room mate and Laura Lamar were feeding Norm information, keeping him in the loop as to Smith's activities. Norm received a tip one day that Smith was going to his girlfriend's house *(stash house)* to pick up two ounces of cocaine to be delivered elsewhere. Norm and Topper jumped in the squad's mini-van and headed to the stash house. They set up surveillance on the house, waiting for Smith to arrive.

Smith showed up at the stash house riding a red and white crotch rocket. He was only in the house a few minutes, barely enough time for Norm to call for assistance from a uniform patrol car. Norm made the decision to arrest Smith before he left the driveway and got on to the street. Smith was already on his bike, putting his helmet on when he saw Norm pull in to block the driveway. Norm didn't even have a chance to stop the van; Smith fired up the bike and took off across the front lawn! Topper radioed in that they were *following* the speeding motorcycle. Legislation regarding police pursuits had changed prohibiting most pursuits, especially if the fleeing vehicle was a motorcycle.

Norm tried to keep up to the speeding bike as Smith sped down the side streets. He didn't seem to handle the bike well in the corners, and Norm was almost able to keep up to him. Smith got wise and pulled out on to the River road. He accelerated until Norm almost lost site of him around a bend in the road. Smith got bogged down in traffic and Norm pulled along side in an attempt to cut him off. There was still no assistance from uniform police, so Topper waved his badge out the passenger window, yelling for Smith to stop.

Smith revved the bike's engine and accelerated in an attempt to make a quick u-turn. He was going too fast for the turn, and his bike slid out from under him, dragging his left leg on the ground. The bike's rear wheel hit the curb allowing Smith to get the bike upright again. Smith cranked the throttle and left Norm and his partner in the dust. Sometimes you win, and sometimes you lose! Jimmy Smith won the game that day. Someone later arrested Jimmy Smith for dangerous driving charge that Norm laid. Norm was called in to interview Smith who just smirked the whole time Norm was questioning him. Norm did get the last laugh that day when he noticed Smith was favoring the leg that had been dragged on the pavement.

The smirk disappeared when Smith was leaving and Norm said, "Take care; I hope your leg heals soon!

If you ever want to rob a bank in Canada and make a clean getaway, use a motorcycle. Police are not allowed to pursue motorcycles, in any instance! Norm and Topper were called in to the big boss' office and told they had to report to driver training school. They were verbally chastised for chasing the motorcycle, especially while driving an unmarked van.

Norm couldn't catch Smith with the two ounces of coke that day, but he managed to make his life miserable. Yes, sometimes the pen can be mightier than the sword! A conviction at Smith's trial for dangerous driving meant he lost his drivers license, and he wouldn't be able to drive his company vehicle to conduct his business.

It was Norm who smirked leaving the courtroom; he gave Jimmy Smith a farewell nod and flipped him the bird just for good measure!

9
Tommy O'Shea

What you never see on television are cops sitting hunched over, behind their desks trying to catch up on days of paperwork. The pace was fast in the Drug Squad, and the cops in the unit were always behind on their paperwork. Search warrants, raids, or drug busts always took precedence with the paperwork left behind to be done another time. There were notes, exhibit reports, statements, search warrants, judicial returns, arrest reports, news releases, and court summaries that had to be done properly to keep the bad guys in jail… for at least a day or two!

It was one of those quiet, catch up on paperwork days when Tommy O'Shea called Norm. Tommy said he wanted to join the team. Tommy admitted right off that he had a lengthy criminal record for B & E's and thefts. He had done some serious penitentiary time up in northern Ontario. He repented and wanted to give back to society by helping the police. Norm signed him up for the team.

Tommy knew the street, and knew it wasn't hard to find dope there. Norm met up with him personally and knew right off he'd fit in. Tommy looked like a biker. He was skinny, with long black hair half way down his back, and he was covered in tattoos. He wore a black concert shirt, ripped jeans, and one of those wallets attached to his belt with a chain. Tommy proudly showed Norm a hidden pouch in his cowboy boot where he concealed a knife *for protection.* Norm explained the difference between the nice to know, and need to know types of information needed to make drug busts, and then sent Tommy on his way.

Different Rats

There are actually two different types of informants the police can use to obtain information. Police agents are one type. Agents are actually hired by police to supply information for money, under a written contract. In return, they have to appear in court and testify as to the validity of the information they provided. Police agents are often used to infiltrate organized crime rings or motor cycle gangs. They can be useful in introducing undercover cops once they have the trust of the organization they have infiltrated. The downside of being a police agent is that they usually have to be moved or relocated later, for their own safety.

The other type of informant is a confidential source; completely anonymous, except to the police handler. They have to prove their reliability, but they never have to reveal their identity or testify in court. Cops have to protect their sources and are actually protected by law in that regard. Judges and lawyers can ask, but a cop does not have to reveal the identity of his source!

Norm saw this put to the test several times, once while he was on the witness stand, testifying at a drug trial. Defense lawyers always tell their clients they will find out who the rat was, and in some cases, they actually charge their clients extra to find out. The informant's identity was *never* put into the police reports; lawyers would just bullshit their clients to gain their trust…and money!

Upon cross-examination during one drug trial, the defense counsel asked Norm the question, "I'm going to suggest to you that John Doe was actually your informant?"

Now, keep in mind there are only two answers to that question: yes and no. The problem for Norm was that the lawyer had the informant's name correct. That was the point where the prosecutor should have gotten off their ass and objected to the question saying it wasn't in the public's best interest for the officer to answer that question. If Norm said no, he would have committed perjury. If he said yes, it could have meant grave danger to the informant.

Norm looked over to the judge and said, "I don't think I should be obliged to answer that question, your honor."

The prosecutor finally caught on and got into a discussion with the defense counsel and judge about the dangers of questioning Norm about his informant. The judge agreed that Norm had to protect the identity of his informant and should not have to answer any question that might reveal their identity.

Blackjack, one of Norm's buddies in the Drug Squad, got the same type of question while he was on the witness stand. That judge didn't like the fact Blackjack wouldn't reveal his source to the court, and he called for a private meeting in his chambers. Blackjack's informant called him during the trial saying he was terrified because the lawyer said he would get the informants name. The informant was still close to the accused and was getting play by play action during the trial. The lawyer and the judge were close friends who actually vacationed together in the winter. The high court judge and prominent lawyer tried to get Blackjack to reveal the informants name, caring more about money, than the person's safety. The rookie prosecutor was intimidated by the judge and veteran lawyer. Even though the judge demanded to know the identity of the informant and threatened Blackjack with contempt of court charges, he stood his ground and protected his informant.

The whole trial was a farce! During the trial, the jury was allowed to hear only *pre-selected* portions of the evidence since they might find it too prejudicial against the accused!

Blackjack had informant information that the bad guy would be delivering coke to someone else...on a certain time and date. The Drug Squad set up surveillance using Blackjack's information and followed the dealer to a corner store where they watched him attempt to complete the drug deal. Norm went after the dealer to catch him with the dope in hand, but he tossed it into the snow near a trash dumpster. After arresting the dealer, Norm followed the guy's footprints in the foot of fresh snow and found a plastic bag containing two ounces of cocaine that he had tossed.

At the conclusion of the trial, the judge addressed the jury before they were sent to deliberate. The judge basically called Norm and Blackjack liars since they described the *exact* location of where the dope was found differently….one said near the N/E corner of the dumpster and the other said the S/E corner…a matter of about six feet! The judge then added that *he* found it highly unlikely that Norm could find the bag of dope amongst all the trash surrounding the dumpster! There had been a fresh snowfall and Norm told the jury how he simply followed the dealer's footprints in the snow when he found the bag of coke.

The one-two punch was delivered when the jury came back from deliberation. The judge told them he wanted to poll the jury as a group instead of asking them individually if they agreed with the verdict. They all nodded to the verdict of not guilty, and then a female jurist in the front row fainted. The judge ordered that the courtroom be cleared immediately. Norm and Blackjack were standing beside the woman when she came to.

She said, "A couple of us thought he was guilty, but we were bullied into agreeing to get the case over with!"

The rookie prosecutor was so upset by the whole trial that he resigned from being a drug prosecutor. Norm and Blackjack told Teflon Tim, thinking the prosecution should demand a retrial. As usual Teflon Tim just shrugged, and then told them to get over it.

007

Tommy told Norm he would do what ever it took to help lock up bad guys, but he hadn't really thought of the ramifications of his actions. Norm only used Tommy as a confidential informant for his own safety. Tommy broke a cardinal rule one day when meeting Norm: he brought his girlfriend along and said she was cool with what he was doing. Norm knew better. If and when they ever broke up, Tommy being a rat would come back to bite him in the ass! Unfortunately, Norm had to say I told you so when Tommy later got dumped by his woman. Things got nasty during the split, and she started blabbing to everyone she knew.

Tommy had his domestic problems, but he had a good job to keep him occupied during the day and then he'd prowl the streets at night. He offered up some small time weed and coke dealers to Norm. Tommy really didn't care about the reward money; he liked the action! He told Norm he felt like an undercover cop; he got off on playing the role. Tommy led Norm to one house where all five of the guys in the house either had drugs on them, or they had outstanding arrest warrants. Norm was able to roll one of those guys, and that guy eventually led Norm to busting Joe Anthony who turned out to be one of Norm's best informants!

Another problem drug cops sometimes run into is trying to protect their rats when they get into trouble. They want to be anonymous, but as soon as a traffic cop pulls them over, they drop the drug cop's name. It's not too hard for the traffic cop to figure out what's going on. It's a dangerous game but one that many rats will play to their own advantage.

Busted & Burned

Norm got a call from the cell block sergeant one night. Tommy O'Shea was in custody, and he asked to see Norm. Tommy was apparently defending the honor of his new girlfriend at a local bar, and he pulled out his boot knife to defend himself. Tommy didn't hurt anyone, but he got his ass locked up for waving around a knife in the bar. Like all informants, Tommy expected special treatment because he *worked for the police*.

Norm had to explain to Tommy how that was not a well-known fact, and that his name was tucked away in a locked cabinet for his own safety. He thought he should have received credit for all the busts Norm made as a result of his information. Tommy forgot about the cash he received as a reward for his information. The prosecutor would expect a fair trade of something substantial if he was to offer Tommy leniency on his knife wielding charge.

Tommy got bail like any other criminal does, and he got back on the street trying to dig up something for Norm. The exodus of Tommy's girlfriend was just the beginning of his troubles. He had a chronic illness that eventually cost him his job. His new girlfriend took him in, but Tommy's physical and mental state deteriorated. Tommy told Norm he was getting addicted to the pain pills the doctor had given him. He said he felt like a junkie but he couldn't handle the pain without the pills.

A few years later, Norm picked up the local newspaper and saw Tommy had made the front page. He was on the outs with his girlfriend, and he tried to win her back by causing a scene outside the store she worked at. Tommy caught everyone's attention by walking around with a gas can, pouring gasoline all over himself. Everyone pleaded with Tommy to put the gas can down, but he continued pouring the gasoline on himself. Before anyone could do anything to stop him, Tommy by he lit himself on fire with the cigarette he was holding.

Tommy was engulfed in flames in a split second. Bystanders tried to put out the fire by using their coats. One of them had a fire extinguisher and managed to put out the fire. A couple people received minor burns to their hands from trying to put out the fire. Tommy's injuries were critical and he was shipped off to a burn unit out of town. That was the last Norm heard of Tommy O'Shea.

A few years later after Norm retired, he struck up a conversation with a bar maid at a local watering hole. It turns out she was the sister of a pair of brothers Norm had chased around and locked up way back in his walking beat days. The woman was a hottie, but unlike her brothers, she never got into trouble. She mentioned that she never had any luck with men and was on the outs with her current biker boyfriend. As she told her tale of woe Norm's jaw dropped to the bar. She said she was Tommy O'Shea's estranged girlfriend when he set himself on fire! She was one of those women who liked the bad boy type of guys. Norm couldn't help pointing out to her that she might consider changing her taste in men.

Poor Tommy, he got burned in more ways than one!

10
The Watsons

Squeaky Sally always came through for Norm. She kept him current with new dilaudid dealers as well as the old regulars. Sally had helped Norm bust Paula Watson on at least three different occasions. Paula had been a long time user who was banging heroin when Norm was popping zits. She started selling dillies to supply her own habit. Paula was better looking in her day when she sold her ass on the street to support her heroin habit. She learned it was much easier to work from home and to sell pills to make a living. Paula had been in the game a long time when Norm finally had his day in court on one of her trafficking charges. She whispered in her lawyer's ear, telling him what questions to ask Norm as he tried to get qualified for the first time as an expert witness. The judge did not qualify Norm as an expert. He had to accept the fact that Paula was simply more of a drug expert than him!

Like Mother, like Father...like Son!

Tommy O'Shea had told Norm about a guy named Jeff who was selling weed; he had a gun and was driving around the city, dealing from his red camaro. Norm later received another tip from a uniform cop that the guy was in fact Jeff Watson, son of Paula. Norm did his homework and eventually got a search warrant to kick Jeff's front door in. The Drug Squad found a half pound of weed, and ammunition for a .25calibre hand gun *(the gun was not recovered at that time)* that Jeff said he knew nothing about.

Jeff was a good looking kid…blonde hair, blue eyes, and well-built. The young girls liked him and his fancy car. Jeff had a huge circle of friends. They all liked to party but not by sticking needles in their arms like his parents.

Unlike his mom who would never become a rat, Jeff went for the cheese right off and joined the team. Jeff was able to help Norm with some of the bigger pieces of the dilly puzzle he had been working on for over a year. Even though Jeff was dealing weed, his family connections kept him in the loop with the Piccadilly Circus. Jeff was completely estranged from his mom, but he told Norm his father Mickey was also using dilaudid and selling it to supply his own habit. Some families are in the construction or restaurant business; the Watsons were in the drug business!

Jeff told Norm that he hated his father because his two younger siblings still lived with him, and they were exposed to all the junkies and the shit going on in Mickey's house. Jeff wasted no time in giving up his father to Norm. Jeff confirmed to Norm that Duke Delaney was in fact, one of the main suppliers of dilaudid in the city. Rumor had it Duke was buying excess pills from a terminally ill cancer patient. Duke was no dummy; he'd befriend a cancer patient and then offer to help them out financially by buying their excess pills from them. Doctors had no problem over-prescribing serious pain medication to terminal cancer patients. It was a futile attempt in trying to improve their quality of life.

Norm was batting .500 with Duke: one bust and one dry warrant. Norm had struck out on one attempt when Duke had the cash but had not yet picked up the pills. Surveillance was always difficult where Duke lived and Norm had to rely on informant information to know when Duke was holding. There were always users going in and out of his place. He also used some of the women, trading drugs for sex. Jeff gave Norm an engraved invitation to Mickey's house where he'd set up a shooting gallery for his dillyhead friends. They were waiting on a delivery from Duke Delaney.

The Gang's all here

Cops have to consider many factors before breaking down someone's door and rushing into their house. They have to make entry plans that take into account foot traffic in and out of the house, and how to approach it un-detected. In this particular case, there were small children in the house, along with some kind of ankle biting mutt. Other needle users would be in there along with Mickey. The possibility of weapons was always a big unknown! Surprise is always the key; it usually takes about six to eight seconds for people to react and realize what's going on when the cops rush in.

The housing projects where Mickey lived were dimly lit; it's always easier to sneak up on someone in the dark. The Drug Squad packed itself into a van and waited in the parking lot for the opportune moment to attack Mickey's house. A taxi pulled into the lot, and two guys headed to Mickey's front door. Norm gave the go-ahead and the team bailed out, running up behind the two guys as they entered the house. The two guys were knocked to the floor…one of them rolled forward and down a flight of stairs just inside the door…oops! Norm shouted, "Police, search warrant!"

Drug cops pointing guns ordered everyone in the living room to get down on the floor. Once everyone was cuffed and under control, it was time to take names and identify everyone that was there. Under the power of the search warrant, everyone in the house was put under arrest for possession of narcotics. Who would actually be charged with what was sorted out later depending on what was found. Norm was pleasantly surprised by all the different people in the house…the gang were all there!

Jeff had been in the house while feeding Norm information. Mickey and his dad Brownie were there…and even Paula, his estranged ex-wife! Norm had to hold back his smile when he saw Squeaky Sally. Duke Delaney was there with a stripper, a former rat of Norm's. There was one other dillyhead Norm knew, and the two taxi guys who were in town from Cornhole, Ontario.

Getting in and getting everyone's attention was the easy part. Searching the house and everyone in it was a major chore! Everyone on the squad had been previously assigned a specific task; they worked as a team. Someone would have to record all the names and check to see if they were wanted or had any arrest warrants outstanding. Other officers were dedicated to search the occupants and the house. A female officer was almost always needed to search the females. If the Drug Squad didn't have one on the team, a uniform officer would have to be called to the scene.

For some unknown reason, it was always really hot in drug dealers' houses. Perhaps it was because *Welfare* was paying the utility bills! Wearing a bullet proof vest and carrying about twenty pounds of police equipment didn't help. The raid on Mickey Watson was also in the winter, so the squad wore warm clothes. Throughout the search, squad members had to strip down, adding clothes and equipment to a pile in a corner as the heat took its toll. Mickey kept a pretty clean house, so the cops didn't have to shake all the cockroaches out of their clothes like in so many other houses they searched.

Sorting Shit

In being the author of the search warrant, Norm got to interview all the occupants of the house, one by one. By speaking to everyone individually, apart from the others, it took suspicion away from anyone who might give up valuable information. Remember that nobody likes a rat, and everyone in the room had to wonder what, if anything, the others in the room said. There was a lot of bullshit to sort through as everyone told their tale of woe, but Norm managed to get at least one little, useful tidbit of info from each person.

Mickey was funny; he made it sound like the gang was all there to watch a movie, but no one brought popcorn. Everyone hates a whiner, and Mickey was a whiner! He told Norm he wanted to help out, but he never really offered any. That was yet to be seen since Mickey took the rap along with the two guys from Cornhole for the 71 dilaudid pills found during the search of his house. Squeaky Sally told Norm she was there to pick up from Mickey. Jeff told Norm that Mickey was waiting for a delivery from someone…one of the guys from Cornhole he thought.

Duke put some more of the puzzle together for Norm. His previous trafficking charges were coming to court soon, and he was starting to sweat. Yup, Duke went for the cheese! He knew Norm had nothing more on him, so why not give up some information on someone else to take the heat off him…he was no dummy! Duke said he was waiting on a supply from one of the Cornhole guys…but not the two guys that were there. Apparently the pills in Mickey's house were only part of the shipment that came down from Cornhole.

Norm worked his magical charm, and one of the Cornhole guys rolled over. He said he was just a runner for two bikers from Cornhole who stayed in a city motel while he did their deliveries. They knew how lucrative the dilaudid market in the city was. They obtained it so cheaply in Cornhole that it was worth the trip. The guy added that the bikers were heavy users, and they might be carrying a gun.

Funny Money

Jeff knew lots of people in different drug circles, and one in the funny money business. He told Norm that Moe Maker was growing weed in his house. Moe was famous in Canada for flooding the country with superior quality counterfeit $100 bills. He is the reason stores actually stopped accepting the large bills from anyone!

Color photocopiers were a wonderful invention, and Moe learned to take full advantage of it. His secret was using top quality paper and different serial numbers. Others had bypassed some of the bill's security features, but Moe became a master at the art of counterfeiting. The R.C.M.P. still use his name when they refer to his counterfeit bills.

Moe had a network of people moving the funny money from Windsor to Montreal and some in the western provinces. Norm later learned from a niece who was tied into the circle just how lucrative the scam was. Moe sold the bills at twenty or thirty cents on the dollar, depending on how much you bought. Then they'd go on shopping sprees, hitting large retail malls, using the large bills for each purchase. They pocketed the change. They even had the balls to return some of their purchases for full refunds of real money! They would also sell their purchases on the black market for fifty cents on the dollar…it was all easy money! Moe eventually got busted, and the Canadian government changed their security features on their paper money.

Jeff's information was good and Norm caught Moe about half way through his harvest of one hundred marihuana plants. He had sold off the first half, but had to take the rap for the remaining crop. He had a real greenhouse set up attached to his house. It was on a dead end street, not really visible to anyone else. Moe won himself some bonus charges; he had another photo copier and was playing with some new funny money. He was still on parole for the previous offences, so he was not allowed to have any of the equipment he was in possession of. Too bad for Moe, a talent wasted.

Double Agents

Like so many informants, Jeff liked to work from both sides of the street. He gave Norm information to work his patch but also to keep the heat away from him and his own criminal enterprises. He gave up his weed supplier Moe, so he decided to get in on the easy cash from the Piccadilly Circus. He already knew all the players, so it was a natural transition to satisfy his greed for easy money. Squeaky Sally and another source gave Norm Jeff's new address and confirmed the fact that he was now getting supplied directly from the Cornhole guys. Good ole Mickey also made a call for some brownie points; he told Norm the Cornhole guys were in town.

Even though Jeff had been giving Norm some valuable information, he was dealing drugs, and he had to go down. Norm and his sergeant the Italian Stallion set up surveillance about two blocks from Jeff's house. Norm had been informed that Jeff was waiting on a delivery, so there wasn't enough information to obtain a search warrant on the house. Norm's real goal was to nab the main man from Cornhole. Surveillance can be long and boring and that day was no exception. Norm and the Stallion were just chit-chatting and taking turns keeping an eye on the house through a pair of binoculars.

Norm was re-adjusting the binoculars and said, "Holy shit!"

He saw two guys sitting in their own car, parked about a half a block ahead of Norm and the Stallion. They were also looking at Jeff's house with binoculars! Norm was even more dumfounded when the car's license plate came back registered to Mack Crow!

"What in hell were these guys up to?"

There were only a couple of scenarios that made sense; they both meant some kind of rip off was about to go down!

Follow the Leader

While Norm and the Stallion pondered their options, a car pulled into Jeff's driveway. The passenger got out, went in to the house, and then returned a minute later. The car backed out of the driveway and Mack Crow followed it down the road. Norm followed Mack and the other car, calling for some uniform assistance. Two cars were now going to have to be taken down at the same time. Norm coordinated things over the radio as everyone followed each other down the road. All the cop cars converged and were in place when the procession stopped for a red light.

Norm yelled, "Go! Go! Go!"

Both uniform and plain clothes cars surrounded and boxed in both of the drug dealers' cars. The occupants were ordered out at gunpoint. People sometimes think the police are over zealous when doing things like that, but in that particular case it was a wise move. Mack Crow and his well-known buddy both had loaded hand guns under the front seat! It was now obvious to Norm that they were going to rip off the Cornhole guys.

The passenger of the other car had bottles full of dilaudid pills from a Cornhole doctor. The prescription was not in his name. The uniform cops also found a hand gun under his seat.

Who knows what would have happened if the cops didn't stop these guys? There could have been a gun fight right there on the street!

Everybody in both cars went to jail, but there was still somebody missing. Norm had to get a warrant for Jeff's house to see just what the Cornhole guys delivered. A search of Jeff's house revealed more of the usual suspects there waiting for their fix. Jeff had taken delivery of some dilaudid. Norm wasn't at the house, but one of the squad called with a surprise…they located the missing .25 cal handgun that Jeff had managed to hang on to since his first bust. Guns and drugs go hand in hand…it's a dangerous game!

Norm learned who the Cornhole doctor was that was supplying the dealers, and he complained to the college of physicians. It took several more months before they finally forced the old horse doc into retirement. He was dishing out pills like they were candy to anyone who wanted them!

Jeff continued to work for Norm and the Drug Squad. The police department didn't like to keep anyone in the Drug Squad too long, so Norm was transferred to another unit. Jeff was introduced to, and handed off to, a new drug cop. Jeff was another dumb-ass who thought he could trust his girlfriend; he brought her to the meeting when Norm handed him off. Norm just shook his head. She had been dealing dilaudid behind Jeff's back while he took care of his weed business. Norm had managed to bust them together on one occasion with thirty-eight dilaudid pills; Jeff said he didn't know about her private enterprise…or the fact she was banging one of the Cornhole guys who was supplying her!

Jeff later paid the price for his misplaced trust when she dumped him. She left a long message on another drug dealer's phone machine. The message was heard over and over and passed on to other dealers and users. Norm's not sure what happened to Jeff after that, but he did hear that someone trashed Jeff's fancy car and then set it on fire! Go figure!

Paula continued to be Paula, living one day at a time, getting high as each day passed her by. She continued to sell to a few friends to supply her own habit.

Mickey continued to help Norm for a while, but then Norm lost track of him after being transferred. Children's Aid stepped in after one of the raids at Mickey's house and took the kids, but as usual they were obliged to give them back.

Norm later received some accolades when the judge hearing the case for the main Cornhole guy quoted Norm from his expert testimony. The judge rejected the joint submission by the crown and defense counsel and sentenced the guy to three years in penitentiary!

11
Joe Anthony

After two years in the Drug Squad, Norm was on fire...kickin ass and taking names! With more than a few regular rats, the information highway led straight to Norm. There were times he wrote and executed up to three search warrants in a single day! That meant he worked long and crazy hours, but he also racked up the overtime. Making arrests meant new opportunities to cultivate even more informants. Norm had watched the veterans in amazement when he first got into the Drug Squad. Now it was his turn to shine and keep the unit hopping. The unit was self-motivated...someone would get a tip, and the unit went into action. All the other cops in the unit had informants too; sometimes the action was non-stop!

Most informants were involved in their own drug sub-culture; each particular drug had its own following. Dilaudid users did not normally use cocaine, and coke users were not normally pot smokers. Drug cops had to be knowledgeable in all the drug subcultures, their informants were the perfect source to obtain that knowledge. One tip led Norm to a body builder who was selling steroids, another drug sub-culture Norm had to learn about before building a case and making an arrest. Once again, steroid dealers/users had their own following, mostly body builders from the local gyms. Norm busted one guy with over $10,000 in steroids but then learned from an R.C.M.P. expert that the amount was not unusual for a top ranked body builder to use personally while in training.

Information from an arrest interview led Norm to a couple guys who were dealing steroids and cocaine. Norm already had a file on Joe Anthony for dealing coke. The other guy was

Benny Bunko. Norm was still busy chasing some of his targets from the wire tap, but the information on Anthony and Bunko was fresh and good. Norm already knew where Joe Anthony lived and what kind of car he drove. Norm didn't know if he kept any drugs in his house, but he knew he made deliveries with his car.

Any Given Day

Working the day shift in the Drug Squad was normally quiet; the cops sometimes had court appearances, or they'd have a chance to catch up on paperwork. Most drug dealers and users don't start their day until late in the afternoon. By starting their day shift at eight or nine in the morning, the drug cops could get a head start on the bad guys. In an attempt to clean things up after his drug wire tap, Norm prepared a search warrant for Jake Lamar's house. The Drug Squad raided the house and locked up the Lamar's. It was still early in the day when Norm got the call that Joe Anthony was holding a pile of coke.

Norm had his hands full but was able to send a couple of drug cops out to watch Anthony's house. He gave them instructions to follow Anthony and arrest him since he'd have coke in the car with him. Norm didn't have enough information to get a warrant for the house at that point. To complicate matters even more, Norm would have to try and take down Benny Bunko at the same time so one man wouldn't warn the other. Norm had enough information for a warrant on Bunko's house, but it took time to put it all on paper and get it signed. That meant no lunch again for poor Norm, not a bad thing considering his weight gain while in the Drug Squad.

The food Gods were on Norm's side. He had to wait for the warrant to be signed, and there just happened to be a sandwich shop in the building. Norm was shoving the mystery sandwich into his pie hole when the cops watching Joe Anthony called. They had busted Anthony with some coke and cash on him. They said there was more in the trunk.

"Shit!" Norm said out loud.

That meant another search warrant to search the car, but it would have to wait...one thing at a time...finish the sandwich first! The day shift was almost over, but Teflon Tim had called in the afternoon shift early to handle all the action! Norm got Bunko's warrant signed. He got another message from the cops with Anthony...he wanted to talk.

That was a first. Nobody ever rolled that quickly!

Norm had the cops impound Anthony's car until a warrant could be obtained for it, and he had them put Joe on ice until he could catch his breath. Then he put another plan into place.

The afternoon shift was put into play, they hit Bunko's place around 4pm. During the search of Bunko's house the Drug Squad recovered two hand guns and two rifles, along with some ammunition, steroids, weigh scales, and cut for cocaine. He was charged with multiple weapons charges.

Joe Anthony's car was eventually searched; the cops found more cocaine and cash in a safe box in the trunk of the car. In total, Joe had almost an ounce of coke and over $8,000 in cash on him and in the car. Norm noticed a safety deposit box key on Joe's key ring, and told him he was getting a search warrant for the bank box.

Joe told Norm he'd find another ten grand in the bank box!

Say it ain't so Joe!

When Norm walked into the interview room, Joe Anthony looked relieved! Joe said to Norm, "It's like you just took a piano off my back."

Norm replied, "What do you mean by that?"

Joe said he'd been dealing for a long time. He was tired of looking over his shoulder, and he had been paranoid about getting caught.

"It's over now" he said.

"What do I have to do to walk away from this?"

There it was. That was the million dollar question. Joe was no dummy…he knew the gig was up and he did not want to go to jail!

Norm explained exactly how he'd have to play the game…how he'd have to give up three other drug dealers or three times the product he had been caught with.

Joe didn't bat an eye. "I can do that!"

"So who do you know, and what can you do for me?"

"I know lot's of people!"

Norm leaned back in his chair, and listened intently as Joe talked about the dealers he bought coke from and other guys he knew who were also selling coke. Joe talked like a professional businessman; he knew the coke business, no doubt. He was confident and well-spoken, not like any of Norm's other informants. Joe was clean cut and well built, his body building efforts showed through his designer clothes. His tanned skin and blue eyes were accented by the heavy gold jewelry he wore.

Joe knew some important people…he either bought coke from them or sold it to them. He didn't reveal his client list but said that a former mayor and prominent city lawyer were on that list. He said he normally got his cocaine from well-known city businessman Michael Cook, who was known for his local charity work. Norm had heard rumors about Cook before but never had enough proof to start a file on him. Joe said he'd buy up to two ounces of coke at a time from Cook or his drug dealer/partner. Cook would never actually touch the coke or money in Joe's presence, but he was always in the room or nearby. He'd broker the deal, keeping a low profile during the exchange.

Playing the Game

Norm was impressed! Joe said he couldn't give up Cook right off, or he'd know it was Joe who ratted him out. Cook was associated to a local biker gang, and Joe feared for his life. He would help Norm to understand Cook's network but couldn't give him up directly.

The conversation had been mostly one-sided, and then Joe said, "So what can you do for me?"

Norm told Joe if he could deliver everything he promised, he might be able to completely walk away from his drug charges. The only catch was that once charges were laid, the prosecutor would have to be told of Joe's cooperation before the charges could be dismissed. A look of pain started to come over Joe's face.

"If you charge me, everyone will know, and I will be of no use to you."

Joe told Norm that Cook knew people in the court house and that they always checked the dockets to see who'd been arrested. If the word got out that Joe got busted, everyone on the street would avoid him like the plague. Norm got the point. If Joe wasn't left in the game, he wouldn't be able to fulfill his obligations. The situation got into an area above Norm's pay grade, so he went to see Teflon Tim.

Norm explained to Teflon Tim that he thought he had a good fish on the line that could lure in even bigger fish, maybe even Michael Cook! Teflon Tim was impressed and he suggested they hold off on processing Joe Anthony. His charges could be laid at a later date. He told Norm to put Joe on a short leash, giving him a month to work his patch in an attempt to make his charges disappear. Norm had been burned by informants with big promises before, but he agreed it was a good idea.

Norm went back to Joe Anthony with the plan. He told Joe the cops would leave him in the game, but he had a month to produce results if he wanted to walk away from his charges. Joe looked like he'd just won the lottery. As a consolation prize, Joe pushed the envelope and asked Norm for his car, cell phone, and pager back! Teflon Tim agreed Joe would need those things to play the game, but the cops would keep his dope and cash as collateral.

The deal was made and Joe Anthony was drafted by the blue team. It had been a very long day, but Norm was sure he had cultivated a very important source.

Cocaine 101

The first thing that made an impression on Norm when he later met up with Joe Anthony was his punctuality. Drug dealers or buyers, or anyone else involved in the business, were never on time! The cops called it *drug time*. Norm met Joe and discussed some of Joe's options for clearing his slate. Joe had a minor criminal record from many years prior for a petty crime, but for the most part he had stayed under the radar. He told Norm things about his personal life and how he got into the drug business. He had a family, but he kept the drug business completely away from them. Joe was serious about his personal health, and he didn't do drugs, with the exception of smoking the odd joint. He never used the coke he sold, and he rarely drank. He was a rare breed as drug dealers go, a businessman to say the least.

Joe had a list of regulars who were long time customers. He did not sell to kids or anyone he did not know. Most of his customers were loyal. That kept Joe in the money, and under the radar. But in Joe's case, someone got busted and dropped his name. Joe asked Norm about that, but he didn't push the issue when Norm said he couldn't discuss any of his other sources. As Joe talked about his coke business, Norm listened and learned. Most of Norm's drug arrests had involved dilaudid or marihuana, with the exception of a few smaller coke busts. Joe explained how dealing in small quantities made him more money, and it helped keep him under the radar.

Cocaine is like any other commodity really; if you buy it in bulk, it is cheaper. The coke gets cut as it passes down the chain, which adds to the profit margin. Joe called it his bread and butter.

Hot Potato

It only took Joe one week to offer up his first fish. He told Norm he'd be meeting a guy who wanted to buy some coke from him. Roger Danby was a nobody, with no criminal record, but he was about to become a somebody. It really didn't matter to Norm, who he was. If he was holding the hot potato, he was going to jail! There are three elements to being in possession: knowledge, consent, and control. If someone knows they're buying cocaine, they consent to buy it, and then they take control…they have *possession*. It is as simple as that. Joe met up with Danby, sold him the coke, and then let the

Drug Squad take him down. Call it a set up if you want…it was!

Of course, in reality, things can't be done that simply. It would have been obvious to Danby he was set up. Joe and Norm hatched a plan where Norm saw the exchange, and then the team stopped both men as they left in the separate vehicles. After surrounding Danby and arresting him, Norm pretended to shout orders over the radio for someone to stop the guy in the other car. Norm then played the heavy with Danby, demanding to know who the other guy was. The trick was to try and take the heat off Joe, to keep Danby's head spinning and guessing as to what just went down. Teflon Tim was there for the take down. His smile said it all when he found the three ounces of coke in the back seat of Danby's car. Teflon Tim saw that Joe was serious about working his patch!

Timing is everything

It was obvious to Norm that Joe could supply the *need to know* information. He told Norm of other dealers he was aware of. Norm's ultimate goal was Michael Cook's organization, but that wouldn't be easy. In the mean time, Joe offered up another small fish to Norm. The bust netted one bad guy, a small amount of coke, and just under $1,000 in cash. There was supposed to be two more ounces of coke, but the cops couldn't find it. Proceeds of Crime legislation had recently been passed, so if the cops could prove the dealer was trafficking or in possession for the purpose of trafficking, the government could seize any cash or property believed to be derived from the criminal enterprise. Joe didn't realize how lucky he was!

Joe called Norm back after the bust. He said the guy had a couple ounces of coke stashed in his car, but it wasn't there at the time of the raid. That guy got lucky!

Joe attempted to set up another guy that was a well-known shit head to the city police. He delivered an 8-ball to the guy. Then the Drug Squad followed and took him down. The guy swore up and down that he didn't have any drugs on him. Norm's partner Blackjack stripped the guy down to his birthday suit in the back of the cop van, but no drugs were found. They let the dirt bag go.

Blackjack said to Norm, "I looked everywhere but down his fucking throat!"

They looked at each other and realized that was the only place he could have concealed the paper deck. A call from Joe later confirmed their fears. The guy was freaking out during the whole search thinking the coke was going to dissolve in his mouth. It was the shit head's lucky day!

The icing on the cocaine cake was delivered to Norm by Joe in the form of Drew Dancer. Joe gave Norm enough information to hit Dancer's house with a search warrant. Norm hit the mother load! Dancer was sitting on over half a pound of coke, about $40,000 worth. He also had an illegal switchblade knife. Joe had told Norm that Dancer was one of Michael Cook's mules, and that the coke belonged to Cook. Dancer knew exactly who Norm was after, but he said he couldn't offer up any names if he wanted to stay alive. Dancer's lawyer begged for leniency by telling Norm he wanted to cooperate, but he couldn't give up any names. Too bad, so sad! Dancer spent two years in jail for Michael Cook!

Joe Anthony had done it; he successfully worked his patch and Norm shredded his whole charge file.

Payback is a Bitch!

Life was good for Joe with the cops off his back, and his business back on track. Unfortunately for Joe, Dancer had told Cook that he believed it was Joe was who ratted him out. Not a word was said to Joe, but one night someone threw Molotov cocktails at Joe's house and car. Joe was lucky. Neither device caused any serious damage. Cook later verbally accused Joe of being the rat, even though he had no actual proof. The sad fact is, they really didn't need any proof, and the accusation is all that was necessary. It was enough to get Joe punched in the head one night in a bar by one of Cook's cronies. Joe suffered a broken nose from the sucker shot.

Maybe Joe's good luck had changed. He told Norm that someone at his gym stole all his jewelry from his locker, about $8,000 worth of gold. Joe was not a violent man, and he wouldn't carry a gun like many other drug dealers. He would just write off some of his customers after they ran up huge debt, and couldn't pay. Joe said it was just the cost of doing business. He had one biker customer who placed an order then pulled a knife when Joe arrived at his house. The biker wanted Joe's money and his dope for free! What goes around, comes around though…as they say. Jesse James raided the biker's house at the end of that summer, seizing several towering marihuana plants that he had growing around his built-in pool in the back yard.

Jesse crashed through the front door so hard he literally scared the shit out of the biker's wife. She was in the bathtub at the time. When the drug cops checked the bathroom, they found her in the tub with an O'Henry bar floating beside her!

Things started to change in the city, and across the country as the bikers took over the cocaine trade. They recruited and expanded their ranks, sending out the message, *if you wanted to deal coke; you'd better deal for them.* Joe's suppliers were drying up and he didn't want to deal with the bikers. A buddy set up a deal with an unknown source for Joe to buy a kilo of coke.

Joe trusted his buddy; he met him and the supplier at a local motel. The unknown guy introduced himself by pulling out a pistol and pointing it at Joe's head! He tied up Joe and his buddy and asked where the $35,000 was. It was a rip off! Luckily Joe had stashed the cash before he got to the motel. The guy pistol whipped Joe when he refused to give it up.

Joe saw his life flashing by as he felt the warmth of his own blood running down the side of his face and neck. The guy threatened to kill Joe, but he never gave it up. Eventually, the guy became frustrated and took off, leaving Joe and his buddy hog tied in the hotel room.

Joe was able to reach a pocket knife he had hidden, and he cut himself free. He looked at his buddy before cutting him free; he wondered if he was in on the whole thing. Once again, Joe chalked the whole experience up to the cost of doing business!

What else could he do? Call the cops and tell them he was pistol whipped when he wouldn't give up his drug money?

That was Joe's life as a drug dealer, he accepted it.

Cokeheads

Joe and Norm met on a regular basis to catch up. Joe wasn't like any other drug dealer or informant. As Norm learned more about the cocaine trade, Joe learned more about how the drug cops and the legal system worked. By staying in touch, Joe figured he got to stay in business. He kept Norm well-informed but he'd also call for the odd favor, like the time he got stopped for speeding. Joe called Norm on his cell phone and then handed it to the traffic cop when he came up to the car window. That was the typical cop/rat relationship; they tried to scratch each other's back.

Although cops and their informants developed a rapport, there was a line that wasn't to be crossed. Informants were just that. They were not your friend or someone you should socialize with in public. It was a professional relationship, and their identity had to remain secret. As much as Norm and Joe liked each other, it would always be just a business relationship.

Norm was always interested in Joe's customer list. Joe had lots of stories related to his business. After getting pistol whipped, he went out west to visit a buddy, his new coke connection. His buddy was affiliated with a five star hotel. He asked Joe to deliver an ounce of coke there for him. Joe obliged and thought nothing of it, until a famous movie star answered the door and invited him in. The movie star told Joe he'd appreciate some discretion. Joe recognized his movie star wife and assured them that they shouldn't worry. They're still married and making movies to this day.

Joe talked some more about the prominent city lawyer who would call him over to supply his party guests. One night, Joe said a few lawyers, one biker, and a few strippers were at the house. Everyone was fucked up when he arrived. They were arguing over what to do about one of the guests who were shot in the foot by the biker! Norm found the story fascinating. He had been questioned by that particular lawyer in court on several occasions. He was one of the city's top lawyers and he handled many high profile cases.

The Elusive Michael Cook

Norm never lost interest in Michael Cook. He paid for his business degree by selling cocaine, and he had friends in high places. Joe provided Norm with the name of another of Cook's mules; he was running cash up north from the city and cocaine back down to the city. Norm was also getting information from Syd, a coke dealer he had busted on the far west side of the city. Syd was buying his coke from Cook's group. He gave Norm some of the same names that Joe did. Before being busted by Norm, Drew Dancer delivered coke to Syd on more than one occasion.

Norm put the mobile surveillance team on the mule, but they didn't come up with anything helpful. Acting on Norm's direction, they followed the mules to Hogtown. Norm called the drug cops in Hogtown but they said a kilo was small potatoes for them. They said they really didn't have the time to look into it.

Norm didn't give up and talked the provincial police into stopping the mule on the way back to the city. The kid still had the $35,000 in cash, but no cocaine. Norm heard a couple different stories as to why the kid never picked up the cocaine. The cops couldn't arrest the kid just for carrying a wad of cash, so they had to let him go.

Syd was able to meet Cook's coke partner face to face. Gary Norris had organized criminal connections across the province. He was tied into some legitimate businesses, so they could launder their drug money. Norm was frustrated but Cook and Norris were out of reach for the city Drug Squad. They were dealing at levels beyond the street team's mandate. Norm had to settle for the little fish in the big drug pond.

Doing the Laundry

Joe Anthony continued to supply Norm with good information that led to more arrests and drug seizures. At the same time, Joe's own coke business was flourishing! Joe said the hardest part about making all that money was how to *launder* it. Laundering money is the process of making *drug* money look legitimate. It can be done in many ways. It has to be done if a drug dealer wants people to believe that their money comes from a legitimate source.

At one point, Joe figured his cocaine fuelled net worth was about $300,000! He said paying cash for everything wasn't all it's cracked up to be; he would get strange looks when dumping thirty grand in cash down on a new car. Buying a house proved even more difficult; who pays cash for a house? Joe used different laundering methods, like buying and cashing in chips at the casino. He had to be careful; they monitored large transactions for exactly that reason.

Joe didn't have a legitimate job, but he decided to claim some income from his criminal enterprise to keep the government off his back. They have confidentiality rules that keep them from disclosing anyone's source of income, so Joe became a tax payer. He hadn't filed a return for years.

Joe gave a buddy who owned a construction company a wad of cash for a company issued pay check and tax receipt. It made Joe look legitimately employed. The heavy flow of drug money eventually forced Joe to invest in a business with a couple employees. Having a business was an excellent way to launder his drug money. Life seemed pretty good for Joe, considering he was a drug dealer!

Women!

After Norm transferred on from the Drug Squad, Joe hooked up with Jesse James, just to keep his union card. Jesse called Norm one day and said that Joe got busted by the provincial police. Joe knew exactly how the game was played and told the cops he wanted to work his patch. They didn't get much when they busted Joe, so it didn't take much to get him out from under the gun.

Getting busted was the least of Joe's problems. He hooked up with a new woman and was in the process of building himself a new house when she got involved in the design. Out of generosity, Joe also set her up with her own business. Joe soaked most of his fortune into the castle he built. One would think that a business to call her own and a new castle would be enough for a woman! Laura wanted more and started sucking Joe's profits up her nose. She preferred the coke over work; she walked away from her business.

Joe had no choice but to carry on the coke business. He eventually made the fatal mistake of using his own product to try and teach his wife a lesson. It was the beginning of a downward spiral that lasted over two years. Joe got to the point where he fell into a deep depression and he physically couldn't get off the couch. The bills stacked up. Laura cleaned up her act enough to get out and pick up the some of the slack; she started doing Joe's deliveries and handling his coke business.

Laura ran the business for some time. Joe finally came to the realization one day that he'd have to leave town to dry out. He made the decision to go and see his buddy out west and dry himself out. Joe was tired of the coke business. He thought he'd invest some money in a grow-op out west, and then get himself a job with his buddy, in construction work. Joe sent coke cross-country to Laura, who kept up the family business.

Laura's independence, and the past strain of their relationship, gave Joe the idea he would be better off staying out west.

Norm hadn't heard from Joe in a long time, but he called one day and said that Laura got busted! She had coke on her and the provincial cops found more in the house. Joe called and asked for some advice from Norm since he wasn't really involved locally, and he hadn't been living in the city in quite a while. Joe may have been a drug dealer, but he was a chivalrous man; he came back home to see how he could help Laura. He would have been better off to stay out west. Laura got pissed, left the house, and then filed a police report saying that Joe had assaulted her three years prior! It was a ploy by Laura and her lawyer to make Joe look like the worst offender so he would take the fall on the drug charges.

Joe was already in a financial tail spin, and the real estate market across the country was in the dumps. He had a fire sale, selling his classic motorcycles, and his other toys. He turned in the keys to the fancy car he was leasing, and he listed his castle for sale. Norm offered all the advice he could, but Joe was really all alone, waiting on the outcome of his court cases. He had no real friends. Joe tried to pick up his coke business again and started to get himself back into physical shape. He started to sell his product again instead of using it himself. Although he took a huge loss, his house eventually sold. Joe tried to do the right thing again and gave Laura more than her fair share.

Just when Norm got to thinking that maybe Joe was getting on with his life, he got a call that Joe had been busted for causing property damage to Laura's house. To make matters worse, he tried running from the cops, and he smashed up his car! Woe is Joe.

Why?

Norm was puzzled. Some time later Norm ran into Joe at the gym; he said he plead guilty to the property damage and did the time to get it over with. Norm just shook his head; he couldn't bring himself to ask Joe why. Looking at Joe, Norm could see that life was finally catching up with him. His blue eyes were glassy and bloodshot from the joint he had just smoked. His hair had thinned; it had receded and was mostly grey. Physically, he looked like he was back in shape but the drama in his life had taken its toll. His permanent smile and charismatic personality were long lost. Joe said he now enjoyed his dog's company better than any woman.

Norm finally asked him why on earth he went out of his way to trash his wife's place. He had always said he wanted to get as far away from her as possible.

Joe said to Norm, "It was like therapy."

Norm still runs into Joe at the gym. One day he told Norm about his time in jail, about a month and a half of the longest time he'd spent on earth! Joe said the jail was filled with young men who don't give a shit about anyone or anything. They bragged about how they couldn't wait to get out so they could get back to things like stealing cars and smoking crack.

Joe was the jail hero when he arrived since he had hooped some weed and tobacco before going inside. The smokers thought he was pretty cool, but a couple of other thugs disagreed and kicked the shit out of him one day for something to do. Joe is no wimp, but he said he could never relax the whole time he was in there; he was always looking over his shoulder. He found it ironic how most of the jail population acted like they were on vacation at an all-inclusive resort. Norm had recalled interviewing dirt bags who called it the *County Hilton* instead of the county jail. They didn't mind being sent to jail because all their friends were there…it was like a family reunion for some of them!

And so, life goes on for Joe. He has no real job, friends, pension, or a light at the end of the tunnel. He is a drug dealer; that's just what he does!

12
Special Projects Part 2: Sting Operations

"The pessimist complains about the wind;
The optimist expects it to change;
The realist adjusts the sails."
-William Arthur Ward

As with all good things, Norm's stint in the Drug Squad came to an end and he was transferred to the Morality unit. Norm's transfer to Morality was a step up the promotional ladder, and it offered a whole new set of challenges. The Morality unit was responsible for enforcing liquor laws in the bars, prostitution, gambling, and sex crimes. The transfer also meant Norm would have to get a hair cut and go clothes shopping…no more jeans! The Morality unit was a suit and tie office; it was a good thing Norm had saved up some overtime cash!

Finding a Niche

One of Norm's duties in Morality was to make regular visits to the bars, checking to see that they were meeting the obligations of their liquor licenses. In Norm's opinion, Canada's liquor laws were, and still are archaic, in comparison to other more liberal countries. But laws have to be enforced, and someone has to enforce those laws. Working the bar detail on the afternoon shift meant you got to dress down a bit…no jacket or tie. The object was to blend into the crowd and not be recognized as cops, in the hope you might catch the bar staff breaking the law.

Norm saw that most of the Morality cops were recognized as soon as they walked into the bar! Norm's experience in the Drug Squad obviously paid off; the bar staff was surprised on more than one occasion when Norm identified himself as a cop. The only good thing about doing the bar checks was that you got to have a few drinks free, on the company!

Chasing prostitutes was only a couple notches up on the fun meter. You had to cruise the areas they hung out in and then set up surveillance once you saw them in action. An added difficulty for Norm in chasing the prostitutes was that some of them were his drug rats! Norm caught one of his rats Mary, in an alley one night with her head buried in a John's lap. The John freaked when he saw the flashlight.

Mary just smiled, rolled down the window and said, "Hey Storm, what's up?"

Norm was with his sergeant, so he had to write Mary up for solicitation. In reality, the ticket was motivation for Mary to call Norm back…she'd have to trade some good information to make the ticket go away. The sergeant wasn't too happy with that, but he knew it's what made the world turn.

The Morality unit also did *John sweeps*, where they'd put an undercover female cop on the street posing as a prostitute. It was like shooting fish in a barrel as traffic backed up with guys trying to pick up the fresh meat on the street. The female cops had to really dress down, most were too attractive to be on the street. Norm even got to go to "John school" to learn all about these new types of stings. The rationale was that if you kept the Johns off the street, you'd be keeping the hookers off the street at the same time. The John sweeps were no big deal to Norm, until he had to arrest one of his old high school football coaches. He said he didn't see the harm in stopping for a blow-job on the way home from getting groceries!

There had to be a niche somewhere in Morality for Norm; he didn't enjoy picking on the bars or the hookers. The city had just passed a new bylaw allowing licensed escorts to advertise and work their trade behind closed doors. The city had also opened a temporary casino…the escort industry took off overnight! The escorts had to register with the city and pay a license fee if they wanted to legally work in the city. Files containing the escort's private information were kept in the Morality office. They had to get photographed and have a police clearance to be licensed.

Norm was trying to find something in the escort file drawers one day and took note at the mess of files and how no one was monitoring anything. One woman had used a fake name and other complaints of non-compliance were coming in to the office. Norm got an idea and ran it by his boss. He asked to be put in charge of the escorts so that they could be better monitored. Norm also ran an idea by the boss for a sting operation that would surely result in some charges, therefore making the boss look good. The boss was an easy sell. It was a way for Norm to opt out of the other Morality crap, and to perhaps cultivate a few more informants!

Sex Stings

Norm got friendly with the ladies who worked in the city licensing office and organized all the escort files. There were over a hundred of them in the beginning. Putting a sting operation together didn't take too much thought. The law prohibited the escorts from working out of their own homes…it was considered *operating a bawdy house*. For their own safety, they requested a name and landline phone number to make an appointment. The women wouldn't discuss sex on the phone but openly told clients the cost was $130 for the first hour of their visit. Any other arrangements had to be made in person once the escort arrived.

Norm ran the sting a couple nights using a hotel room the first night and the party room of a buddy's apartment building the second. All it took was a bunch of phone calls, making appointments with the escorts about a half hour apart from each other. Some of Norm's co-workers got in on the fun by ordering up their own escorts. Norm even called a male escort; he didn't want it to seem like he was just picking on the women! The women usually arrived by taxi or had a hired driver/security man drop them off and wait outside. One of the drivers questioned was actually an escort's husband…how weird is that?

Do you say, "Hi honey how was work tonight?"

The escorts showed up for their appointments one by one…only to be pissed off or disappointed when they found cops waiting instead of their Johns. They also had to produce their escort license on demand. A few of the girls thought the sting was a good idea; there were a lot of *freelancers* in the trade who were not licensed. They just wanted a fair playing field. Norm got quite an education in just a few nights…the women were very interesting to talk to. The woman with the husband driver also had five kids at home! She said her husband appreciated the fact that she brought in more money in a week than he could in a month! The women said that the Johns were from all walks of life. Granted most of their calls were for sex, but there were some guys who were lonely and just wanted to talk. Others were from out of town and needed a date for the night.

The boss was happy, the escorts were mostly happy, and Norm was happy. Within a few days, some of the escorts started calling Norm to rat out other prostitutes who weren't complying with the bylaw or who were selling drugs…right up Norm's alley!

The escort industry grew like a wildfire, and the city made a killing on the licensing fees! Some people started their own escort companies, hiring escorts to work for them. The phone book yellow pages were soon flooded with huge ads for escort services. Between the casino, the escorts, and the abundance of strip bars, the city gained a reputation as the *Tijuana of the north.*

Fixing the Broken Wheel

Another part of Norm's job in Morality was investigating sexual assaults. The child abuse cases were the worst. Norm didn't have any kids, but it didn't stop him from wanting to cut a guy's balls off after hearing the details of the abuse. It was always difficult to listen to two completely different sides of the story and then try to make an informed decision that would affect someone's life forever.

One young girl and her mother had Norm convinced her boyfriend raped her…until he heard his side of the story. Norm doubted the girl's version, but had to arrest the boy on the word of the girl. She eventually recanted the day after Norm put her boyfriend in jail. She said she lied so her mother wouldn't be mad at her for having sex!

Lucky for Norm, the Morality and Break & Enter units were combined in a department re-structuring. The Pawn Shop unit was also brought into the mix. The new group was called Street Crimes. The days off rotated, meaning officers worked with different partners all the time. One day they'd be investigating a B & E and the next day they'd be locking up someone under the mental health act. There was no consistency, and that drove Norm crazy.

There was one guy in the office that looked after all the pawn and second-hand shops in the city. City bylaws required the second-hand stores to obtain identification from customers who were selling their goods. They also had to submit the paperwork to the police so they could check to see if the property was stolen. It was a daunting task! There were hundreds of items sold every day; each serial number had to be checked manually against lists of stolen property. It's no wonder the old guy doing the job went off on a long-term sick leave. Stacks of paperwork piled up on the poor bastard's desk; nobody did his job while he was gone.

Norm worked on a B & E investigation that led him to a pawn shop to recover some stolen property. The rightful property owner discovered their stolen jewelry at a local pawn shop. The investigation gave Norm a better insight to the pawn shop business. It also gave him an idea!

Norm's boss had an office meeting one day; he said he was looking for someone to take over the pawn job. Everyone looked over at the thousands of sheets of paper piled all over the corner desk; nobody wanted the job. Norm thought about the offer that night then went to see his boss the next morning. He told his boss he'd take on the job, but there were some conditions attached. Norm told his boss he would only take the job if he could do it his way…and that meant starting from scratch. There was no possible way to catch up on the months of paperwork that had piled up, so it had to be stuffed into boxes and filed away!

Norm also wanted to modernize the job with a better computer system, one that would search records automatically, look for stolen property, then pass on any hits to Norm. To sweeten the pot, Norm asked his boss to let him work different hours so he could overlap the pawn shops' operating hours and the office afternoon shift. It was better for communication and for the flow of information. *Norm also hated getting up early.* Norm thought the idea of having his own desk and his own specific job would be cool and nobody would bother him with all the other shit going on in the office! The boss was sold on Norm's ideas; of course, it would make him look good!

A part of Norm's deal was to let him use two of the co-op students assigned to the office; they really hadn't been doing anything useful anyway. Norm put the two kids to work and had them haul all the paperwork down to the vault. The files had to be kept in the case they were ever needed as evidence...how anyone in particular would ever be located would be someone else's problem! While the kids were busy, Norm met with the computer programmer and the woman in charge of data entry.

While the computer geeks worked on Norm's plan, he went out to introduce himself to all the pawn shop owners. Norm told them of the new automated system coming into effect and how they'd have to do their due diligence in completing the paperwork properly. Some owners didn't give a shit previously, and no one did anything about it. Norm's research showed that 50 % of all property going through the pawn shops was stolen, and the police didn't recover even one percent of it! Some of the shop owners weren't happy, but they knew it was better to cooperate with the police than to have them snooping around your store every day.

Here's how Norm's new system worked: All pawn and second hand shops had to be licensed by the city. A requirement of that license was that they had to request ID from all their customers, record all purchases including serial numbers, and then deliver the completed forms to the police. Norm would then skim through the forms daily, selecting items that had the possibility of being stolen. The students then entered those items into the city police computer system which automatically interfaced with a national data base for stolen property. Any hits on stolen property would then be sent back to Norm. The system worked! One or two hits a week started to roll in, Norm kept busy visiting the pawn shops and seizing stolen property from their shelves. The sellers were arrested, and some people actually got their stolen property returned to them!

Spinning

Norm's new pawn system could pretty well run itself as long as an investigator kept up to the daily paperwork, and the students kept up with their data entry. Norm found out the hard way he needed someone to replace him and the students when they weren't around. Although the boss promised he'd have someone look after things, Norm returned from a vacation to find his desk buried almost half as deep as when he took on the job! Nobody did a damn thing while Norm was gone! That was unacceptable. Norm trained another investigator to fill in for him and had the data entry clerks take up the slack between the coming and going groups of co-op students.

Co-operation between Norm and the B & E Squad led to the targeting of a group of *B & E boys* who were terrorizing the city. A provincial police investigator who visited regularly came into the office, compared notes, and agreed some of the same dirt bags were wreaking havoc outside the city. A joint force operation *(J.F.O.)* was put together to combat the problem. Because of his past surveillance experience in the Drug Squad, his knowledge of the B & E boys, and perhaps as a bit of a reward, Norm's boss assigned him to the J.F.O.

Norm was teamed up with the provincial investigator, and their mobile surveillance *(Spin)* team. The city Spin team would also be phased in and used on occasion to follow the specific targets that were known to be doing B & E's across the county. This meant Norm got his own car that would become his office for two months, while he worked with the J.F.O.

Mobile surveillance was always fun for Norm; it was the static surveillance that was a killer. There was nothing worse than getting stuck in the back of a freezing cold van in the middle of winter, having to piss in an empty juice bottle! As Norm had learned in the Drug Squad, Spin teams used a whole different language to communicate over the radio. With the provincial spin team, it was a different language but with many similarities. Not getting *burned* was the whole object of a good spin. That means using at least five cars, so that different surveillance techniques can be used while watching the specific targets. The goal was to catch them in the act of committing a crime.

On one occasion while being the eye Norm saw the target leave his residence on a bicycle. He lived outside the city. This guy was an experienced thief who did heat *checks* before heading out to do a B & E. Norm was parked about a half a block from the target's house on a side street. The target rode out of his driveway and went about a half a block in the opposite direction. He then circled back, riding past his house towards the street Norm was parked on. He looked in Norm's direction, rode a ways down that block, and then turned around again.

Sure enough, he turned on the side street and rode towards Norm. This guy knew his neighborhood, a guy sitting alone in a car parked around the corner from his house would not look right…he would have to assume it was a cop! Without hesitation, Norm threw his coat over the mobile police radio, grabbed his clipboard, and bailed out of the car. There was a new house under construction across the street, so Norm walked up the driveway, and then grabbed a hard hat off the back of a pick-up truck. Norm walked up to some guys working in a trench beside the house, and pretended to be taking notes on the clipboard. The workers glanced up at Norm but continued their work. The target stopped right beside Norm's car and looked in the window. He looked all around in the car, and then gazed over in Norm's direction. Norm started babbling to the workers about a baseball game that had been on T.V. the previous night. The target got off his bike and stared at Norm and the workers for what seemed like an eternity…it's a good thing Norm had watched the game and had something to talk about!

The ruse worked and the target rode off into the neighboring town. Following a bicycle without being compromised turned out to be too much of a challenge for the Spin team. This guy was good! He'd purposely ride around the block, doing heat checks to see if anyone was following him. At one point, he placed his bike up against a tree and walked in between some houses. Unfortunately for police, you actually have to catch someone committing a crime before you can arrest them. In this case, that meant seeing him break into a house, letting him steal something, and then arresting him with the goods on the way out. That was much easier said than done!

The Spin team tried to surround the neighborhood and box the target in, but he came back out from between the houses and rode back to the commercial district. The team leader said he had the eye, and that the target went into a variety store. Norm had some doubts about the skill level of the team leader and one other cop. They continually drove back and forth past the store…instead of pulling in and parking somewhere. Even with his doubts, Norm was still shocked when the target came out of the store with a disposable camera and he snapped pictures of the two Spin team guys as they whizzed by…trying not to look conspicuous! The gig was up. The team was officially burned!

Pawn Stars

Norm kept the Pawn unit running smoothly and even had the city beef up some of the bylaws to put tighter restrictions on the stores. The opening of the casino brought a half dozen new pawn shops with it, some of which had shady reputations for practices like knowingly buying stolen property. With information from one of his rats, Norm was able to obtain a search warrant to recover some unregistered stolen property from one downtown pawn shop. The owner had not been reporting his purchases of stolen property and fudging the serial numbers on property he was reporting. The licensing committee felt sorry for the guy and only gave him a thirty day suspension.

Reactive policing has been the norm since the inception of crime fighting. This was frustrating for Norm; he firmly believed in proactive policing…stopping crime before it actually happened. Norm's rats played a huge part in that pursuit. A seminar on property crime was held up in Ottawa; Norm was ordered to attend. There were a lot of great ideas kicked around at the conference. Norm made some good contacts and came away with a couple ideas. One idea was to further computerize the local pawn industry, linking individual store computers with a national police system. The cost would have been mostly covered by the store owners. Norm presented the idea at a meeting with them. That's as far as he got.

The other idea was a pawn sting operation where the police open their own pawn shop. It had been done successfully in another city. Norm thought it was a great idea since the thieves would be bringing their stolen property directly to the police. Police always had difficulty in obtaining information on whoever was fencing stolen property or where it all went. There was some honor among thieves, not like druggies! Norm's buddy in the provincial police was really interested in the pawn shop idea, so Norm put together an operational plan and proposed a J.F.O. between the city and provincial police. Norm knew that bringing in manpower, and more importantly money, from the provincial police would make the project easier to sell locally. Norm's boss was an easy sell, but Norm had to convince Ash Kist who was now the Deputy Chief. He was more concerned with the possible overtime hours, so Norm had to make promises he wouldn't blow the overtime budget. Hence, *Project Copshop* was born.

Norm knew what it took to run a pawn shop, and he scoped out a few prime locations throughout the city. The provincial police brought in a few cops from out of town to help run the shop; they had to be someone who wouldn't be recognized in the city. A location right in the heart of Motor Town was picked for the store…the rent was dirt cheap, and there were plenty of criminals in the hood. An apartment on the outskirts of the city was rented for a safe house; the undercover cops *(UC's)* needed a place to stay at night. The two UC's both had fake ID with the first name of Joe so the new store was called *Just Joe's*.

What the provincial police promised, and what they actually delivered was far from the same, but Project Copshop got off the ground and opened for business. The two UC's were not happy about being assigned to the project. It was a decision made after their former boss was transferred. Norm learned he was basically getting their *has-beens*, but they would have to do. The lead provincial investigator that was supposed to be Norm's partner was re-assigned to other duties. The cop that replaced him was soon dragged into the daily store operation because the two Joe's were in over their heads. They were clueless about setting up and maintaining a store. Norm couldn't help with the store because he might be recognized in the hood, and that could have compromised the whole project.

The crew managed to work out the kinks and the neighborhood punks started poking their noses into the store. The business was barely operational when the guy from the phone company installing the phone offered to sell the store a bunch of stolen phones! Norm visited the police property room in order to fill the store shelves with recovered property that was to be sold at auction. Getting the store set up and cutting through all the red tape was a difficult task, but not as difficult as keeping the whole project a secret. Cops are nosy by nature, and everyone wanted to know what Norm was up to! Norm spent more time working from a laptop in the safe house, rather than in the office, just to avoid all the questions.

One of the local B & E boys went into the store one day and sold the guys a set of golf clubs…there was no doubt he'd never even set foot on a golf course! The guys tried to get the thieves to admit the stuff was stolen…they said they wanted to know so they could keep it *off the books* so the cops wouldn't know. The transactions and conversations were all being recorded on a surveillance camera. Others started to bring in their jewelry and what ever else they thought they could get a buck for. The UC's started hanging out in the local bars, drumming up business, and just getting known in the hood.

A hardcore, well-known criminal went to the store one day and asked the guys if they were interested in one hundred brand new Ford car radios! The guy worked at Fords and had been stealing them off the line one at a time for months. He said he'd sell the whole lot for $4,000. One of the Joe's said he'd have to see a sample, and he was able to get the model and serial numbers. Norm had to scramble but was able to hook up with the head of Fords security to see if the radios were missing. Fords security said they'd cover the cost of buying the radios, so the deal was set up. Joe 1 went to the bank to get $4,000 from the project *buy account*. Norm was horrified when he returned and showed him four one thousand dollar bills!

"Who the hell would use such large bills for any kind of street deal?"

It was too late to change the money; the time and place for the deal was set. Joe 1 said he needed a few minutes...he had to get his police stuff out of the undercover pick-up truck!

"What the hell is the matter with you?" Norm asked out loud.

He learned that Joe 1 had been sneaking out of town at night with the truck going home to see his family. He even attended one of his kid's soccer games! Joe 1 obviously didn't understand his priorities while working *undercover.* The deal was made, and Joe 1 bought all the stolen radios.

The dirt bag said, "What the fuck am I supposed to do with these?" when Joe 1 handed him the four crisp new one thousand dollar bills.

Bikers and Politics

Just Joe's was accepted as a normal business in Motor Town, and the UC's were accepted by the locals in the neighborhood bars. Joe 2 had done an about face and really got into his role. He was walking and talking the biker part. Joe 2 even got an invite to the local biker clubhouse...he was ecstatic. It was one of his life long goals as a UC...to be able to infiltrate a biker gang. Norm was losing his patience with Joe 1, so the news from Joe 2 was a welcome reprieve. The six month project was almost at the half way point and the time had come for an evaluation from the brass.

During the inception of the project, changes had taken place with the upper echelon of both police forces. A new chief was hired in the city, and the provincial police shuffled around some of their brass who were overseeing Project Copshop. The project team told the brass how they were just starting to see some good results and how Joe 2 had been invited into the local biker clubhouse. This was the same place where their president has been murdered a few years earlier. A heated discussion ensued while the team defended the project and tried to explain how the biker infiltration could lead to great new possibilities. The brass balked, citing officer safety concerns. Joe 2 fumed; he was willing to take the risk. His superiors were not.

Norm couldn't offer up many criminal charges for the stolen property bought so far; it was difficult to prove many of the items were actually stolen. According to the Crown Prosecutor, they would have had to rely on recent case law from similar situations to make the case. Manpower and money are always major issues within police budgets; that meant the end of Project Copshop. Once again Norm had his project shut down before its time…too bad so sad! Joe 1 was happy to go back home. Joe 2 was pissed off that he missed out on a good opportunity, but he had no choice in the matter.

New businesses came and went in Motor Town, so it was not unusual to see a store go out of business. The prosecutor wasn't sure about the reasonable expectation of securing convictions in the handful of cases, so it was decided to keep the integrity of the project intact. No one was arrested or charged. The store was closed up and the remaining property was returned to the property room to be auctioned. All the cops involved in the project were sent back to the units they had originally come from. Norm was not a happy camper; once again the political powers to be put the kibosh on one of his projects. Norm went back to his old pawn job in Street Crimes. It was business as usual with the bikers and criminals in Motor Town.

13
Mattress Mary

Mattress Mary could have been a nurse. She could have been a loving wife and mother of three children. She could have been a successful clothes designer. Instead, at an early age, Mary was chosen to be a victim of child abuse. Her mother's boyfriend taught her all about sex at the ripe age of ten! Her mother didn't believe her accusations, so Mary became a runaway by the age of thirteen. She was book smart, but she soon traded in her books for street smarts. She was a pretty blonde girl with blue eyes and a nice figure. She could have easily been the high school prom queen. Instead of an academic high school, she went to the school of hard knocks.

Mary learned that she could put what her abuser taught her to good use to get some of those things she wanted in life. The problem was that Mary hated her life, so she turned to drugs to make her feel better. The problem with her drug addiction was that she had to find money to buy the drugs. Mary knew how to manipulate the system and received government assistance. The money was never enough to feed her addiction, so she took to working the street, trading her body and self esteem for drug money.

The Italian Stallion

One of Norm's sergeants in the Drug Squad was known as the Italian Stallion. Someone gave him the nickname after seeing him in the showers…he was hung like a wild stallion! The Stallion liked to brag how many bow-legged women were out there because of him. He was a legend in his own mind.

There was one other thing that the Stallion was known for in the Drug Squad; he had a lot of informants. The strange thing was most of them were females. The running joke in the office was that he *had* to be banging them.

The Stallion got a lot of calls from a rat he called M.M. The tips were usually related to crack dealers. Her tips were always good and the Drug Squad busted a lot of crack dealers on M.M.'s information. Like the majority of rats, M.M. was loyal to her handler and only dealt with the Stallion. Norm stumbled across some photos on the Stallion's desk one day and figured out that M.M. was in fact Mattress Mary. The Stallion kept pictures of Mary before and after her crack addiction. The two women in the pictures didn't even look related!

One night the Stallion said to Norm, "Let's go Storm, we gotta go meet M.M." They drove into the downtown projects where Stallion pulled into an alley, and Mary jumped into the van.

She looked at Norm and said, "Hey big fella, you gotta smoke for me?"

Stallion pulled a cigarette out of a pack he kept for Mary. He introduced her to Norm. Mary reached over Stallion's shoulder and grabbed the whole pack before Stallion could put them away.

He just shook his head and said, "What have you got for me Mary?"

"Fat Fiona's got a little nigger named "T" running for her, I'm gonna hook up with him."

Without missing a beat, Mary looked at Norm and said, "I hate niggers. You couldn't pay me enough to suck a nigger cock!"

Norm choked…must have been the cigarette smoke. Mary went on to tell the Stallion that she had to order up through Fat Fiona, who would in turn send T to meet Mary with the rock.

Mary looked at the Stallion, "You got fifty bucks so I can buy a rock?"

The Stallion and Mary bickered back and forth like an old married couple. The Stallion lectured her that he wasn't supporting her drug habit. Mary took a long drag on her cigarette and blew the smoke in the Stallion's face.

"Okay, let me off up the road so I can find a John and make some money."

The Stallion wheeled around the corner. The van was barely stopped when Mary jumped out.

"I'll call ya later" she said, as she hopped out and ran across the street.

The Stallion just shook his head again and said to Norm, "Are you hungry? Let's get something to eat."

The Stallion was always on some kind of fad diet. He took Norm to his favorite Chinese restaurant. The Stallion wasn't even half way through his house special fried rice when his pager started vibrating.

He looked at the display and shook his head again, "Guess who?"

"Shit, that was a quick trick!"

The Stallion and Norm wolfed down their food, and then went to meet Mary again.

She jumped back in the van again and said, "Okay, I got money, I need to get high!"

The Stallion said, "There's no way you did a trick that fast?"

"He was a two minute wonder!" Mary replied.

The Stallion told Mary she had cock breath. She leaned forward and blew on the side of his face trying to gross him out.

The Stallion said, "Fuck-off Mary! Where's the crack bastard now?"

Something's burning

The call was made, and Mary hooked up with T. The Stallion and Norm got a good look at T and the car he was driving. Mary ran back to the van and told the Stallion to drop her off down the road. Norm then heard the click of Mary's lighter and thought she was lighting up another smoke. He caught a weird smell in the air, like burning Styrofoam. Norm looked back and saw Mary sucking on her crack pipe. She was smoking her rock right there in the van with him and the Stallion. Norm looked over at the Stallion. He just shook his head again and drove on.

T was busted later that night with a pocket full of crack. The Drug Squad knew he was running for Fat Fiona, but they couldn't prove it. Her turn would have to come another day. Mary disappeared into the night…getting high…doing tricks…and getting high. It was the circle of life for Mattress Mary. She was a crack whore.

High & Dry

Norm got a call at work from the Italian Stallion one night. The Stallion was at home, but he told Norm that Mary was holed up in a flea bag motel. She was on the wagon and drying herself out. The Stallion was concerned about Mary since she had been on a five day bender…that meant no eating or sleeping ...just sucking on the pipe *(in more ways than one!)*.

He asked Norm if he could check in on her at the motel. Norm was only doing paperwork, so it was no big deal. It was a bit weird, going to a motel to check up on a crack whore! Granted, she was a good informant, but in reality she was a suffering human being, someone cops are sworn to protect.

Norm called the motel first to see if Mary was still actually there. The front desk put Norm through to her room. Mary answered the phone and Norm asked how she was doing.

Mary replied, "Oh, hey Storm! I'm okay but I could really use a cup of tea!"

Her voice was raspy, but quiet at the same time; she sounded like a little girl. She was usually loud and bouncing around like the energizer bunny. Crack does that to you. Norm told Mary he'd pop by with a tea.

Mary said, "You're such a sweetie. Can you bring me a pack of smokes too?"

That was the Mary Norm knew. She tried to get whatever she could take, and take whatever she could get! Norm drove out to the motel, stopping first to grab Mary some smokes and a cup of tea. Mary was tucked into bed when Norm walked into the room. She got up to fix her tea and to light up a smoke. Norm chuckled at the Donald Duck flannel jammies Mary was wearing. She looked like a zombie from the Night of the Living Dead goes to Disneyworld.

Mary said, "Thanks for the tea, sweetie."

Norm and Mary fell into a conversation about nothing that turned into some sort of confession on her part. She spoke softly and told Norm how sick she was. Not just from the crack binge, but how her body was starting to shut down from all the different ailments she had. She listed the first part of the alphabet and all the different hepatitis strains she had, along with her kidney and liver problems.

As Mary talked, Norm couldn't help but wonder what kind of men would actually pay this poor broken down woman for sex. Norm had heard from Mary and Squeaky Sally, how some men would want to ride them bareback even after they were warned about the possibility of being infected with whatever diseases they had. Yes, according to these women, some men really are that stupid! Mary juggled her tea, her smoke, and the T.V. remote from hand to hand as she told Norm about her shitty life.

She didn't go into detail about what her stepfather did to her and her sister. Mary never talked about her sister; she didn't see her much. She mentioned her last failed relationship; Norm remembered Mary's lesbian lover Michelle. The guys in the office would joke and call it the Mike and Dyke show. They were always feuding, Mary would take off on a crack binge and Michelle would call the Stallion; giving up Mary's crack connections in hopes of finding her and getting her back home.

Norm listened like a big brother while Mary babbled on. She slowly crept deeper and deeper under the covers as she spoke.

She looked up at Norm said, "Thanks for coming by sweetie, I gotta crash now."

Mary reached up to give Norm a hug. He bent over the bed, and she steered her lips towards Norm's. Norm politely turned a cheek and gave her a hug. It was sad to say, but Norm couldn't stop all those diseases from racing through his mind.

Something about Mary

Mary was a crack head, and she made no bones about how much she hated black men. The ironic part of that is all of the crack dealers in the city at that time were black! At least that's the way it started when the crack was introduced to the city. It was like the gold rush days of yesteryear; young black Americans would flock across the border looking to get rich! One lawyer accused Norm of being prejudice and racially profiling his young black client.

The courtroom fell silent when Norm answered the question and said, "Yes."

Before the lawyer could regain his composure, Norm told the court that every crack dealer he had arrested was black. Most of them were American. It was the simple truth.

Mary never really made any money being a rat. She mostly traded information for a quick fix. Sometimes she'd have a prostitution charge to work off. She would call the Drug Squad when the Stallion wasn't working or just ignoring her calls. Mary would give her information to whoever answered the phone in the hopes she could trade up for a rock somewhere. When the Stallion transferred out of the Squad, Mary worked with others, becoming a squad rat. It was always all about Mary. Like any crack head, she said or did anything to get that next high!

When Norm transferred out of the Drug Squad to the Morality unit, it was Mary who he found sexually engaged in an alley one night.

There was another time when Norm was doing surveillance in Motor Town, watching the undercover police pawn shop. Mary came up from behind Norm, opened the passenger door, and jumped in the front seat.

Before Norm even realized who she was, Mary said, "Hey Storm, have you got a smoke?"

That was Mary. Every time Norm saw her, it shocked and saddened him to see how much she had deteriorated physically.

The last time Norm saw Mary was a couple years before he retired, while he was investigating Arson in Motor Town.

She looked like a sixty year old woman. She was all skin and bones, and her once pretty face was hollowed and sunken in. Mary was dying a slow and miserable death. She looked over at Norm from the sidewalk and offered up a half a smile. Norm nodded in response as Mary walked away down the sidewalk. Norm watched as she disappeared around the corner and he wondered …what would become of Mary?

Life can be cruel. Mary is a living example of it!

14
Politics and Promotion

"Nearly all men can stand adversity, but if you want to test a man's character, give him power."

– Abraham Lincoln

It took 20 years, but Norm Strom was finally promoted to the rank of sergeant. It took Norm longer than most, but he earned the promotion all on his own, and he owed no one! Norm refused to cheat on the promotional exams like many of his co-workers and thought promotions should have been the reward for good work. Unfortunately, that wasn't the case with the promotional system that was in place. Norm had no aspirations of climbing the company ladder, but a promotion meant more money, and more job opportunities.

Norm made the decision a few months prior to his promotion to lose some serious weight and to get his ass back into shape. The process took almost a year, but Norm lost a shit load of weight through proper diet and exercise. That meant no more fast food, beer, or wine! It was tough, but Norm got buff!

The first order of business upon being promoted was to be welcomed to the management team by the Chief of police. As Norm's luck would have it, his old buddy Ash Kist rose through the ranks to the Chief's position. Kist was the man who said Norm would never get a plain clothes job if he had anything to do with it! Six years later, after working in plain clothes doing investigations, Norm was now a member of Kist's management team!

It was a routine welcome aboard speech given by the Chief in his office; Kist told Norm what was expected of him as a supervisor and leader in the organization. He congratulated Norm on the promotion and asked if he had any questions.

Norm couldn't resist, he just had to ask, "Yes Chief, now that I'm part of your team, I was just wondering what it is that you don't like about me?"

The chief had obviously gotten better at playing poker over the years; he didn't turn red like the last time.

"I have no problem with you at all Norm."

"I've been curious all these years chief, I'd like to know if it is something that can be fixed."

"I don't know what you're talking about Norm."

It was important for Norm to know his allies and his enemies, but the chief wouldn't reveal his hand. The game was a draw, but Norm had no doubt the chief was holding a couple aces.

The New Centurions

Being promoted to sergeant meant that Norm would have to get a hair cut and put a uniform back on. He was told by the big boss that he had to take his turn back in the monkey suit like everyone else. Well not really everyone else, a few of Kist's golden boys managed to stay in plain clothes, being promoted to detective instead of sergeant *(they are the same rank).* Norm's hard work in drugs and B & E didn't make any difference to the brass; he was just another body to fill a position.

Norm had always promised himself that if he ever got to be a sergeant, he would lead by example and try to pass on valuable lessons that he had learned from his past experiences. The majority of the patrol officers Norm would be commanding were much younger and had no investigative experience. Norm wrote out a whole list of tips on different investigative topics and planned to give his platoon a tip each and every day before they hit the streets. Norm wanted to share his expertise and to help them to become better street cops. So each day at roll call, Norm would offer a "tip of the day" after reading out the assignments and bulletins.

Norm noticed right from the start that something had changed since his uniform days. There was no more camaraderie among the platoon! Each man and woman seemed to be out for themselves; it was a new breed for sure. Norm asked the platoon what socializing they did as a platoon.

One of the guys said, "We don't do anything together."

"What, you guys don't go out for beers together?"

"Nope, we've never done that!"

Norm firmly believed that he needed to sit down a share a few cocktails with someone in order to really get to know them and eventually trust them. Getting someone out of their working environment and loosening them up with a couple drinks, was a sure way to let their true personalities show through. Norm's first order of business was to coordinate a night out for the entire platoon. There were some cops who didn't talk to others and some that said they didn't drink or see the need to go out. Norm really didn't care if they drank or not, they were all going to go out as a group!

The only way to get everyone out for the night was to do it when everyone was actually at work *(the platoons were set up in such a way that everyone had the same days off)*. Norm arranged for one of the other platoons to cover for his at the end of an afternoon shift. This meant that everyone would have to put in a chit for two hours off. Some of the platoon was not happy about taking time off to go out with their co-workers, so Norm spelled out the rules to them. Everyone would put in a chit, and everyone would attend! For those who thought they'd just take the time off and go home...Norm said he would process their chit. For anyone who went out with the group…Norm would hold on to the chits for a while, and then they would eventually just disappear! It was basically a bribe, giving them free company time to go out together as a group.

Norm's plan worked. Everyone showed up, even a couple guys who never socialized with anyone. Some beers and wings and a lot of laughs were had. One of the guys even asked Norm what the "tip of the day" was going to be the next day. Another said what a great idea it was getting together and going out. The smiles on their faces and the jocular mood told Norm it was the right thing to do. He had managed to bring the platoon a little closer together, letting them know who the people backing them up really were. In police work their lives sometimes depended on each other! That lost camaraderie some how found its way back to Norm's platoon. They even came to work with a smile on their faces, and most of them actually seemed eager to learn something new each day!

Leading by example was part of Norm's game plan, but he soon found out that things had changed out on the street. The patrol cars were now all computer dispatched; there was minimal chatter over the radio. Norm would have to search the computer to find out where and what calls his people were on. In the old days, you knew what everyone was up to just by listening to the radio. With the new system, no one knew what anyone else was doing. The system isolated everyone out on the street. In Norm's opinion, it was dangerous when nobody else knew what you were up to. It was also boring just watching calls pop up on a computer screen and not being able to hear all the action going on.

There was also a new breed of cop on the street, they were being hired older and with families. Men and women in their thirty's or forty's were trying to do a job Norm found difficult at twenty! Their minds were on their families at home and not on the job at hand. Cell phones were becoming popular, and one guy shocked Norm when his phone rang out loud and he actually answered it while on a service call. Some were afraid to get involved, for the fear they might end up getting their asses sued. The old street wise cops were gone, replaced by report takers. Calls for service were endless; Norm's platoon went from call, to call, to call. There was no down time for writing tickets or for hunting down bad guys.

Going Back

Norm worked as a patrol sergeant for about six months, and then he jumped at the opportunity to get back into plain clothes. He applied for a detective spot on the B & E Squad in the Street Crimes office. Norm came out of the interview with a good feeling. His old Street Crimes boss was on the interview panel and told Norm he was a shoe in. The next day, one of the golden boy's names appeared on the transfer order. The boss just shook his head and told Norm that he had the job when he left the room; the decision had been made higher up…Ash Kist again? As fate would have it, the golden boy got himself in trouble several years later. He was caught on video beating an innocent man, and he lost his job!

Another plain clothes posting came up, this time for an opening in the Drug Squad. Norm's buddy Jesse Williams was being transferred out, so he and Norm basically switched jobs. Norm was back in Drugs, this time as a sergeant, and once again working for Teflon Tim. He knew most of the cops who'd be working for him, and he had worked along side a few of them in the past. The other sergeant in the squad was Norm's old Drug Squad buddy Blackjack. He and Norm would now have to supervise the cowboys, instead of being one of them! Blackjack gave Norm the heads up right away as to who the troublemakers were. He had already butted heads with a few of them; he wished Norm luck and welcomed him back to the squad.

New Sherriff in Town

Teflon Tim also welcomed Norm back; he said there was a new breed in the Drug Squad too…they had to be hand-fed their work on a silver spoon! Go figure, they were glorified secretaries on patrol; they never had the time or desire to investigate anything. The Drug Squad was supposed to be a training ground for investigators, but the new breed thought they knew it all coming in. Tim told Norm the squad was splintered into three separate groups, who all hated each other. He asked Norm to look into that and see what he could do…the joys of being a supervisor! Teflon Tim also asked Norm to give him progress reports on any changes that might come about.

Most people can be supervised, but it's much easier to supervise a person than to supervise an ego. There were a few too many big egos in the Drug Squad. All the search warrants, seizures, arrests, and projects that Blackjack and Norm had under their belt meant nothing to the new breed. They took short cuts in any way they could and always looked for the easy way out. A few of the lazy bastards actually used a template for their search warrants; they just changed the names and addresses in the information to obtain the warrant. Not all lawyers are completely stupid; Norm warned them what would happen if they got caught. None of the squad gave two shits about their investigative files; they only wanted the easy busts. Blackjack told Norm he had some of the same concerns, but his help was unwanted and his suggestions were ignored.

As asked by Teflon Tim, Norm kept him in the loop by leaving tape recorded phone messages letting him know what was going on during the night shifts when he wasn't working. The squad started to rebel against Blackjack and Norm; they acted like children and turned to playing little games like paging their sergeants with each other's phone numbers or the *gay* hotline. They even sent a pizza to Blackjack's house one night. After some time, Norm helped bring the squad closer together as a whole, but he some how alienated himself at the same time. This all should have been no surprise to Norm who had gone through some of the same crap, back when he had sergeants over him in the squad.

The Italian Stallion told Norm, "What goes around comes around!" He was right.

Passing the Torch

Some new blood was introduced to the squad in the form of transfers, and things got a bit better. Norm still had a few active informants and would rely on them to drum up some action for the office. To try and get their feet wet, Norm signed off on a couple informants, letting the new recruits work with them. He saw potential in one guy and gave him some of his old files with big fish like Michael Cook, so he could learn to do some digging. A younger Drug Squad cop tried to take down Cook after Norm left the unit. Norm warned him that the money and drugs would never be in the same place at the same time, but he tried anyway. Cook was nowhere near the $35,000 that was recovered, and no drugs were found. The money had to be returned.

One of the provincial police sergeants had tried to get a J.F.O. going with Cook as one of the targets, but he couldn't put an attractive enough package together to convince the brass to run the project. About a year later, the R.C.M.P. took a run at the same group who was deeply connected to the outlaw bikers in the area. Norm took his protégé along to the meeting, and he ended up being seconded to the J.F.O. They later took down some of the bikers and put a dent in their cocaine business, but Cook remained unscathed. He had moved out of the city and taken on a larger role within the criminal enterprise.

Some of the new blood did well in the Drug Squad, but there was still a small group that had something against Norm; he could never figure out what it was. Even more frustrating was the fact that one of the guys was actually partners with Norm in uniform one year! It wasn't until about a year later when Norm transferred out of the Drug Squad that he found out what the problem was. Jesse had transferred back into the unit again and they told him Norm was a rat! Good old Teflon Tim called the guys into his office one morning, played his phone message, and said,

"Here, listen to what your sergeant had to say about you!"

Unbefuckinglievable! Tim completely sold out Norm, trying to win favor with the guys even though he had asked Norm to try and fix things! That explained why Norm got the cold shoulder from the squad. Norm had bent over backward for the squad and even looked the other way a few times when they broke the law, while trying to enforce the law. One night, the whole squad decided to give themselves half the night off so they could go drinking while Norm wasn't around. Unfortunately for them, Norm later ran into two of them in a bar…while they were supposed to be working. Norm called a meeting and disciplined them by docking them accrued hours from a book kept in the office…it didn't cost them a dime in cash. Once again, Teflon Tim caved in when they whined, and he put the time back in the book for them. Norm knew he had lost all respect in the squad, so he put in for a transfer.

Norm got the next opening in the B & E Squad, and he went back to Street Crimes as a sergeant/detective. It was once again a supervisory role, but he was also expected to conduct and lead property crime related investigations. The Street Crimes office consisted of the B & E, Morality, Auto Theft, and the Pawn Shop units. Norm was right at home since he had worked in most of these areas before. His boss was transferred out and Norm's old training officer Andy Green was put in charge. Norm's connections on the street were of great help in solving some break-ins and recovering some stolen cars. Norm had also worked with the Morality sergeant in the past so the two men were able to work in harmony when Norm's hooker informants wanted to trade information for the withdrawal of their charges.

Street Crimes was a good home for Norm, he liked the shifts and the fact he got to wear jeans to work once again!

15
Louie the Wap

Louigi Finghetti was probably born and raised an upstanding Catholic boy who went to church every Sunday and even did his time as an alter boy. Somewhere along the way, he fell off the path of God; his quest was to see how many of the commandments he could break. Norm knew Louie was a con man the moment he met him. He pretended he was another one of those do-gooders when he called Norm, saying he wanted to get his girlfriend back on the path of the righteous. With several years experience in handling informants, Norm knew better. It was protocol to check police records for any prospective informant; Louie had a bit of a criminal record, one conviction was for Arson. He was hired to set someone's car on fire and burned himself in the process.

Louie liked to yap on the phone, but Norm insisted they meet so he could get a better feel for the anxious caller. Louie met up with Norm and climbed out of a beat up old pick up truck with a wheel barrow and some shovels in the back. Along with the truck and its load, Louie had "typical Italian" written all over him. He had the southern Italian wavy black hair that was starting to recede back on his well-tanned forehead. His two day stubble beard probably looked sexy to some women, but Norm thought it just added to Louie's disheveled look. He even wore the wife beater white tank top with his torn jeans and work boots. The young man introduced himself as Louie the Wap. He said he was self-employed in the cement business…go figure!

Love is blind

Louie told Norm his girlfriend was a coke head, and he was afraid her two small children were being exposed to a life that he didn't think was fair to them. It was obvious to Norm that Louie was infatuated with his girlfriend as he described her and the fact she had been a stripper when he met her. There it was...lonely guy in bar falls for stripper; how cliché! Anyhow, Louie seemed sincere in his concern for his drug abusing girlfriend and the welfare of her children. It was difficult for Norm to figure out exactly where Louie fit in since he said he was actually living at his mom's but staying with his girlfriend. Maybe the girlfriend washed his balls and mom washed his laundry…who knows?

Louie was another sucker in that long line of do-gooders who thought he could stop his girlfriend from doing coke by getting her dealers busted. It really didn't matter to Norm since his job was busting drug dealers. Norm was a sergeant in the Drug Squad when he met Louie. He had considered handing him off to one of his subordinates but frankly, none of them were deserving of a free handout at the time. Norm had the time, so he followed up on Louie's information and staked out his girlfriend's place whenever Louie said she had placed an order for coke. It didn't take Norm long to figure out that Louie was partying right along with his girlfriend Patty. The more he called and talked to Norm, the more Norm was convinced of his earlier suspicions that Louie was a smooth talking con artist.

Norm got the impression that Louie trusted Patty about as far as he could throw her; she was a stripper turned shooter girl after all, and somewhat of a con artist herself.

If anyone's ever been to a strip club they'd have noticed the shooter girls have more body contact than most of the strippers. They don't take their clothes off but basically they dance all over you and your lap while trying to feed you a watered down shot with a fancy name like *sex on the beach.* Norm believed Louie's real fear was that Patty was trading sex for coke when he wasn't around. He said she never had the money for the stuff, and he was always lending her cash. Either way, Louie was intent on setting up Patty's coke dealers. Some of the things Louie said led Norm to believe that he wanted the dealers busted so he didn't have to pay the cash he owed them; dealers will sometimes "front" their customers the dope until they have the cash to pay them. It's kind of hard for the dealers to collect money owed to them when their in jail or everyone finds out they got busted

Louie called Norm frequently, but he could never seem to put Norm and the coke dealers on the same page. In the meantime, Louie let the cat out of the bag in regards to other guys he knew who were dealing coke…his own buddies or dealers that had nothing to do with his girlfriend. Some of the names Louie dropped easily caught Norm's attention since they were well-known to the Drug Squad. The one guy was a high level dealer with outlaw biker connections, and another was a part owner in a local business. Norm tried to steer Louie in their direction instead of constantly stalking his girlfriend's dealers.

Louie the Wap finally came through with a noon time phone call to Norm saying Patty was taking delivery of two 8-balls, or a quarter of an ounce of coke. Time passed slowly and the information changed, as those things often do in the drug world. It wasn't until 8pm that Norm was able to put the grab on a guy who left Patty's house with an 8-ball of coke. He wasn't the original dealer, but he had the hot potato and got busted with it. It wasn't a total waste of time, since Norm made some overtime cash and Louie was paid a $50 reward for his tip.

Money Motivated

A taste of cash was all Louie needed to keep him calling. Within three weeks, he was on the horn again with Norm, this time ratting out the DJ at the bar where Patty worked. Louie said that the DJ was dealing coke to the staff and patrons in the bar, including Patty. Once Patty made a buy Louie dropped a dime to Norm to say she scored and that the DJ was holding. Norm pinched the DJ with twenty-three grams of coke, individually packaged for sale, along with a bit of weed, $250 in cash, and his pager. At that time, powder cocaine was selling on the street for $100 per gram. Louie had hoped to get Patty busted too, but her search came up clean. That tip earned Louie a C note.

There were three ways that informants could make money from the police. As mentioned in an earlier chapter, informants could become police agents and sign a contract to be paid money for their information and involvement. The drawback was that they would later have to testify in open court. The easiest way for an informant to make money was to anonymously call "Crimestoppers" and give their information over the phone. Crimestoppers did not record the calls and issued the informants a personal identification number. The informants could call back later using their ID number to see if the police took any action. If arrests or drug seizures were made the informant, was directed to a specific business location where they identified themselves by their ID number, and they were given an envelope with their cash reward.

Louie the Wap was a registered city police informant. That meant that Norm had signed him up, and his name went into a special vault that was only accessible by the officer in charge of the intelligence unit. After making an arrest and/or seizure, Norm had to submit a report to the officer in charge of the Investigations Division requesting a cash reward for the informant. Whether it was Crimestoppers or the police directly, the rewards were usually minimal. Crimestoppers was privately funded, so big busts could net informants up to a maximum of $1,000! Norm only had one case where such a reward was paid out, the Drew Dancer bust. The police reward money came from unclaimed found or seized property that had been auctioned off. It was difficult to get an informant any more than a couple hundred bucks from that source, no matter how big the bust was.

Bigger Fish to Fry

Louie the Wap was on and off with Patty, but he relished the fact he was still banging her. She had taken up with some bikers who were also banging her. It seemed she would spread her legs for who ever had the coke. Norm asked Louie if he was double bagging when he fucked Patty but he just laughed in response. He was able to supply Norm with some information on the bikers and some other coke dealers the Drug Squad was interested in. In the meantime he gave up Patty and some other guy to Norm one night. Norm was able to arrest them in the guy's car; they were both in possession of a small amount of cocaine. Louie was probably pissed that he hadn't banged Patty in a while!

The R.C.M.P. had an interest in one of the high level suppliers Louie was connected to. Norm took one of his keener Drug Squad guys to a meeting with the Mounties and shared the information he had on the drug kingpin. The young city cop became part of their J.F.O. Norm introduced him to Louie so that he could get information directly from the source. He would have loved to be part of the J.F.O but Norm's rank meant that he wasn't eligible. The project went almost a year, and the kingpin was taken down with a bunch of his cronies. The Mounties seized his house, boat, fancy cars, and motorcycle, along with a whack of cash, under the proceeds of crime act.

The Mounties let Norm continue to use Louie in an attempt to get one of the smaller players involved in their project. The theory being that if Norm was able to get one of the smaller fish, he might lead them to the big fish. The mid-level dealer was partners with a guy whose family owned a local sporting goods store. Louie told Norm that a lot of the deals were made after hours in the store in a party room upstairs. On one particular night, Louie told Norm there was a half a pound of coke coming to the store to be separated between the two partners. The Drug Squad set up surveillance and waited for all the players to be in place.

Murphy's Law applies to drug work; if something can go wrong, it will. Piecing together Louie's information and trying to identify the various targets in the dark proved difficult. Norm acted on the information he had and raided the store. Only the younger brother of the coke dealer was at the store, and it seemed he wasn't involved. The store was huge, and a search came up empty. As it turned out, one of the dealers had the exact same type of car that the brother had, and the Drug Squad missed the bad guys leaving with some of the dope. Louie later told Norm that the brother who got away flushed three ounces of coke down the toilet when he figured the cops were coming for him.

Things didn't work out as planned that night, and to make it worse, one of the drug cops left his notebook containing highly sensitive information in the store. He wasn't able to retrieve it until the next day; it was not a good thing. As fate would have it, the younger brother was arrested a few years later for several charges of attempted murder. He was H.I.V. positive, and he had infected several city women. He knowingly infected the women, not caring about the consequences. It seems the innocent looking little brother was the real bad ass in the family. It came out in the media that the mother even knew about his condition; nobody did anything to stop him. He was convicted and will be in jail for a very long time!

Project Pop Shop

Norm had been itching for a good project to sink his teeth into, and Louie helped deliver the goods. He told Norm about a downtown variety store that was buying/selling/trading stolen property and drugs.

Louie said, "You can get a coca-cola and cocaine at the same store!"

He also said that he heard the brothers who ran the place were also selling guns. When describing the store's location, Louie said one brother also ran a massage parlor next door.

Louie chuckled and said, "Ya man, you can get high and get off!"

He said the owner, or one of his girls would sell you weed or coke along with the massage. George liked getting massaged there because the girls offered him a *happy ending.* That's all Norm had to hear…it covered all the bases for a Street Crimes project…drugs, guns, and sex! Norm ran the idea of a project by his boss Andy Green. Andy liked it and ran it by his boss. He told Norm to write up an operation plan.

An operational plan can be simple or complex, depending on the type of investigation. It is like a flow chart in words, describing how you will go about conducting an investigation. It has to include the personnel and equipment to be used, as well as the target(s) and what exactly the criminal activity is that the project will focus on. It's a playbook for the brass so that they know exactly what the context of the investigation is and what the proposed outcome will be.

Since drugs and guns were really beyond the scope of the Street Crimes branch, Norm brought his buddy Jesse from the Drug Squad on board, along with someone from the Provincial Weapons Unit. Norm not only needed manpower from the other units, he needed buy money. The mandate in Street Crimes would cover any stolen property purchased but not drugs or guns. The provincial unit had lots of money earmarked to take illegal guns off the street, so Norm took advantage of that. Norm also had to bring the Spin Team on board for surveillance on the targets and different locations involved.

With all the different units, manpower, and money in place there were only two things missing…a lead investigator and an undercover operator. Norm was a supervisor in Street Crimes, and he suggested one of his investigators, Mickey D, take on the roll of lead investigator. That meant he'd have to do all the grunt work while Norm supervised and oversaw the whole project. Andy Green's boss didn't except Norm's suggestion for an out of town UC and he went with one of their own guys from the Drug Squad. Cheech had taken the UC course and acquired a little drug experience, but it is always a risk doing undercover work in your own city. Norm agreed on the condition he could act as Cheech's handler. The handler is responsible for the UC and their actions.

Getting In

The most difficult part of an investigation for an undercover operator is getting next to, or being accepted by, the bad guys. They have to dress for and play a role, according to the situation at hand. In this case, the variety store was the main target, with the massage parlor next door a secondary target. Two of the three brothers who ran the store were the main players; one of them ran the massage parlor and also dealt drugs from his house. Cheech's job was to befriend these guys and eventually make some buys from them. You would think an introduction from Louie the Wap would be the way to go but then he'd have to testify in court later on. That would not be good for Louie.

Using the background information from Louie, Cheech took on the identity of a local street urchin who was looking to make a buck any way he could. To make the project operational, Norm had to have briefings in advance with the bosses and then with everyone from the Street Crimes, Drugs, and Surveillance Units who were involved. It was a dangerous gig for Cheech; officer safety was paramount!

Cheech was given a special pager that was actually a transmitter. The cover team could listen in on any of Cheech's conversations. Cheech would use a special code word in the case of an emergency, and the cavalry would rush to his rescue. Norm also requisitioned some gold bling and electronics from the property room. The bling was for show, and Cheech would try to sell the electronics as stolen property.

One Stop Shopping

On Cheech's first visit to the store, he scored an 8-ball of coke for $200 and two electronic calculators. He was in!

Cheech made arrangements with one of the brothers to come back later in the week and buy a quarter ounce of coke *(2 8-balls or 7grams)*. On the second visit Cheech tried to unload a camcorder at the store. He bought a quarter ounce of coke and ten ecstasy pills for $520. The goal for the rest of the project team was to see exactly where the stolen property and drugs were coming from and going to. The team had to follow the brothers and their friends back and forth from the store to various houses in the city.

On Cheech's third visit, he traded the camcorder and $100 cash for a laptop and an X Box. During his conversation with the one brother, Cheech was offered more ecstasy, cocaine, and guns. The project team made the decision to try and buy more cocaine and guns. They would attempt to see where the stuff was coming from at the same time. Cheech returned to the store for the fourth time and bought a .32 caliber hand gun for $450 and an 8-ball of coke for $220. He left a laptop at the store for a future trade. The target also told Cheech he could have sex next door at the massage parlor if he wanted. He also offered Cheech larger amounts of coke and more guns. Mickey D checked the gun Cheech bought and found it had been reported stolen.

Cheech went back to the store a fifth time and was able to buy an ounce of cocaine for $1,400. The project team made the decision there was enough evidence to search the store, massage parlor, and one house. There was also enough evidence to arrest two of the brother for drug trafficking and possession of stolen property. The three search warrants were all executed at the same time on the same night. Cheech had ordered up some more coke just prior so the team would have the chance to get some more of the drug off the street. The cops found some weed and cash while searching the store, along with the electronics Cheech had traded them. More cash and stolen property was seized from one of the brother's house. Three women were arrested at the massage parlor and charged with various drug and prostitution charges. Two of the three brothers were charged with a shit load of different charges!

Mickey D almost pulled out what little hair he had left trying to wrap up the project and complete the mountains of paperwork that went with it. Norm was in his element, loving the high pressure, and multi-tasking that went along with such a gig. He thrived in such work environments!

Norm didn't hear from Louie the Wap after Project Pop Shop. He got his reward and stayed in touch on and off with the younger Drug Squad guy Norm introduced him to. The last Norm heard of Louie he was doing a stint in jail. Louie's life was set, like the cement he worked with. It would always be the same. He did whatever he could to make a quick buck…and to trowel his way through life.

16
Fraudsters

"I hated every minute of my training, but I said, 'Don't quit.' Suffer now and live the rest of your life as a champion"
– Muhammad Ali

Just when Norm was enjoying a good run in Street Crimes, the powers to be decided that one of their golden boys needed some investigative experience, and they gave him Norm's job. His own buddy Digger Daniels actually called Norm on the Labor Day holiday weekend to give him the good news. Norm was up north on his annual fishing trip with the boys when he got the call. His old car partner and buddy wanted to congratulate Norm personally on his transfer to the Fraud Squad.

It was the last place Norm wanted to go…he had even spelled that out on the fancy new "skills inventory" forms everyone had to fill out months earlier. The form was basically an interdepartmental resume where you listed your job experience and where you might like to work in the future. Norm specifically checked the box specifying he did NOT want to go to Fraud.

The horrified look on Norm's face was so obvious that one of the guys handed him a beer and asked him what had happened. Norm had checked the box for the Arson job. Daniels tried to make Norm feel better by telling him that the Arson Unit actually worked out of the Fraud office. They filled the Arson job with another golden boy who had absolutely no investigative experience. It made no sense at all, but the brass did that kind of thing to give some people more experience before their next promotion. Fraud had been known as a dead end position for mostly senior guys that nobody else wanted. Norm was in shock and took some extra vacation time before returning to work.

It had been a rough year for Norm personally, they say shit comes in threes and Norm had his triple whammy. He separated from his wife, his dad had a heart attack, and his mom got cancer. The separation became a divorce. His dad recovered with a double bypass, but Norm's mom died of cancer. There was one point where he actually got to visit them both on the same day in the same hospital. Norm's strength came from the fact that each event distracted from the other. He was the eldest sibling and had to be strong for the others. Work was a distraction too…it kept Norm's mind off his personal life.

The New Fraud Squad

Norm showed up for his first day in the Fraud Squad with his left arm in a sling. He had been out on his motorcycle and had a spill, fracturing his left elbow. It was strictly an office job, so Norm figured he might as well suffer on company time. Once again, he had to trade in his jeans and break out the dress shirts and ties. There had been quite a few transfers while Norm was away…they did that every once in a while to shake things up and to stop stagnation in areas where some people worked forever.

Norm had worked with his new boss before; he was not happy with all the transfers either. He said he was trying to give the Fraud Squad a new image and turn things around. That task seemed pretty well impossible since there was a two year backlog of fraud files! That meant that Norm had thirty files stacked up in his computer queue, waiting to be addressed.

Norm had one thing going for him; his new boss had previously been the Arson investigator, and he was not happy about the new guy who had no investigative experience. He knew Norm was interested in the job and he asked Norm if he wanted to be the guy's backup *(it was normally a one man job)*. The boss hoped that Norm could offer the new guy some investigative support, an area where Norm had years of previous experience. It was an offer too good to refuse. Norm knew that by taking the offer that the Arson job would be his some day

Fraud was complicated, probably one of the reasons that nobody wanted to work there. The files were long and involved, sometimes with hundreds of pages of documents to read over. The only saving grace was that the lengthy paper trail eventually led to the criminal who instigated it. Norm was completely overwhelmed at first. He got to go to the police college for a two week fraud course, which helped him get a better understanding of the crime. Norm also knew everyone in the office, having worked with them at some point over his career.

The workload was heavy, but for the most part everyone carried their own weight. Norm did what he always did; he dug in and did his job. It wasn't long before Norm got called in to assist the Arson guy…he needed a search warrant and had never written one. Norm had about 150 search warrants under his belt, so he became the tutor.

Magic Plastic

While Norm tried to figure out just exactly what Fraud was all about, the other guys in the office conducted show and tell with some of their investigations to bring Norm up to speed. One of the guys was just finishing up a huge counterfeit investigation where the fraudster had mastered counterfeiting various government documents and American Express travelers' checks! Norm was amazed at the quality of the documents, and he would never have detected them on his own. Even more amazing was the fact that the head of security from American Express said the counterfeit checks were the best he'd ever seen! The checks were in Canadian funds, and that's how the dummy got caught. An alert sales person finally noticed the guy spelled *Canadian* wrong on the top of the checks. Prior to getting caught, he cashed in about $200,000 in phony checks. He traveled and bought all kinds of stuff including two vehicles!

Norm got called into his boss's office one day and saw his buddy Jesse sitting there with one of the other Fraud guys. Jesse said one of his informants got busted for a bunch of arrest warrants, and he was looking to trade information for a get out of jail free card. Norm and the Fraud guy were well aware of whom this long time criminal was; he was a target on their joint wire tap when Norm was in Drugs and he was in the B & E Squad. The information he wanted to trade was all fraud related so Jesse brought it to the Fraud Squad. Karl Crest was in the cell block waiting to be interviewed, so Norm's boss told him to do the interview with one of Jesse's drug investigators.

Norm thought he'd heard it all after twenty-five years on the job, but he was in for another lesson in crime. Karl Crest had been a thief most of his life. He told Norm he was stealing credit cards and selling them to a guy named "Roy" on the west side of the city. Karl also had a girlfriend who was *skimming* credit cards at a local restaurant. Crest said she was given an 8-ball of coke a week for skimming the cards. The girl carried a mini credit card reader in her apron, and she would swipe the customer's card through the device before swiping it again at the cash register. This was all new to Norm; he was in awe!

Karl said he'd take the skimmer to Roy who'd download the credit card info to his laptop in the back room of the store there that was run by his buddy Nazim. Karl had given Roy at least fifty stolen credit cards!

The deal was that Karl would supply information and work with Norm if he could get released on bail. The assistant crown attorney was not impressed with the information alone; he wanted Karl to swear to a written statement before he would consider releasing him. Even though Jesse vouched for Karl, Norm had been burned by informants before, and he knew that if Karl got released, he'd probably never hear from him again. He had to milk Karl for all he was worth before letting him out of his sight. Norm grabbed Karl as soon as he was released from jail and took him for a ride.

On the way to Roy's place, Karl told Norm he also had a guy working at major electronics store who'd let him use the stolen credit cards to buy plasma TV's and other electronics. Karl would then sell the electronics on the street for up to fifty cents on the dollar. Norm drove Karl right to Nazim's store where Roy worked in the back. The deal was that Karl was supposed to get Norm a sample card from Roy, but he was uncomfortable when Karl showed up. The word may have gotten out that Karl got busted, and Roy said he didn't have any cards to give Karl.

Credit *Card skimming 101:* Karl would steal someone's wallet and credit cards. Roy would take the cards and run them through his skimmer, obtaining all the information that is encoded on the black stripe on the back of the card. Roy could then take that information and transfer it to any new blank card, or one that he had previously wiped clean. He had software that would tell him the limit on the cards. Roy would then sell the cards to guys like Karl who would go on shopping sprees for merchandise. They could then sell the goods on the street for cash. The scary thing is that a guy like Karl could have a Visa card with his name on the front, but all the information on the back belonged to someone else. It was a very lucrative scam!

Norm had a lot to think about and even more follow-up to do on the people and addresses Karl gave him. Norm spent the whole next day trying to absorb all the new information. Karl never checked in with Norm…that was no surprise! Another day passed with no word from Karl but one of the drug cops called Norm with more information on Roy and "Nazim," the guy who ran the store. Norm now had enough information to start up a search warrant for the store and Roy's apartment above it. The boss was impressed. With the exception of searches on bank records, fraud guys never used informants or did search warrants on houses.

Hip Deep

While Norm was busy prepping his search warrants, the office got a call from uniform officers who arrested two guys with a bunch of cloned debit cards and a whack of cash…all in twenty dollar bills. They had been caught in the act at a local bank machine, using the cloned debit cards to withdraw cash from people's bank accounts. The cops caught the guys with seventeen blank debit cards and $7,000 in cash. They had grounds to believe there was more evidence in their vehicle, so that meant getting a search warrant. Guess who was volunteered to write the warrant? The shit was piling up in the fraud office, and Norm was in it hip deep! After all was said and done seventy-one cloned cards and almost $30,000 in stolen cash was recovered. The Fraud Squad got noticed…the brass was ecstatic! They even put on a show and tell news release for the media. *(The cloned debit cards worked the same way…stolen personal information was encoded on the magnetic strip on the cards, giving access to the bank accounts. PIN numbers were also stolen and attached to the cards)*

Norm had no time to bask in the glory; he had two more search warrants to finish in order bust Roy and Nazim at the variety store. Norm absorbed and learned as he went along; it was on the job training for sure! The Fraud and Drug Squads raided the variety store, arresting Roy and Nazim. The cops seized clone cards, stolen cards, two laptops, fake ID, credit card info, and debit machines. Norm later learned how these guys put a special chip into debit machines, to steal card data. They hid a mini camera somewhere close by to catch people punching in their PIN's. Nazim was running the variety store, and Roy was running a credit card factory!

No job is finished until the paperwork is done; in Fraud, it seemed the paperwork was never done… it just got deeper and deeper! Norm didn't mind...he was seeing some action, getting out of the office, dealing with informants, and actually having fun! It was really no surprise, but neither Norm nor Jesse ever heard from Karl Crest again! After every arrest, there is an interview where the accused gets a chance to confess or help out the police in consideration for a lighter sentence.

Roy was willing to give up everything he knew, but he wanted something in exchange.

17
Roy Rogers

The informant information that Norm received was as complicated as the fraud investigations he was involved in. Sure the paper trail led to the bad guys, but it always led to more and more paper! The names were getting more complicated too…it was the Lebanese, Romanians, Arabs, and Nigerians who were behind the fraud scams. In Nigeria, some government officials were involved in the scams and actually encouraged their people to get involved to stimulate the economy! The scams were devious and forever evolving. Some of the email spammers were relentless with their mailings telling people things like they had a family inheritance or they won a huge lottery in another country.

Norm worked on one case where an elderly woman got sucked into giving scammers almost $200,000; all in the hopes she could claim her sixty million dollar Spanish lottery windfall! Norm tried to tell the woman it was a scam before she gave all her money away, but her greed got the best of her. The woman's daughter called Norm after her mother blew all of her life's savings. She said her mom was actually upset that she ran out of money and that she wouldn't be able to claim her prize!

Virgin Territory

It was a continuing education for Norm. When he arrested the Romanian named Roy Rogers, he had nothing to say. After a night in a jail cell, he told Norm he would tell him everything he wanted to know. The only condition was that Roy wanted to be deported back to Romania! It was a strange request considering Roy had defected from there to the U.S. and then snuck across the border into Canada. Roy said he missed his girlfriend back home, but Norm didn't buy that, figuring there had to be a lot more to it. Regardless, Norm reached out to one of his Immigration contacts and put the wheels in motion.

Norm sat down in the interview room with Roy and opened his notebook. The interview rooms contain only a table and two chairs. For an interrogation, keen investigators arrange the furniture in such a way that they can openly confront a suspect while questioning them. Two of the chairs can be placed facing each other at one corner of the table, with the suspect facing the camera. The second investigator sits at the opposite end of the table taking notes of the conversation and suspect's body language. With no table in between the investigator can move his chair closer to the suspect to apply emotional pressure by getting into their personal space. In a normal interview where a potential informant wants to supply information, the investigator can simply sit across the table from them, letting them feel more comfortable; really, that table is a safety barrier.

Roy sat there attentively on his side of the table, waiting for Norm's questions. Norm started with the preliminary tombstone information like his name and date of birth. That information was already in the official reports but it's an interviewing technique that helps put the subject at ease. The man sitting across from Norm was thirty years old but he looked forty-five. His name was Romanian and difficult to pronounce in English.

He said to Norm, "Everyone just calls me Roy."

"I always wanted to be a cowboy like Roy Rogers!"

Roy was slight in stature, soft spoken, and he had a thick Middle Eastern accent. His head was almost completely bald, and his only facial hair was his five o'clock shadow. Roy's teeth were heavily stained from his cigarette habit. He asked Norm if could have one. Cigarettes used to be a great tool for police investigators; it would relax many suspects and help them to spill the beans. The law had changed and Norm told Roy he was sorry, that there was no smoking in the building. In reality, Norm wasn't sorry. He hated sucking in second-hand smoke!

Card Players

Roy wasted no time in rambling off the names of other guys he knew that were involved in credit card fraud. He started talking about M.S.R.'s, P.M.R.'s and data chips, technical stuff that was way over Norm's head. Norm interjected telling Roy he was just a dumb cop and asking him to explain things in layman terms. Roy spoke about two particular young guys in the city who were running illegal credit card factories from their homes. According to Roy, it could be easily done with a laptop computer and a few things obtained over the Internet.

The M.S.R. is simply a credit card reader, similar to the machines you see in any business but without all the fancy buttons. It looks exactly like the machine you see in hotels when they program your room key. The P.M.R. is the miniature version that can be easily concealed in a pocket or apron. They can be easily purchased online. It was obvious to Norm that Roy was no dummy, and he knew what he was talking about! He said he got into the business back home in Romania with a group of fraud artists. Roy said that most of Europe had switched to chip cards to alleviate most of their credit card fraud. Canada had not switched over to the new technology, so it was virgin territory for enterprising criminals.

Roy said that the two main fraudulent card makers were Drew and Bogart. He believed that Drew had a debit card machine set up in a local corner store somewhere and he was skimming credit card information. He was paying one of the store employees to let him run his scam. Roy said Drew had blank and stolen credit cards in his house. He didn't know the address but described the house's location to Norm. Roy said that Drew had a credit card embosser, but he believed that Nazim's brother Basheer was in possession of it.

According to Roy, Bogart was some kind of kid computer genius. He started hacking computers in his early teens and was "phishing" by the time he was seventeen. Bogart would copy a bank website and try to lure people into logging on with their personal data. He would pump out 10,000 emails at a time, so even if he got three or four card numbers, it was a good day. Hackers like Bogart didn't do it for the fun of it; he did it to make money!

Roy said that Bogart had organized crime ties in Romania where he would swap stolen credit card information with his contacts there. Locally, he had a buddy named Rony who was helping him make fake identification to be used for some of their scams. Some of the cards that Roy got from Karl Crest went to Bogart for reprogramming. He would get $300 bucks a piece for them. Roy said Rony and Bogart also had some kind of Wire scam going where they were raking in thousands of dollars every week! He said they acted like little gangsters; they went to local night clubs buying cocaine and expensive bottles of champagne while they entertained their friends.

Norm filled two pages in his notebook with details from Roy; his work was cut out for him doing follow-up for the next few days! Norm pumped Roy for all the information he had…it was difficult talking to him once he got to the county jail. Norm had to make appointments to visit Roy at the jail. A guard would bring him into a tiny interview room to visit with Norm. Between his whispering and his thick accent, Norm could barely understand him at times. According to Roy, even the guard posted outside the door couldn't be trusted; he feared for his safety there if anyone found out he was a rat. His fears were not unfounded; Norm glanced out the little window at the guard on one occasion and saw he was leaning in with his ear near the crack in the door.

Roy Rogers eventually got his wish. He didn't get to ride off into the sunset; he was deported back to his native Romania. Roy gave Norm his email address and said he'd stay in touch, but he never did.

18
Bazaar Brothers

While Norm was busy checking police records and chasing leads on Roy's information, Nazim Bazaar called. He should have offered Norm some cheese with all the whining he did on the phone! Nazim went on and on about how he was just trying to run a business and keep his head above water. He had already been given the team speech by Norm when he got arrested, but he talked in circles, not really saying anything worthwhile. He gave Norm the same information that he had already gotten from Roy. All of Nazim's information seemed to be second hand and basically useless to Norm. Nazim persisted though and called back on another day, saying he wanted to meet Norm in person.

Norm always liked to arrive early when meeting an informant...it was a safety thing as much as it was a curiosity thing. Cops can get set up by their informants, so if Norm was meeting someone new while working alone, he took precautions to avoid any potential problems. Norm usually told his boss or one of his co-workers where he would be meeting the informant. He learned that most informants were late for a meeting, so arriving early wasn't a problem. Norm told Nazim to meet him in the parking lot of a public park on the far west side of the city. Norm got there early and positioned his car so he could see Nazim or anyone else coming into the lot.

It was only a couple minutes past the meeting time when a dark colored, ghetto cruiser pulled into the lot and made its way over to Norm's car. The car's windows had dark tinting, but Norm could see that someone else was with Nazim in the car. Nazim and the other guy got out of the car...they had similar Middle Eastern features, but they looked like night and day. Nazim was impeccably dressed with tan slacks and dark brown dress shirt. His wavy jet black hair was gelled and slicked back. Nazim was clean shaven, but it looked like he was one of those guys who had to shave twice a day to achieve that look. Norm could smell his cheap cologne as he climbed into the back seat.

The other guy was a contradiction; he had the home boy, jock look going on. He wore clean white, expensive sneakers, grey track pants, and a pro basketball jersey. His hair was spiked, and he had a neatly trimmed Fu Manchu moustache.

Nazim shook Norm's hand and said, "This is my brother Basheer; he can tell you what you want to know."

Basheer reached over the seat and shook Norms hand; the smell of his sport cologne overpowered his brother's.

Basheer said, "It's nice to meet you Norm, how can I help my brother?"

Norm was impressed that Basheer was stepping up to help his brother. Nazim either didn't understand exactly how the game was played, or he really didn't know anything. This was not the case with Basheer…he immediately dropped some of the same names that Roy did but he gave more details and admitted he had dealt personally with them. Where Nazim had a thick accent, Basheer spoke clear and precise English. Within minutes, Norm was convinced that Basheer would be able to help him take down some of the guys making fraudulent credit cards.

Norm let Basheer finish his speech and then directed him to focus on one guy at a time. Norm still had lots of follow up to do on these fraudsters, so he told Basheer to keep in touch and see what else he could dig up on the guy named Drew. Basheer said he would do whatever it would take to help get his brother out of trouble.

Norm felt that Basheer was sincere so he asked him, "As a show of good faith, how 'bout you give up that embosser you have tucked away somewhere?"

Basheer looked a little surprised, but he cracked a smile and said, "Sure, no problem Norm!"

Dominos

Karl Crest was the first domino; when he fell, he knocked over Roy and Nazim Bazaar. The dominos were lined up waiting to fall, and Norm was there waiting to catch them! His backlog of other fraud files was put on the back burner, but his boss didn't care…the Fraud Squad was getting noticed. The brass even popped by the office to see what was going on; normally no one came by to visit. The rest of the crew in the squad loved the action; it gave them a chance to get out of the office and to make some overtime!

Norm's boss laughed out loud after one long overtime shift and said, "They don't know what to do upstairs, the Fraud Squad never had an overtime budget before!"

While Norm was browsing computer screens and police files, Bogart's name popped up as a person of interest with the Mounties. A phone call to their financial crimes office put Norm in touch with one of their investigators. He told Norm that Bogart's father showed up at the Mountie office one day with his son's computer. Apparently, dad told the cops that he felt his son was up to no good…spending endless days and night in his room on his computer. His son also came into a pile of money that he didn't have a good explanation for.

The Mountie told Norm he was welcome to take the computer since he had it for a year and hadn't had a chance to look at it! Apparently, fraud cops everywhere were backlogged and fighting a losing battle. Norm gave the computer to one of the in house computer technicians so he could run a special software program to retrieve any files hidden on the hard drive.

Norm already had rough plan on how to take down the rest of the card players when Basheer called back. He created a file called *Card Players* to keep all the different names straight. Basheer had been to visit Drew and got the information that Norm needed for a search warrant at Drew's house. Drew was even kind enough to show Basheer some of his hiding places for the stolen credit cards and electronics he had!

Search warrants changed dramatically over the years; a two page document that used to contain a one paragraph appendix had turned into a short novel containing a dozen or more pages, depending on the complexity of the case. In the court's opinion, a man's home was his castle, and the cops needed abundantly clear and precise grounds as to exactly why they wanted to search someone's castle. The days of visiting judges at their homes were long gone so cops had to use *Telewarrants*, applying to an unknown out of town judge via a fax machine.

Like everyone else, Norm missed those good old days! On one occasion during his early Drug Squad days, Norm caught the judge late in the day as he was on his way out the courthouse door. As a courtesy, the cops would call the judge first to tell them a search warrant was being prepared. The judge was in a hurry to go somewhere, so he told Norm to meet him at the side door.

The veteran judge looked Norm in the eye and asked, "Do you have really good information on this one?"

"Yes sir!"

Norm didn't have time to fill in the appendix that was normally attached to the warrant.

The judge looked at it and said, "Don't burn me on this."

To Norm's astonishment, the judge signed the blank search warrant!

As the judge hurried away, he said, "Just make sure you leave me a copy after you fill it in!"

The Fraud Squad raided Drew's place and recovered a whole bunch of stuff. He had stolen and blank credit cards hidden all over in his basement apartment. He actually had blank bank cards that just needed the numbers embossed on the front. Drew had a skimmer machine and a laptop to hook it up to, and the electronics he had bought with stolen credit cards. It was a good bust, and Basheer had proven that he was a reliable informant. As a bonus, Norm's sixteen hour day earned him some big overtime!

Drew had been arrested before, he immediately told Norm he wanted to help himself out and work his patch. He spit out two names like he was discarding cherry pits, guess who…Bogart and Rony! Norm wasn't sure exactly what Drew might be able to come up with to take them down, so he told him to start digging and call when he had something substantial.

Jack of All Trades

Basheer had successfully worked his brother's patch and was now collecting some extra cash as a reward for Norm's successful search warrants and arrests. Basheer took a liking to Norm.

He came right out and asked Norm one day, "So what else do you want to know?"

"Why, what have you got?"

"Cigarettes, drugs, you name it…"

Norm, always curious, "Who do you know selling drugs?"

Basheer grinned from ear to ear and said, "How about Fat Fiona? I play poker with her all the time."

Basheer rambled on about Fat Fiona and how he knew that she stashed her crack at a certain friend's apartment. He had more clout and connections that Norm was aware of. Not bad for an illegal immigrant who had only been in the country for a couple years!

Norm felt like a secretary, scribbling pages of notes while Basheer filled him in on who was into what. He gave Basheer directions on what he needed to pursue people like Fat Fiona and the cigarette guys. Norm explained that Fraud was now his job, so the other information would have to be passed on unless Basheer wanted to work directly with other cops. He said he was content with Norm handling him and his information. Nazim would show up for the odd meeting with Basheer, but he was pretty well useless to Norm. Regardless, Norm humored him and pretended to appreciate his input.

The cigarette info was passed on to the Mounties, and Norm went directly to his buddy Blackjack with the drug info. Blackjack was in charge of the Drug Squad and he said that Fat Fiona managed to stay in their good graces by playing both sides of the fence, supplying mostly useless information to the Drug Squad in the hopes of keeping them off her back. In reality, the Drug Squad always wanted to nail her, but she was a smart cookie and always one step ahead of the cops.

Mixed Smoke Signals

It was physically impossible for Norm to look into everyone and everything that his informants told him about. Basheer was in deep with some Middle Eastern guys who were bringing truck loads of illegal Indian cigarettes into the city. The loads were worth up to fifty thousand dollars each, and they were distributed among a group of variety stores across the city. The crime didn't fall under Norm's jurisdiction, so he introduced Basheer to a Mountie investigator. Basheer eventually helped them take down one of the major players involved, but he told Norm they fucked him out of his reward. There wasn't much Norm could do about that; it was obvious Basheer wouldn't be calling the Mounties back!

Norm knew Basheer was a middle man, being involved in some drug deals as well as some illegal cigarette deals. He just wasn't sure how deeply Basheer was involved. Basheer called Norm one day asking him to meet at a local coffee shop. Norm got to the location early as usual, so he went in for a bit of lunch. Basheer showed up on foot about 10 minutes later carrying a paper bag from a fast food restaurant. He asked Norm for a lift home and if he could throw the bag in Norm's vehicle in the mean time. Norm pointed to his grey van parked outside in the parking lot, and then went to the bathroom.

Basheer told Norm that Bogart had hooked up with a new Russian guy and that another kid he had been doing the wire scams with was now selling cocaine. It was some of that nice to know information that Norm already knew...he had gotten the same from another source. Basheer could see that Norm wasn't too excited.

He leaned in closer and said, "I know where you can find a gun!"

That caught Norm's attention. Basheer told him who had the gun and where it was stashed. Norm knew very well who the guy was; he was a well-known criminal whose specialty was breaking into homes and stealing high end jewelry. Norm and Basheer continued their conversation while they walked to the parking lot and got into the van. Norm pulled out of the lot and started heading towards Basheer's place. Basheer was fidgeting and looking all around under the front seat.

Norm asked, "Are you looking for the seat belt?"

Basheer's face had gone white.

"No, I'm looking for the thirty grand; it was in a paper bag right here under my front seat!"

"What thirty grand?"

Basheer was freaking out. He started to stammer.

"I had thirty thousand dollars in a paper bag; I put it under the seat when you were in the coffee shop!"

Norm was not a guy who got excited easily, but he could feel his heart starting to pound a little faster as he pulled over off the road. Both men fell silent as they frantically searched the van for the missing bag of cash.

After coming up empty handed, Norm looked at Basheer and asked, "What the fuck were you doing carrying that kind of cash?"

Basheer looked like he had just lost his whole family in a horrific car crash.

"It's part of a cigarette deal, they'll kill me if I don't deliver that cash!"

Norm did what any good Sherlock would do; he returned to the scene of the crime. To his astonishment, there was an almost identical van that was parked in the spot next to Norm's! Norm looked at Basheer; the color was starting to come back to his face.

"I don't know, maybe I put the bag in the wrong van?"

Norm parked down the street leaving Basheer in the van. He wasn't about to start rifling through someone else's van, so Norm went back into the coffee shop. There was some kind of commotion behind the counter near the kitchen…a woman with two young children was babbling away to the manager. Norm understood what had happened, but how could he explain that he was a cop and all that cash belonged to his informant?

Before Norm could say anything, a patrol car pulled into the parking lot, the manager had called the police. Apparently the woman couldn't believe what she found; she was afraid and didn't know what to do with the bag full of cash. Norm spoke to the cops and pointed out the similar vans. He tried to explain the situation, but officially the cash had to be seized and a police report filed. Norm went back to his van to break the news to Basheer. He also called his boss. Poor Basheer, he wondered out loud what would happen to his daughter and pregnant girlfriend when he fled the country, fearing for his life.

Norm went to see his boss, and then his boss's boss to see what could be done. The word had spread by the time Norm got to the station; the general opinion was that the bag of cash was drug money, and it should be forfeited to the government coffers so it could pay for some retiring politician's retirement. Norm argued that the bag of money was actually found property and that the rightful owner should have claim to it like any other found property. No matter what anyone thought, there was no proof of any kind that the money was tied to drugs or any other crime for that matter. The big boss agreed that in fact, Basheer was the rightful owner of the cash, and he was entitled to claim it.

Basheer was a happy camper! The boss said the money could be returned to him, but it had to be counted in front of him, and on camera. It meant that Basheer would have to go to the cop shop to get his money, but that was fine with him. He probably would have crawled over broken glass to get that cash back!

Bugs

The light at the end of the tunnel was shining brighter each day for Norm. His retirement was approaching fast. He had to try and finish up his outstanding files and re-assign those he couldn't. In Norm's job, you couldn't just walk out the door. Some of his investigations were ongoing and had been so for months. Harley Davidson and the other guys in the office inherited some of Norm's files.

Norm had to introduce the last of his informants to new handlers. Some of them weren't happy about that, but such is life. Basheer was Norm's last reliable informant…he was a proven plethora of criminal information. He reminded Norm of the guy with a gun that Norm never looked into. Norm handed the investigation off to the detective squad and the SWAT team. Why anyone would want to resist a bunch of guys in dressed in fatigues and carrying machine guns is a mystery. Norm dropped by during the search and waited in the hallway. The screaming and yelling brought neighbors out into the hallway. Norm flashed his badge and told the neighbors everything was under control. The dummy lost the fight, and a hand gun was recovered during the search of the guy's apartment.

Basheer told Norm about a local variety store that was selling drugs and illegal cigarettes. Norm let the Drug Squad handle that one. As it turned out, the guy was into kiddy porn too! Norm let the other squads handle the work, but he made sure Basheer got paid for his efforts. By Norm sitting on the sidelines, it meant he wouldn't have to return after retiring when the cases went to court.

Basheer was well-connected. He told Norm he met some guys up north who showed him a shipping pallet stacked with pounds of weed. They were looking for someone to help them move the stuff. He had another gang affiliated guy offer him an opportunity to smuggle cocaine into the country. This guy wanted to use Basheer's girlfriend as a mule. The gang guy would send single girls off to an island in the Caribbean and then have them return with a special suitcase, lined with cocaine. Norm tried to get the Mounties interested, but they said it was more of an *international* case, whatever that meant.

Norm had to introduce Basheer to one of the new Drug Squad guys; he couldn't be the go between forever. Basheer told Norm and the new guy about some guys with guns…it was the fraudster Drew and his brother. Apparently his brother was connected to a terrorist organization, and they were selling the guns to financially support the terrorist group. The new guy's jaw kept dropping as Basheer filled him in. Norm had to remind him to keep making notes.

The last gift to Norm from Basheer was a group of hard core B & E boys who had preyed on the city for years. Norm had locked some of them up years earlier when he worked in the B & E Squad. The seasoned criminals had done some time in jail, learned from their mistakes, and honed their skills. The Mobile Surveillance Unit struck out with the crew on many occasions…they were too good at evading the cops. The B & E Squad was also stymied by the crew; they knew what they were up to but couldn't figure out how to get them.

One of Norm's buddies in the B & E Squad got a boner when Norm told him how to get them. Basheer was right in with these guys; he would buy some of their high end stolen jewelry. He told Norm the location of the store where they fenced a lot of it. These guys were serious players. The ring leader was the guy with the gun who the S.W.A.T. team beat the shit out of. Obviously, he wasn't deterred. Basheer said the crew knew how to pick out houses where there would be high-end jewelry and electronics. One of their methods was to scope out houses with certain kinds of satellite dishes. They knew that certain ethnicities liked satellite service from their own countries. Some of these same people liked high-end jewelry. They kept the jewelry and sometimes large amounts of cash in their homes. The crew preyed on those people in the city, and across the county.

Basheer gave Norm a list of some property the crew had recently stolen; he bought a laptop from them. The B & E Squad confirmed the property had been stolen from a couple houses outside the city. Basheer asked Norm why the cops couldn't catch the crew. Norm asked the B & E Squad the same question. It was the same old story…the crew was too good; they didn't know how to catch them.

Basheer asked Norm, "Why don't you bug their cars?"

That was the million dollar question. The crew switched cars and license plates all the time. The cops found it almost impossible to do surveillance on the crew even when they knew what cars they were driving.

"I can tell you what cars they have and where they're at."

Norm was impressed. Leave it up to Basheer to tell the cops how to catch bad guys! The force had a couple tracking devices collecting dust, so Norm suggested they use them. His buddy applied for tracking warrants, and Basheer supplied the cars and their locations. The crew had two different cars stashed in parking lots. When they went out to do a B & E, they drove to that area then swapped vehicles. The stash vehicles were not known to the cops.

With Basheer's help, the B & E Squad bugged the cars and got lucky a couple nights later. The tracking device allowed them to keep their distance without being detected. They followed the crew into an upscale sub-division and then sealed off the area. When the crew tried to leave the area with a car full of loot, they were taken down by the cops. They had broken into a couple homes and had stolen some jewelry and electronics. Thanks to Basheer, the crew was on its way back to jail.

Bye Bye Basheer

Unfortunately for Basheer, he would soon be seeing his friends in jail. Not long after Norm retired, Basheer's new handler called. He said another Drug Squad guy busted Basheer at his store with a substantial amount of coke and some weed. He played both sides of the fence, and he got caught. He called Norm one day whining, saying he should get credit for all the help he gave the police. Norm reminded him he was being paid for the information. He also told Basheer he was out of the game so he could no longer help him.

With Basheer getting busted, Nazim lost the store. It was just a front; they never really sold anything legal there anyway. Somehow, Nazim managed to get some more financial backing and he opened a pizza place on the other side of town. It wasn't long before that went belly up. Some time later, Norm ran into Nazim managing another variety store. He was working for someone else, but it is what he knew. Unlike his brother Basheer, Nazim had no problem trying to earn an honest living.

Basheer never got his Canadian citizenship, and by being arrested, he never would. The last Norm heard Basheer was going down for his drug bust, and he would be going to jail for a while. He could have tried to skip the country, but he had two kids with his girlfriend. Basheer was no different than many of Norm's other informants; they played the game in the hopes the cops would leave them alone. They get a false sense of security thinking they can't be touched… they become fearless.

Basheer was a grand master at playing the game, but in the end, even a grand master loses the odd game!

19
Rony the Geek

Drew called Norm to fill in the blanks with regards to Rony and Bogart's criminal activities. It was obvious to Norm that Drew was withholding pertinent information and was trying to play both sides of the fence; he didn't want to go to jail, but he didn't want to rat on his friends either! Norm had enough info on Rony to satisfy the judge and get a search warrant for his house. Bogart was very careful, so it was difficult for Norm to get enough information for a warrant on his place. Norm prepared warrants for both places anyway, hoping he could find the last piece of the puzzle for Bogart while searching Rony's place.

The Fraud Squad hit Rony's place first thing in the morning. Rony left in his car before Norm could get the warrant signed, so the cops had to follow him around until it was signed and they could arrest him. They brought Rony home and he cordially showed Norm where everything was. He handed over $11,000 in cash, seventy fake Canadian citizenship cards, two cloned credit cards, a laminating machine, and a laptop computer. Right from the minute the Fraud squad walked into his house, Rony said he wanted to cooperate. The cops also found a pile of Wayfar wire transaction slips. Rony said he'd give Norm an inculpatory statement admitting to everything if his wife could be left out of it. They just got married, and he didn't think she'd be too impressed.

Rony gave up Bogart, giving Norm enough to get the search warrant for his place. Norm just had to add a couple paragraphs to the warrant, and they hit Bogart's place the same afternoon. His girlfriend Brittany answered the door, and she was presented with the search warrant. While questioning her as to Bogart's whereabouts and checking her ID, Norm found out she had lied about her name. That was no surprise; people had been lying to Norm ever since the day he was hired. Her name was really Cassandra, and Norm requested she call Bogart to come home. Cassandra was a beautiful and well-developed young girl who knew full well what Bogart was up to. He had made her fake ID so she would appear to be of legal drinking age.

Norm spoke to Bogart on the phone; he was cocky, but he said he was coming home. During a search of his place the cops seized $2,300 in cash, four computers and a whack of software, a M.S.R. credit card reader, a forged U.S. passport, cloned credit cards, and a pile of Wayfar wire transaction slips. Norm later seized two more of Bogart's computers from a repair shop. He remained cocky, saying he used to do credit cards and the Wayfar wire scam, but not anymore. It was all lies.

Fraud Lessons

Rony was chomping at the bit to get himself out of hot water. He told Norm he'd come in to the cop shop and open the files on his computer that had been seized. These young fraudsters were all computer savvy and used passwords or hid selected files. Drew had managed to hit a button on his computer before Norm grabbed it; he shut it down and hid all the files. Rony kept his word and attended the Fraud office for show and tell on his laptop. He had files showing some of the work he had done with fake ID, but more importantly he had pictures of Bogart and some of the other guys who were involved in the Wayfar wire scam.

Once again, Norm was amazed at how easily the young punks could make loads of cash! Rony said they would go online using a fake name, pretending to sell certain items like electronics. When someone wanted to buy the item, they'd have them send the money via Wayfar wire. Wayfar wire would issue a code word or number to identify the person picking up the money. So the buyer would wire X amount of dollars to Joe Schmoe in Timbuktu for their purchase, expecting to take delivery of the item later. These kids were ballsy enough to accept multiple buyers for the same item. They would then take their fake ID to one of a number of Wayfar wire offices in the U.S. and claim the cash. The glitch in the system was that anyone who had the proper ID and code could claim the cash anywhere in the world!

It was a lucrative scam; Rony said Bogart used him and several other buddies as pick-up guys. He figured that Bogart was making two or three thousand dollars a week. That was big money for anyone, let alone a couple of twenty-one year-olds! Bogart never had a job and apparently didn't need one, with the money he was making illegally. Rony had worked in an electronics store, and he had his own music business. Admittedly, he was in it for the money. He had no record and was a good kid from a good family. He was clean cut and always dressed well. Rony had a bit of a wimpy look; he was definitely a computer geek. Norm was impressed with his manners and punctuality when he said he'd call or meet up with him. Rony the Geek stayed in touch with Bogart and reported back to Norm with anything that was going on. Norm's case on Bogart was weak, so another arrest would have sweetened the pot.

The more Norm learned, the more things appeared over his head. He was dealing with a whole new generation of sophisticated cyber criminals. Since the Wayfar wire scam was taking place in the U.S., Norm had to call the Secret Service and set up a meeting with a couple of their agents. Rony agreed to work with the Secret Service and attended the meeting. They wanted him to continue the scam across the border with them in tow doing surveillance. Norm let that play out while he tried to catch up on his own pile of paperwork. It was fun kicking in doors and busting the bad guys, but then it all had do be written up in triplicate!

Double Trouble

It didn't take long for Bogart to get back in business. Rony said Bogart went out and bought a new laptop right after leaving the cop shop. Norm had spoken to Bogart's father the day he was arrested. The same man, who was so concerned about his son that he brought his computer to the cops, was now complaining that the cops were picking on his son. Rony said Bogart's father changed his attitude when Bogart started sending some of his money daddy's way. His mother wasn't impressed with the situation. Bogart got himself arrested again one night when his parents got into a violent domestic, and he got in between them. Norm had a good chuckle when he heard, but his ultimate goal was to nail Bogart for fraud again.

Rony kept Norm in the loop and said that Bogart was working with a new guy named Ramundo. He was another young Romanian with a record for human trafficking! How many guys can brag about having a charge like that on their record? Rony said Ramundo was now programming cards with Bogart; they were buying electronics with the cards, and selling the stuff on the street. According to Rony, Bogart was getting the stolen credit card info, and then giving it to Ramundo who was loading it on to blank credit cards. Rony gave Norm the name of the store and the last date and time the Romanian boys pulled one of their scams. Norm had received some of the same information by Basheer Bazaar; he said the Romanian was a serious player!

Norm made a trip to the Wallyworld store and sat down with their security guy to watch surveillance tapes. After about an hour of recorded tape, Norm recognized Bogart as he strutted in the front doors. He was with a guy and girl that Norm did not recognize, but the guy fit the description of Ramundo that Rony supplied. The store's security system was state of the art. The cameras followed Bogart right to the electronics department. Two other guys joined the group; they all chatted with each other, then Ramundo and one of the unknown guys each bought an iPod with a credit card.

Security was able to pinpoint the transactions and give Norm details on the credit card that was used. The card belonged to an Italian woman from Italy, her card info had been stolen there and transferred to a blank card here…courtesy of Bogart's Romanian connections. The card should have been flagged at the checkout, but Norm learned the clerk was in on the scam. He interviewed the clerk who admitted to the crime and said Bogart had promised her a free iPod for letting the card go through. The security guy did some of his own homework and brought Norm evidence of another crooked clerk and more stolen credit card numbers.

Rony told Norm that the gang had also been shopping at another Wallyworld location where they scammed two plasma TV's. Norm viewed the security tapes from the store and identified Bogart as one of the fraudsters involved…finally his greed got him caught on camera.

The Bogart files and paperwork forced Norm out of his office and into a project room across the hall. Months of investigation on Bogart and his scams was represented by the boxes of files and reports. Norm spent countless hours adding up the transaction slips from the wire and credit card scams; they totaled over a half a million dollars!

Happy Birthday!

About an hour before the end of Norm's shift, on the eve of his birthday, Rony called. He said Bogart and Ramundo and some friends were all going shopping! The first obstacle for Norm was that they were going in two groups to two different stores. The second obstacle for Norm was that the day shift was ending, and he'd have to scramble to find enough bodies to make up two surveillance teams. Norm's boss gave him the nod to work late. He called on his drug buddies to make up one team and some of the fraud guys to make up the other. With enough cops ready to roll, Norm had to get the security personnel from both Wallyworld stores on board.

Darkness fell over the city, the street lights came on, and the fraudsters went out to play. Rony confirmed the game was on, so Norm jumped in as quarterback. He put the Drug Squad spin team on Ramundo, and he took Bogart with the Fraud Squad guys. Norm called the play out to both spin teams as well as relaying the action to the security at both stores. They had their security cameras set up and waiting. Norm had his game face on! He juggled his cell phone, the drug radio, and fraud radio in his two hands while he kept everyone in play. He used his knees to steer the car.

Norm knew what store Bogart was heading to, so he raced ahead and got a good spot in the parking lot. It was like listening to two hockey games at the same time, with the separate announcers calling out the action. Bogart had another guy in the car with him; they both entered the store. Norm alerted the security guy who said he had them on camera, and he was recording the action. Ramundo had a guy and girl with him and they hit the other store. The security system wasn't as elaborate at the second store, but the girl assured Norm she'd be watching them from the time they entered the store.

Bogart and his buddy each bought an iPod using cloned credit cards. Norm had a hard time getting direct information from the second store, but the spin team stayed with Ramundo when he left the store. Norm was hoping the two cars would meet up somewhere, but it wasn't the case; he gave the order to take both cars down and arrest the occupants for fraud.

The cops swarmed Bogart and his buddy as they went to get in their car. The iPods were seized, but the cops saw more stuff in the car. Suspected property obtained by crime that is in plain sight can legally be seized, but a search warrant is required to legally search the remainder of the car. Norm wanted to do things right; the car was impounded until a warrant could be obtained. The same thing applied to Ramundo's car. The evening's tally was five arrested, two cars impounded, three iPods recovered, and some receipts for other electronics. When the action died, the clock showed 2:30am; it was an eighteen and a half hour day for Norm. He had to get some sleep so he could prepare three search warrants in the morning…on his birthday!

The next morning search warrants were executed on the two cars, and Ramundo's apartment that was directly across the street from the cop shop. Ironically, from his living room, you could see right into the Fraud office across the street! During the searches the cops recovered Bogart's laptop, an M.S.R., P.M.R., and eighty fraudulent credit cards! After all was said and done, it was only a twelve and a half hour day; Norm still had time to go out and grab a few birthday cocktails. He had a lot to celebrate!

A Dead End

Most people think that when a bad guy gets arrested for committing a crime, he goes to jail and that's that. Many of those people are completely shocked when they hear the person got out on bail...even if the guy committed murder! It is our justice system…everyone is innocent until proven guilty…and sometimes it takes several months, or up to two years for the case to go to trial. Unless the prosecutor can show why the accused shouldn't be released, he can get out on bail. That was the case with Bogart. Although Norm got to testify at his bail hearing, Bogart was set free pending his trial date.

According to Rony, Bogart needed some money, so he got right back into the wire scam. Wallyworld security called Norm and said they went back through their security tapes looking for other transactions by Bogart and his buddies. They found an additional eighteen occurrences. They fired three of their clerks that had facilitated the fraudulent transactions. It was another month before Norm was able to finish loading up the five file boxes and take them over to the courthouse. Norm laid seventy-two charges of fraud against Bogart, mostly for local stuff since the wire scams and some stolen cards originated in other countries. You couldn't expect some poor woman from Italy to fly to Canada to be a witness in a fraud case.

Bogart's file changed hands a few times in the prosecution office…nobody there wanted it, or really had the time to peruse the five boxes of paperwork. Norm returned from a vacation to find that Bogart went to court and made a deal. Without consulting Norm, a young prosecutor took a guilty plea to two of the Wallyworld charges with the condition *all* the other charges would be dropped! That's how the wheels of justice grind. Bogart had to make restitution in the amount of $1,500 to Wallyworld; he received one year of house arrest, and another year of *double secret probation*...he was already on probation for his previous charges. That was it! He systematically ripped people off for hundreds of thousands of dollars, and he was punished by being told to stay home...where he could easily continue his criminal activities!

Norm was furious...it's no wonder he drank! There was no doubt in his mind...crime paid! To rub a little salt in Norm's wounds, Bogart's lawyer called and asked for some of his property back. Norm had to return a few things that the police weren't able to keep as part of the case. Bogart stood on the other side of the steel cage in the property room with a stupid grin on his face. Norm tried not to acknowledge him while he contemplated how he could reach through the little window in the cage, pull Bogart through it, and pound the snot out of him! Such is the life of a crime fighter...once again, Bogart got the last laugh.

Rony continued to work for the Secret Service for awhile but they eventually moved on to bigger and better things. Norm called the head of security for the Wayfar wire company, but they really didn't care...it wasn't their money that was being stolen.

Rony called Norm from time to time with tidbits of information; he just liked to be able to help out. He had learned from his mistake and moved on. Norm last heard from Rony just before his retirement. He called to say he was a proud father; his wife had just given birth to a baby boy. Norm jokingly asked if they were going to call him Bogart.

It was a few years after Norm retired, when he received a call from his buddy Harley Davidson.

"Did you hear about Bogart?"

"No...why?"

Harley laughed, "He committed suicide out west!"

Norm started to laugh too…"You're shitting me right?"

Harley laughed even harder…"No, he shot himself in the back of the head, then buried himself face down in a shallow grave!"

Norm pictured Bogart lying there with that cocky grin on his face. He smiled.

Norm got the last laugh after all!

20
End of the Storm

"Old soldiers never die; they just fade away."
-Douglas MacArthur

As if Norm wasn't busy enough chasing fraudsters. He started to get called in to do Arson investigations too. At least he had a day of rest after Drew's raid. The boss called him in to work at one in the morning for his first solo Arson investigation. Some nut bar had trashed his entire apartment and then set it on fire. The fire inspector had determined it was Arson before Norm got there. Norm had seen a lot over the years, but this guy won first prize for creativity! He had torn up, smashed, and broken every thing in his apartment. Dishes, furniture, everything! There was ketchup and mustard smeared all over the walls. He plugged the toilet with a towel, then pissed and shit on top of it. He put the smoke alarm in the bath tub, and then covered it with a whole can of shaving cream, Q tips, and cigarette butts. He cut the phone line and every other visible wire in the apartment.

When Norm interviewed the guy at the cop shop, he said he wanted the place to burn! That was his confession. He had used lighter fluid to start at least three separate fires in the apartment. Luckily the nut bar didn't know enough to ventilate the fire, and it ran out of oxygen before it could spread to the other units in the building. No one was hurt. Norm had to get a search warrant to legally collect any evidence at the scene. That meant working through the night and all the next day. Thank God it was Friday, and he had the next two days off!

A Candle in the Wind

Norm had investigated more than a few fires while assisting and training his predecessor. They say you never forget your first time. How could Norm? He got called in on Christmas Day! There was an explosion at a local restaurant and foul play was suspected. At any fire scene, it is the captain's responsibility to determine the cause of the fire. The fire department had Fire Inspectors who specialized in finding the origin and cause of the fires, so the captains would usually call them in. If the Inspector found that a fire was deliberately set, he called the police Arson Investigator.

Norm threw some Christmas cookies in his pocket and said farewell to his siblings at the family gathering. Showing their sympathetic nature, they raised a glass, wished him luck, and told him they'd save him some turkey! Norm had never seen an explosion, but the scene was exactly what you would imagine it to look like. The building's brick walls were blown out into the neighborhood and a big part of the roof was lying on the floor. It looked more like it got squashed…like taking your foot and stomping down on a tomato! Miraculously, no one was injured from the flying debris. Some of the cement bricks flew right across a busy six lane road. Since it was a holiday, there wasn't much traffic, and the restaurant was closed.

Norm's boss was already on the scene and briefed him on his arrival. He showed Norm around the field of debris, and then walked him to the front of the store.

"Look here, this is the best part!"

There was about two feet of block wall that remained, protruding from the ground. Just inside the wall on the floor was a red glass candle…still lit! It was exactly as the first firemen on the scene had found it. That candle was the ignition source for the fire. The investigation showed that someone removed the cap from the main gas line in the store and placed the lit candle at the front of the store. Natural gas is lighter than air. That means that the gas filled the upper part of the store first. When the concentrated gas worked its way to the open flame of the candle…KABOOM!

The concussion from the explosion was felt up to two miles away! The force of the blast took out the salon next door, along with the flower shop beside that. Bricks and glass flew up to a half a block away. Even with all that damage, Norm could tell that the building was locked and secure before the explosion. The deadbolt extensions on the doors showed they were in the locked position. All the broken glass was on the outside of the building. If anyone had broken a window to get in, the broken glass would be on the inside. Since the building was secure and the gas line cap didn't remove itself, it was a no-brainer that someone blew the place up.

As is the case with the majority of Arsons, investigators have to consider the owner as a suspect. In this case, someone needed a key to get in and out of the restaurant, the owner could easily be that someone. It didn't take long for that idea to begin circulating around the crime scene. Neighbors, customers, and employees gathered in a parking lot across the street. The rumor mill started to churn. The rest of that day and the next were spent interviewing employees and potential witnesses. The restaurant's owner was conveniently out of town and couldn't be reached.

One Lucky Bastard

The explosion was big news, and the local media covered the event. Norm used the media to ask for any witnesses to the explosion. A few days later, Norm got a call from a guy who said he was there at the time of the explosion. He said he was afraid to come forward earlier because he was afraid the police might think he was responsible.

The guy told Norm he had forgotten his jacket at the restaurant the night before. He went to retrieve his jacket but found the shop was closed when he got there. He pulled up beside the shop in the parking lot, then got out of his car and looked in the window. He said he pressed his face up against the glass to see if his coat was inside. Realizing he couldn't get in anyway, he turned away and opened his car door. Just as he was bending over to get in his car…KABOOM!

The shock wave sent the guy sprawling face first across his front seat. He turned to look over his shoulder, and a giant orange fireball rolled over the top of his car. He ducked back down and trembled as chunks of debris rained down on his car. He managed to get the passenger door open and he ran away from his car. The guy was in shock. He started to freak out thinking he might get blamed since he was the only person around. He got back in his car and drove away.

Norm hadn't said a word the whole time the guy told his story. It was incredible!

It was miraculous!

Norm looked at the guy and exclaimed, "You have to be the luckiest bastard alive! You should go out and buy a lottery ticket!"

The guy grinned sheepishly and shrugged his shoulders. Other than a few scratches and dents on his car, the guy walked away almost completely unscathed. He told Norm that he had been having some hearing problems since the explosion…"No shit!" Norm thought to himself. If the restaurant exploded a minute earlier when the guy was looking through the window, pieces of him would have been scattered throughout the neighborhood.

The owner finally contacted Norm and was interviewed. He pretended he had no idea what happened, but he showed no signs of shock, anger, or sorrow. His answers to the questions seemed rehearsed. Everyone knew he was having financial difficulties, but he vehemently denied that he blew his coffee shop up. He agreed to a polygraph test, but it came back inconclusive. Even the polygraph technician agreed the owner was guilty, but the machine wouldn't back him up. The technician felt the owner had rehearsed his answers and was possibly on medication that kept him calm during the test.

There was one piece of evidence that Norm thought might hang the owner…the candle. There were no finger prints on the glass, but the owner said it did not belong in the restaurant. He had no idea where it came from. Norm scoured all the stores in the area and found the exact same candle in a store only a few blocks from the restaurant. The bar code confirmed the candle had been purchased there. Norm was almost giddy when the manager told him all the check-outs were monitored and recorded on video. The manager brought up the video footage for the day before the explosion…the monitor was blank! The manager thought about it for a second then said that the explosion had knocked out their power and set off their alarm. It was not Norm's lucky day. The explosion also fried their computer hard drive!

Norm interviewed the owner's wife and got the same results. Neither one of them showed any signs of emotion what so ever…it was a bit weird, they were a bit weird. Even though everyone thought the owner was guilty, and some of the evidence suggested he was guilty, it could not be proven *beyond a reasonable doubt*. That is the threshold in Canadian law. Norm quickly learned that Arson was a very difficult crime to prove. It was fairly easy to find the origin and cause of the fires and that they were intentionally set. The difficulty lay in trying to connect the evidence to the person responsible.

Dr. Death

Whenever Norm's phone rang in the middle of the night, it was for a fire call. Norm was a one man Arson Unit, so any time the fire department needed an Arson investigator, Norm got the call. The staff sergeant in charge called Norm late one night, sending him to investigate a fatal fire, not too far from Norm's home on the east side of the city. Norm had brought the Arson van home that night, so it was a short drive. He had talked his boss into letting him bring the van home. When Norm got called in, he had to drive all the way downtown to pick up the van and his equipment, and then drive out to the fire scene. Norm sold the idea to his boss by pointing out he was wasting overtime dollars driving back and forth.

The fire scene was at a senior's apartment complex. The buildings were fairly new so Norm was surprised when he arrived. The fire was already out when Norm arrived, he was briefed by the Fire Inspector. The Inspector believed the fire had been caused by careless smoking, but there was a fatality, so the police had to be called. There were hundreds of cigarette burns on the furniture and floors. Norm looked around the living room and kitchen while the Inspector briefed him; strangely, there was only minimal smoke damage. The Inspector knew exactly what Norm was thinking. He tapped Norm on the shoulder and pointed to the bedroom.

The bedroom was cooked, and so was the poor old man in it. He was lying on the edge of the bed with his feet on the floor; it looked like he had been sitting there. His pants were down around his ankles. He was burnt to a crisp. Norm couldn't help but notice the man's penis...what was left of it was sticking straight up…like a half a hard on! There was a garbage pail full of cigarette butts right beside the man. The Fire Inspector believed a lit butt started the pail, then the bedroom curtains on fire. The bedroom door was closed so the fire flashed through the room, but burnt itself out when it ran out of oxygen.

A metal walker was still standing right in front of the victim. He couldn't walk well and needed the walker to get around his apartment. While Norm was examining the body, a fireman came into the bedroom with a grappling pole and he started to poke the ceiling right above the body.

"What the hell are you doing?"

The young fireman looked a little stunned that someone would question him.

"I'm looking for hot spots."

Norm barked back at him, "I'll call you if I see one, now get out of my crime scene! And that goes for you guys out there talking about the ball game in the living room!"

Norm could hear some grumbling as they cleared out of the apartment. A police sergeant stuck his head in the apartment door as they left.

"Hey Norm, the media is driving me crazy out here, what should I tell them?"

Norm sighed, "Tell them I'll let them know when I know."

The Forensic specialist then came into the apartment. She was a rookie in the unit, a pretty girl. She already had her camera in hand, Norm told her to get a few shots of the apartment.

Norm waited for her to finish, "The victim is over here in the bedroom."

Norm led her into the bedroom. The Fire Inspector was standing near the victim taking notes. The forensic gal took some pictures of the bedroom and victim.

Norm pointed to the victim's penis and said, "Make sure you get a picture of this."

She was a bit shocked and immediately blushed.

"Why do you want me to do that?"

Norm looked her dead in the eyes and bluntly said, "That's the cause of the fire."

The Fire Inspector smirked, but the forensic gal just focused on the half boner and took a few pictures.

She took the bait, "And how's that?" she asked.

Norm still had his poker face on, "Can't you see? Look, his pants are down around his ankles…he was sitting on the edge of the bed masturbating…it caused a spark and he set himself on fire!"

The Fire Inspector burst out laughing; he fumbled to catch his notebook as it almost fell into the pail of cigarette butts. Norm couldn't help himself and joined in the laughter.

"Asshole!" she said.

Norm's first fire victim became his first autopsy. Being the investigating office, he got to attend the autopsy while the victim was carved up at the morgue. Norm had dealt with many arrogant doctors before, but the coroner was very courteous and helpful. He dissected the man's esophagus and showed Norm how smoke inside could tell him whether the victim was overcome by smoke or fire when they died. He also pointed out a spot on the man's brain where there were signs of a past stroke. Norm found it all fascinating. It didn't bother him at all…not like a live victim, bleeding and screaming for help.

Norm's smoking masturbator was his first in a string of fire fatalities over the next few months. The Fire Inspectors started calling Norm Dr. Death.

The Mountie Rat

Norm got a call from one of the local Mounties one day. He was a drug investigator who had some information from a police agent that he wanted Norm to hear. Norm grabbed Harley and sat down with the Mountie in an interview room. Norm's retirement was just around the corner, so he was teaching Harley Davidson his job. Harley had worked some fraud cases with Norm, and the two of them got to be buddies on and off the job. Norm got to like sleeping in during his last year on the job; Harley would be Norm's wake up call some mornings.

The Mountie told Norm and Harley that he was using a police agent for a drug investigation he was in the middle of. The Mountie had a taped conversation between his agent, an Arsonist, and a local business owner who wanted his business burned down. The business owner called the Arsonist about torching his business. When the Arsonist went to meet the owner to discuss the details, he brought along his buddy…who just happened to be working for the police as an agent. He taped the conversation. The owner's business in Motor Town wasn't doing too well financially. He wanted it torched so he could collect the insurance money and get out of debt. The owner said he wanted it done in the next two weeks while his partner was out of the country.

The information was good, but was problematic. The agent was only part of the meeting and wasn't going to be involved any further. Nobody knew exactly when the Arson would take place, or if it would at all. Regardless, Norm had to report it to his superiors and let them make the decision how to handle it. Norm already knew the answer; there was no way they would set up twenty-four hour surveillance on the place for who knew how long. So that was it; submit the report and wait to see what happens.

Told ya so

Shit happens…and so it did. About two weeks later, Norm got a call; the business in Motor Town was on fire, and so were the attached buildings. It was a spectacular fire! The buildings were right across the street from a fire station; they didn't have far to go after getting out of bed! The Fire Inspector told Norm not to hurry, the fire was still roaring. Norm's job really didn't start until the fire was out and the scene could be examined. He had learned through experience that it didn't hurt to blend in with the crowd of onlookers. People like to talk; it was surprising the little tidbits of information you could pick up listening to the scuttlebutt. Like at the coffee shop explosion…people always have their own theories. Besides, a spectacular fire is fun to watch!

Ironically, investigating Arson was an interesting way to end Norm's career. He liked to play with fire as a kid and accidentally set the field behind his house on fire…twice! On one occasion, Norm's mom chased him up a tree threatening to burn his fingers to teach him a lesson. Norm stayed in that tree all day. His buddies brought food up to him, but he had to come down at some point. When Norm went home his mom held his fingers over a burner on the stove until he felt the sting of the heat. The pain Norm felt was a lesson for sure, but he was always fascinated by fire.

It was colder than a witch's teat the night of the fire. It was the damp cold that drove Norm into the fire station for a bowl of hot soup. The poor firemen froze their asses off fighting the fire across the street while Norm enjoyed a bowl of chicken noodle soup, with his feet up, watching a news broadcast about the fire. Harley had joined Norm at the scene; it was his turn to take the reins. He was the new guy, so Norm relaxed and watched the fire from the window.

There were half a dozen different businesses sharing a turn of the century building complex. All the owners were devastated, except for one. Harley and Norm already knew where to start the investigation. Because of the extensive damage, a provincial Fire Marshall was called in. He ruled the fire Arson. It was no surprise to anyone. Harley and Norm interviewed the partner who was out of town, first. Within the first five minutes of the interview, they knew the soft spoken man had nothing to do with the fire. He had owned the business for years; he put his life into it. He knew there were money problems, but he'd worked through them before.

Of course the younger partner who contracted out the fire denied everything. The law requires that you have to advise a person of their rights when they go from a person of interest in an investigation, to a suspect. Knowing what they did going into the investigation, Harley and Norm read the young owner his legal rights. He offered to take a polygraph but never kept his appointment.

Norm was frustrated. It looked like another business owner was going to get away with Arson…and this guy was on tape hiring someone to do the job! After consulting with the Mounties, Norm and Harley took a different approach. Their drug investigation was just wrapping up, and they had the business owner tied into the Arsonist in their drug case. They arrested the men on drug conspiracy charges. Norm wanted to do the same for the Arson. Maybe he couldn't prove the Arson itself, but he could prove the men conspired to commit the Arson.

It was Norm's last kick at the cat, probably the last arrest he'd make on the job. He went at the owner hard. He had obviously talked to a lawyer. He openly admitted having a previous conversation with the Arsonist asking him *about* burning his place, but he said he never *actually* asked him to do it. It was bullshit, and everyone knew it! The Mounties watched from the other side of the two-way glass; Norm and Harley had the room. Harley was running the investigation, but Norm piped up as the bad cop. He called the owner a liar and weasel and coward and threw in some F bombs to try and rattle the guy. It wasn't like TV; they don't always confess at the end of the show.

The Arsonist was a smart guy, he'd played the game before and wasn't about to admit to anything. The case relied on the testimony of the agent and the tape, but it was not proof of who actually set the fire. End of story.

Fading Away

Norm had thought about retirement from the day he was hired. Granted it was a great career, but it was always just a job to Norm. He had seen too many guys ruined by letting the *job* consume their lives. He saw guys pass away before they could even collect a pension check. Norm always promised himself that would *not* be him. Norm considered a couple potential job offers, but he didn't want to start another career. Norm took the advice of some other retirees and planned to do nothing for at least a year.

Norm was a single guy who loved to socialize and travel. He had done many all-inclusive vacations in the past, and some solo motorcycle trips. With having three hundred and sixty-five vacation days a year, it would be the perfect opportunity to travel some more. Norm had a buddy living in Cambodia who extended an invitation to come and visit. It would give Norm a chance to see other places in Southeast Asia like Viet Nam and

Thailand. So, a plan was hatched; Norm would fly half way across the world a week after his retirement.

It was hard not to look back as Norm looked ahead to his future. It had been a good haul, but thirty-one years of looking at the ugly underbelly of society was enough. Norm always tried to have some fun on the job, but at the same time, he gained a reputation for *getting the job done*. Even as a supervisor, Norm never asked anyone to do something he wasn't willing to do himself. He never did find out what Ash Kist had against him, but for the most part Norm was well-liked. He owed no one. Norm worked with many partners and made many friends over the years. In the end, he came away from the job with a handful of *true* friends.

There were too many arrests to count, but then there were those like Michael Cook who would never be brought to justice. C'est la vie. Norm locked up more than his share. Norm learned over the years that justice was better vetted on the street, than in the legal system. The people who lived in neighborhoods like Motor Town never called the police; they always took care of their own problems. Then there were those who called the police for things as trivial as their neighbor's dog shitting on their lawn.

The biggest change Norm witnessed over the years was in *people*; many started caring a lot less, showing no respect for anyone, including themselves. It was sad to see how some people treated others, including the police. Norm always believed in treating others, the way he wanted to be treated. It was the recipe for his success, especially with his informants. Deep down, everyone wants to be respected.

The job paid well, and the pension plan was good, so Norm knew he could live comfortably after retirement. Norm had always invested his money wisely; he started investing when he received his first police pay check. A divorce settlement stung a bit, but he was single and had no children to support. That meant Norm could spend all his money on himself! Norm had the option of staying on the job another five years to boost his pension by ten percent, but he appreciated that there was more to life than work. In the end, Norm knew he wouldn't miss the job…it was just that…a job. He had no regrets. He surely wouldn't miss being called in to work in the middle of the night!

On Norm's last day of work, there was a coffee and cake party for him. Too bad Norm didn't drink coffee or eat cake…it was the thought that counted. Norm put out an open invitation to everyone for cocktails after work…that was more Norm's kind of party! People from the civilian, uniform, and investigative offices attended both parties. Richard Cranium and the new Chief said a few words at the coffee and cake party.

The Chief paused at the end of his speech and asked, "Norm, you don't seem too worked up or emotional about this?"

"No Chief, I've been planning this since the day I was hired."

A parting speech is customary; Norm kept his short and sweet. He thanked all those who attended, and he said he would miss them. At the time he thought he might miss the job too, but that really wasn't the case. Norm walked the gauntlet, shaking hands and giving hugs. Even Norm's ex-wife attended the party; Norm always preferred to have friends over enemies. The Dickhead gave Norm a copy of his personnel file that included his commendations and trivial complaints. He was also presented a picture of himself the day he was hired; Norm looked like he was twelve years old.

Unlike many former retirees, Norm still had his health, and his hair! The many years of stress only grayed his sideburns a bit. That was important to Norm; to be able to walk away from the job healthy, and financially sound. The friends that Norm made, and left the job with, were a bonus. It felt weird handing in his key card, gun, and badge, but Norm knew he made the right decision as he walked out the door for the last time. Crime, such as life, would go on…and so would Norm Strom.

The End

Glossary

8-ball – 3.5 grams of cocaine
Bareback – having sex without a condom
Battering ram – a steal device for breaking through doors
Beater – an old or beat up car
B & E – a break and enter
Check day – day welfare recipients receive their checks
C.I. – confidential informant
C Note – a one hundred dollar bill
Crimestoppers – tip line where callers earn cash rewards
Dillies – dilaudid
Embosser – machine to stamp credit card numbers
Excalibur – the nickname for one officer's leather baton
Eye – person on surveillance who can physically see the target
Fix – the act of injecting drugs into a vein
Heat score – something that attracts the cops
Hesitation mark – a practice line before the real cut
House Arrest – sentenced and confined to your own home.
Informant – one who supplies information to the police
John – a prostitute's male customer
Junkie – drug addict
Kit – an addict's tools for injecting themselves
Mountie – common name for member of the R.C.M.P.
M.S.R. – device that reads encoded information on credit cards
Mule – one who carries drugs for others
Normie new guy – the new guy
Paddy wagon – police prisoner van
P.I.T. – a vehicle nudging maneuver used to end a police chase
P.M.R. – miniature credit card reader
Rat – an informant or one who informs to the police
R.C.M.P. – the Royal Canadian Mounted Police
Richard Cranium – dick head

Roof Goofs – guys who do roofing
Shooting gallery – where addicts hang out and inject drugs
Skimming – obtaining personal information from credit cards
Spin – conducting mobile surveillance on someone
S.W.A.T. – special weapons and tactics
Target – the person who is being watched
Trick – a sex act.
U/C – undercover officer
Voluntary deportation – driven back across the border.
Working a patch – supplying information to work off charges.

Cast of Characters

In order of appearance

The Police

Norm Strom or Storm…*Main Character*
Jesse James…*Norm's best friend*
Andy Green…*Norm's training officer, boss*
Ted Masterson…*Body removal guy*
Mad Manny…*Uniform cop*
Franky…*Uniform cop*
Marty James…*Uniform cop*
Poncho…*Uniform cop*
Tommy Gunn…*Occasional uniform partner*
Cuckoo Connors…*Uniform cop*
Buck Flynn…*Partner in Motor Town*
Digger Daniels…*Partner in Motor Town*
Richard Cranium…*Uniform cop, boss*
Ash Kist…*Boss, Chief*
Blackjack…*Drug cop*
Tanker…*Drug Squad Sergeant*
Bongo…*Drug cop*
Missy…*Drug cop*
Banger…*Drug cop*
Matty Allen…*Uniform, plain clothes cop*
Teflon Tim…*Drug Squad Boss*
Topper…*Drug Cop*
Kirk Westwood…*Detective Sergeant*
The Italian Stallion…*Drug Squad Sergeant*
Cheech…*Undercover cop*
Mickey D…*Plain clothes cop*
Harley Davidson…*Fraud/Arson Detective*

The Informants

Crazy Jerry…*Norm's old buddy*
Squeaky Sally…*Drug Informant, Prostitute*
Hanna & Helen…*Drug Informants*
Cracker Jack…*Drug Informant/Crack head*
Ronny the Robber…*Informant*
Danny Dugan…*Drug Informant*
Jeff Watson…*Drug Informant*
Tommy O'Shea…*Informant*
Mickey Watson…*Drug Informant*
Duke Delaney…*Drug Dealer/Informant*
Danielle Delaney…*Dilaudid user*
Laura Lamar…*Informant*
Joe Anthony…*Drug dealer/Informant*
Syd…*Drug dealer/Informant*
Louie the Wap…*Informant*
Roy Rogers…*Fraudster/Informant*
Rony the Geek…*Fraudster/Informant*
Nazim Bazaar…*Informant*
Basheer Bazaar…*Fraudster/Dealer/Informant*

The Criminals

Duchene Brothers…*B & E Boys*
Donny Gates…*Convicted* murderer
Paula Watson…*Dilaudid dealer*
Brownie Watson…*Father of Mickey Watson*
Jamal…*Cracker Jack's brother*
Dwayne, Darnell, Tyrell…*Fila Boys/Crack dealers*
Fat Fiona…*Crack dealer*
Rick…*Crack head*
Jimmy Smith…*Cocaine dealer*

Craig Santos...*Marihuana dealer*
Jake Lamar...*Cocaine dealer*
Austin Grey...*Cop killer*
Ma Barker...*Dilaudid dealer*
Mack Crow...*Dilaudid dealer/Ma's son*
Laura Anthony...*Joe's wife/cocaine dealer*
Michael Cook...*High level cocaine dealer*
Roger Danby...*Cocaine dealer*
Drew Dancer...*Cocaine dealer/mule*
Gary Norris...*Michael Cook's partner/dealer*
Karl Crest...*Fraudster/Crack head*
Drew...*Fraudster*
Bogart...*Fraudster*
Ramundo...*Fraudster*

Author Bio

Edmond Gagnon grew up in an automotive town, swearing that he would never work in a factory. He worked in a warehouse after finishing high school. The office manager called *Ed* in to see him one day and asked where he saw himself down the road. *Ed* couldn't see himself behind a desk in the office and told his boss he considered being a police officer. *Ed's* boss told him to use his lunch hour the next day to go and apply for a job at the police department.

Ed retired as police Arson detective. He investigated a myriad of crimes, from simple shoplifting to fatal Arsons. He began his career as a respected street cop, and retired as a seasoned detective. As an investigator he learned the art of writing a good story. It was *the story* after all, that convicted the criminals. Over his 31 year career *Ed* cultivated and worked with numerous police informants. Those informants gave *Ed* valuable information that led to arrests, the recovery of stolen property, illegal narcotics and guns.

Upon his retirement *Ed* travelled extensively, writing about his adventures and misadventures. *Ed* visited other countries around the world, and explored the back roads of North America on his motorcycle. He put a collection of travel stories together, then wrote and published his first book called "A Casual Traveler." *Ed* wrote the book so that he might share his travel experiences with his family and friends. His readers complimented his writing, saying he made them feel like they were right there with him.

The day that *Ed* retired a co-worker commented on the number of informants that *Ed* had. That comment gave *Ed* an idea for another book. Everyone has a story to tell. *Ed* heard many stories from other people during his career, but he thought he should tell the stories of the people he knew as police informants. These people are necessary to the police, yet they have to remain anonymous for their own safety. Each person has their own reason for becoming a police informant, but they all share a dangerous existence.

We call such a person a "Rat."

CPSIA information can be obtained at www.ICGtesting.com
Printed in the USA
LVOW080349250613

340013LV00001B/13/P

9 781626 464414